I0680598

Sixth Sense

by

Marilyn Baron

A Psychic Crystal Mystery
Book One

Sixth Sense

Cover Art by *Debbie Taylor*

The Wild Rose Press, Inc.
PO Box 708
Adams Basin, NY 14410-0708
Visit us at www.thewildrosepress.com

Publishing History
First Crimson Rose Edition, 2013
Print ISBN 978-1-61217-933-9
Digital ISBN 978-1-61217-934-6

A Psychic Crystal Mystery, Book One
Published in the United States of America

"The plane is going to crash!" a woman shouted. "You need to do something."

Jack jolted forward, ready for action. *A plane crash!* Then his police training kicked in. *Stay calm in a disaster.*

"Could I get your name, please?" He reached across the desk and picked up a pad of yellow sticky-notes.

"It's Katherine Crystal. But my name isn't important. Vince Rivers and his son are on a plane, and it's going down."

This call was getting stranger by the minute.

"The movie star Vince Rivers? Are they on a commercial airliner?"

"It's his private plane. Vince Rivers is the pilot."

"When is this crash going to happen? And where?"

"I don't know when it's going to crash, but soon, and somewhere in Georgia."

"Can you be more specific about the location?"

Dead silence.

"Let me get this straight," Jack stated. "You can't predict when or where this crash will happen?"

"That's not how it works."

"How what works? Do you have inside information about this incident? Is the crash weather-related? Is it terrorism? On what facts are you basing this call?"

"I saw it in a vision."

"I see." Jack exhaled, rolled his shoulders, laid down his pen, and flexed his right hand. *Another lunatic. Predictable.*

Praise for Marilyn Baron

SIXTH SENSE won the Georgia Romance Writers 2012 Unpublished Maggie Award for Excellence in the Paranormal/Fantasy category.

~

Marilyn is also Winner of First Place in the Suspense Romance category of the 2010 Ignite the Flame Contest sponsored by the Central Ohio Fiction Writers chapter of Romance Writers of America, as well as Finalist in the Georgia Romance Writers Unpublished Maggie Award for Excellence in 2005 in the Single Title category.

~*~

"Baron offers a bit of everything...There's humor, infidelity, murder, mayhem, and a neatly drawn conclusion." *~RT Book Reviews (4.5 Stars)*

"Expertly handled relationship... a page-turning journey... a riveting read." *~Anna K.*

"Wonderfully witty writing...sharp characterization and...brilliant dialogue...humorous asides and...the quite fantastic twist at the end...left me with a real lump in my throat...highly recommended. Worth more than 5 stars if that were possible." *~Andrew Kirby*

"Ms. Baron's portrayal of her heroine's thoughts, feelings and actions was spot-on. Five stars! Highly recommended!" *~Pam Asberry*

"[*UNDER THE MOON GATE*] is a surefire blockbuster...a treasure trove of mystery and intrigue. It sparkles with romance. The thrills and chills are unrelenting, and the writing is witty and engaging...I couldn't recommend this more." *~Andrew Kirby*

Acknowledgments

Thanks to my critique partner, Anna Doll,
for her help with this manuscript,
and to Haywood Smith and Debby Giusti
for their advice and support.

Other Books by Marilyn Baron
Available from The Wild Rose Press, Inc.

UNDER THE MOON GATE

~

DESTINY: A BERMUDA LOVE STORY
(prequel to *Under the Moon Gate*)

Chapter One

Atlanta Police Department
Mini-Precinct in Midtown

Beauregard Lee Jackson Hale was a shit magnet. No doubt about it. And he could feel a mighty shit storm blowing his way.

"Hey, Wolf Man Jack, cover the front desk while I take a leak."

Jack grimaced and walked by the empty waiting area toward Sarge's desk. It was a fluke he was even in the precinct this late at night. He'd dragged in from the field to fill out some paperwork. Just his luck, after the day from hell, Sarge's pea-sized bladder needed emptying. Sergeant Anthony Lisle's bathroom breaks were legendary around the stationhouse.

"Don't worry, Hale, it's dead around here. I'll be right back." *Famous last words*. Sergeant Lisle rose from his chair and stretched his stubby legs as he reached for the remote to lower the volume on the flat-screen television set mounted over his desk. As an afterthought, he grabbed a magazine from his inbox. *Reading material*. A sure sign Sarge was in it for the long haul.

Jack shook his head, picked up the report he was working on, replaced the sergeant at his desk, and slapped the file down on the hardwood surface. Atlanta in the middle of the night was anything but dead. That's usually when the crazies came out.

He looked around the empty, dimly lit squad room of the Atlanta Police Department's newest mini-precinct and felt like Gulliver in Lilliput. Everything about this place was small. The chairs were designed for grade-schoolers. His six-foot-four-inch frame dwarfed the furniture. The whole precinct could fit into his one-bedroom-plus-den apartment. How thirty police employees squeezed into this cramped space was beyond comprehension.

He couldn't wait for his undercover assignment to be over so he could move back to more mundane crimes like auto theft, burglary, robbery, drug arrests, and run-of-the-mill shootings and homicides. Cases that had a conclusion. Cases where perpetrators actually got caught. And tried. *And* convicted.

Ever since he'd grown a beard and gone on the trail—the stone-cold trail—of the Midtown Strangler, he'd suffered ribbing from the guys at the precinct and brought a negative publicity hailstorm of epic proportions down on the department.

If he'd had any success in catching the twisted bastard, things might be different. But the killer had brutally strangled five Atlanta College coeds, right around the corner from where Jack lived in his high-rise Midtown condo. And right under the noses of the officers in Zone Five, the same mini-precinct the mayor had opened precisely to protect the students at Atlanta College. *Protect and Serve*. He'd done a hell of a job. He hadn't protected shit. He certainly hadn't protected the five young girls whose dead bodies had been found naked in their dorm rooms right down the street. Now, after easy pickings on the Midtown campus, the killer had vanished, like a phantom, into thin air, left the planet without a trace, with no leads and little chance of capture. At least he'd stopped killing…in Atlanta. Maybe he'd moved on to greener pastures.

If he were alive, Jack's father would have stopped the killer dead in his tracks. Sometimes his dad cut corners and didn't always follow the rules. But he did what he had to do to get the job done.

Jack inspected his reflection in the stainless steel coffee tumbler mug on Sarge's desk. In the scheme of things, whether he looked like a homeless wacko wasn't high on his priority scale. He needed a change. He needed a shave. But he had promised himself he wouldn't shave until he caught the strangler. And that wasn't happening anytime soon. The investigation had hit a brick wall. An insurmountable, Berlin-style, brick wall.

Sarge had ordered him to resurface. It was a good thing, too, because he needed a bath. He needed a woman. He'd been so deep undercover even his mother wouldn't recognize him. He needed to check in on his mother. He hoped he hadn't forgotten her birthday or another important date. Since his father had been murdered, it had been up to Jack to make sure those special occasions didn't go unrecognized. What he really needed was a secretary to keep him organized.

Jack picked up a pen and reached across the desk to answer the phone that wasn't supposed to ring.

"Fifth precinct. Detective Hale. How can I help you?"

"The plane is going to crash!" a woman shouted. "You need to do something."

3

Jack jolted forward, ready for action. *A plane crash!* Then his police training kicked in. *Stay calm in a disaster.*

"Could I get your name, please?" He reached across the desk and picked up a pad of yellow sticky-notes.

"It's Katherine Crystal. But my name isn't important. Vince Rivers and his son are on a plane, and it's going down."

This call was getting stranger by the minute.

"The movie star Vince Rivers? Are they on a commercial airliner?"

"It's his private plane. Vince Rivers is the pilot."

"When is this crash going to happen? And where?"

"I don't know when it's going to crash, but soon, and somewhere in Georgia."

"Can you be more specific about the location?"

Dead silence.

"Let me get this straight," Jack stated. "You can't predict when or where this crash will happen?"

"That's not how it works."

"How what works? Do you have inside information about this incident? Is the crash weather-related? Is it terrorism? On what facts are you basing this call?"

"I saw it in a vision."

"I see." Jack exhaled, rolled his shoulders, laid down his pen, and flexed his right hand. *Another lunatic. Predictable.* Atlanta was full of them, and Jack was already drowning in a reservoir of bad feelings about so-called psychics. When he was ten, a psychic had taken advantage of his widowed mother and bilked her out of most of his father's police pension. He'd had his fill of psychics, and he definitely did not believe this

4

deluded drama queen on the phone.

"What do you want me to do? Tell Vince Rivers he can't fly his jet anymore?"

"Do whatever you have to do to save them."

Whatever you have to do. That had been Jack's father's motto. And his dad's cop credo had proven to be a sure-fire formula for getting himself killed. His father had been a maverick, a cop's cop. Everyone in the precinct made allowances for Jack's cautious, plodding, by-the-book code because of his father. They also made the inevitable comparisons. And by any measurement, he came up short. The consensus around the precinct was: Jack could never fill his father's shoes.

"If we grounded a plane every time a psychic made a prediction, nobody would fly," Jack pointed out. "Law enforcement agencies can't act on premonitions or crackpots calling in with false claims."

"I'm not a crackpot."

Jack scratched his beard. There was probably a family of fleas setting up house on his face. He was dog-tired, and he didn't believe this conversation was happening. The woman's story had as many holes as Bonnie & Clyde's bullet-riddled getaway car. All he wanted to do was hop in the sack and spend the next day, maybe the next week, in blissful peace and quiet. No serial killers. No psychics.

"Tell me, Miss Crystal, if that's really your name, do your premonitions always come true?"

"Yes."

"Why did you call the Atlanta Police Department?"

"I didn't know how to get in touch with Vince Rivers. Even if I did manage to get through, he probably wouldn't believe me. I thought if a law enforcement agency contacted him he would take it seriously. But you were my last resort. I've called all the local news stations and the *Atlanta Journal-Constitution*, the national networks, CNN, everyone. No one will listen to me."

Bingo. She'd called all the networks? She was nothing but a run-of-the-mill publicity hound. She wasn't genuinely concerned about the lives of a man and his son. She was trying to make a name for herself, like all the rest of her kind. This chick was bugging the hell out of him. Where was Sarge? Probably whacking off in the head. Sarge had endless patience. Jack's had just run out.

"Now you listen to me, Miss Crystal. I know your type. I've dealt with psycho-broads like you before."

"I'm not a psycho."

"What if you're wrong?"

"I'm not wrong. Do you promise you'll do something about this?"

"Yes," Jack assured her as he released the last of his strategic politeness reserves to place the phone gently in its cradle, when what he really wanted to do was slam it in her face.

Any one of his fellow officers would have done the same thing in his place. Some hysterical woman calls out of the blue in the middle of the night with a premonition that Vince Rivers' son was about to die in a private plane crash.

All his questions had been reasonable. All her answers had bordered on fantasy.

The department got prank calls from psychos and psychics on a regular basis. He couldn't be expected to take all of them—or any of them, for that matter—seriously.

He didn't make a practice of lying, but this was one promise he had no intention of keeping.

Jack bounded out of his chair, took the sticky note with the woman's information, promptly crumpled it up, and aimed for the wastebasket. *He jumps. He shoots. He scores!* He didn't alert the authorities. He didn't pass the message on to his superiors.

When Sarge finally returned to his station, with a smile on his face, Jack *did* go on a coffee break, eat a stale doughnut, and try his best to forget about the whole sorry episode.

****

Katherine gripped the receiver and squeezed her eyes shut, but she couldn't get the picture of the crash to disappear. The mid-sized Gulfstream private jet was a burning hunk of metal, a wreckage of parts scattered like pick-up sticks in random disarray over an oily slick on the ground. The pilot, actor Vince Rivers, stunned, staggered out of his cockpit, still miraculously intact, a glint of moonlight reflecting on his pale, baby face and in his glacial blue eyes.

She tried to speak, but was overwhelmed by another clear vision of the movie star shouting for his son and sobbing as he covered the mangled body of the innocent young boy with his trademark black leather jacket. In her recurring nightmares, Vince Rivers survived. Ocean Rivers did not.

Katherine's parents had warned her, drummed it into her head since she was in grade school, not to reveal her premonitions to anyone. For some unexplained reason, they were vehemently against her using her sixth sense or advertising the fact that she had psychic abilities. They didn't want anything but visions of sugarplums dancing in their daughter's head. But this vision was too powerful to ignore, and a young boy's life was at stake. This was the right thing to do.

Katherine knew with certainty that the jerk down at the police station wasn't going to do anything. She'd heard the contempt and the doubt in his voice. Well, she was going to march right down there and shake things up, *make* him listen.

Katherine stripped off her nightgown, dressed hurriedly, took the marble stairs two at a time, and slid behind the wheel of her blue BMW. Revving up the motor, she sped around the long circular driveway and made a left at West Paces Ferry Road, past the Governor's Mansion and onto an eerily deserted Peachtree Street. Maybe she'd get arrested for speeding. Then someone would listen to what she had to say.

****

"Sarge, I'm done here," Jack said, dropping his papers into a folder as he turned in his completed report. "I'm headed home. I've got some time coming, so I'll see you next week."

Jack hoofed it out of the squad room, his mind already wrapped around a bottle of ice-cold beer and a warm bed, when he ran smack into five feet four inches of soft, sweet-smelling woman.

Man, he was either really beat or sex deprivation was kicking in, big time. How could he have failed to notice her? She was about as hot as any woman he'd ever seen. Her thick black hair fell in a mass of ringlets he wanted to tangle in his hands as he held her full, pouty lips captive and kissed her senseless. He could gaze into those violet bedroom eyes forever. Not to mention a peaches-and-cream complexion he'd like to slowly lap up with his tongue. Though she looked like a disheveled gypsy, she was as tiny as a fairy, a very well-developed fairy, and she was madder than a starving pit bull.

The gypsy was dressed in a navy pencil skirt and a white form-fitting shell that left nothing to the imagination. Oh, and the pink necklace was a classy touch. He was having trouble not imagining Miss Junior League naked, under him, dressed only in that goddamned string of pearls. The mystery woman was the kind of glamour girl you ran into once in a lifetime. And now he was stuck with a hard-on the size of Greater Atlanta.

"Excuse me, I'm looking for Detective Hale," the vision said breathlessly.

He must be dreaming.

"Honey, I think I've been looking for you all my life."

"Are you seriously trying to pick me up in a police station?" the sexy stranger snarled.

"It's as good a place as any," Jack replied, baiting her.

"Do I look like a prostitute to you?"

"No, but we are in the red-light district."

"What kind of a cop are you?" she accused. "I need help. And that jerk Detective Hale blew me off."

"You mind telling me why you want to see that jerk…er, Jack Hale?"

"I called earlier to report a plane crash, and I know he didn't take me seriously."

"You're Katherine Crystal?"

"Yes." Katherine glared, balling up her fists at her side. "Now I recognize your voice. *You're* Detective Hale."

It was the nutcase on the telephone in the flesh. Another psycho psychic the world could do without. Tempting or not, he was going to show her the door and get a jump-start on his much-needed vacation.

"Look, lady, you can waltz your pretty little butt out of this precinct. Nobody is interested in your wild rantings. You're wasting our time and the taxpayer's money when we could be working on more important cases."

"Like the Midtown Strangler?"

Jack yanked on his shirt collar. "Damn."

He didn't have to take this shit. What right did she have to come in here criticizing the way he did his job? The woman might be the hottest piece of ass he'd come across in a long time, but she was not his type. End of story. Psychics were off limits. In a way they *were* like prostitutes, only they fucked with your mind, not your body. Major buzz kill. He'd be taking a shower alone when he got home—a cold one.

"Yes, I know about that *unsolved* case," Katherine said. "So does everyone else in the city. You can't seem to catch him, and until you do, no one is safe. Did you call my report in like you promised?"

Did everyone in the world know he had failed to apprehend The Midtown Strangler? Was it trending on Twitter?

"Look, I'm off duty, so you can just talk to that nice officer sitting over there at the desk," Jack said, pointing to the front of the squad room. "Sarge, you're in for a real treat. This woman has something she wants to get off her...um, chest."

He needed to get away from this kook. Her manicured nails gripped his arm and attempted to spin him around. He stopped in his tracks. The prognosticating pixie was surprisingly strong.

"I'm talking to you, Detective Jack Hale," said the diminutive stunner. "And you'd damn well better listen, or you're going to be sorry."

"Is there a problem here?" Reacting to the raised voices, the sergeant got up from his desk and walked toward Jack and his visitor. "If you have some issues to work out with your girlfriend, Hale, you'd better take them out of the precinct."

"He's not my boyfriend." Katherine turned her attention away from Jack and toward the man approaching her. "I'm Katherine Crystal. I called in to report a plane crash, and he ignored me. Are you his boss? I want you to reprimand him."

"I'm not the captain, but what's this about a plane crash?" Sergeant Lisle asked.

Jack jerked a finger at Katherine. "This psycho, I mean *psychic*, claims Vince Rivers' plane is going to crash in Georgia and his son is going to die. I humored her, but of course she's making the whole thing up just to make a name for herself."

"Ma'am, I'm Sergeant Anthony Lisle," he said, extending his hand and nodding politely in Katherine's direction. "Is what Detective Hale said true?"

"Yes."

"Well, young lady, don't you worry, we're going to get to the bottom of this," Sarge assured, covering Katherine's tiny hand with his big meaty one.

So, Sarge had charm. Who knew?

"When is this crash supposed to happen?"

"That's just it. I had this vision, but I don't know. It might already have happened."

"Sarge," interrupted Jack. "It's a *vision*. Nothing concrete to act on."

"I haven't seen anything about it on TV," reasoned the sergeant. "We haven't had anything reported, except for your call." Sarge narrowed his eyes and glared at Jack.

Jack flinched. How could Sarge believe this soothsayer that he'd known for one minute over a cop whose family he'd known for years? Then he gave Katherine Crystal a second look. The reason was obvious. Sarge was a man, and she was a perfectly put together woman. What guy wouldn't respond to that?

A rush of uniforms swarmed into the squad room, causing a minor commotion and jostling Jack and Katherine while they vied for Sarge's attention.

"Sarge, you've gotta come see this," shouted one officer. "Turn up the volume on your TV. It's breaking news." Being the tallest person in the room, Jack strode over to Sarge's desk and adjusted the volume on the television before Sarge could get to the remote.

Crowded around the TV, the group looked up at the steaming wreckage on the big screen.

"Vince Rivers' plane just crashed at the DeKalb-Peachtree Airport," said one of the officers. "We got the call to assist."

"Is fire-and-rescue on the scene?" inquired Sarge.

"Yes, and the place is crawling with reporters."

"Okay, we've got to get down there," Sarge directed.

It hit Jack like a punch in the gut when he saw the headline scrolling across the screen:

Vince Rivers Injured in Private Plane Crash.

Ocean Rivers Dead.

Chapter Two

Midtown Atlanta, Three Weeks Later

Jack paced the highly-polished hardwood floors in his Midtown condo like a caged panther. The place looked like a pigsty. He'd ordered in pizza four nights in a row and finished up the last bottle of beer. Now he'd moved on to the hard stuff.

He'd tossed and turned but hardly slept since the news of Ocean Rivers' death went viral. Holed up in his condo for a week after the crash, he'd avoided work because he didn't want to deal with people. But life as a hermit crab was not all it was cracked up to be.

He couldn't get the TV images of a devastated Vince Rivers walking behind the tiny white casket at the cemetery out of his mind. And Vince Rivers struggling to keep his distraught wife from jumping into the grave after it.

Predicting the death of Ocean Rivers could have been a lucky guess. Jack did not believe in psychics, but maybe this Katherine Crystal was for real and he was foolish for ignoring her warnings.

Dammit, that Crystal woman was messing with his head. She was all over the news. Every time he turned on the tube he saw her face. Her unforgettable face. He couldn't stop fantasizing about her long dark ringlets, those violet eyes and pouty lips, and the rest of the irresistible package. He thought maybe it was the beer talking, but even when he was cold stone sober he couldn't stop thinking about her.

The media had dubbed her *Crystal Ball Kate* and they couldn't get enough of her. He couldn't blame them. She was making the rounds of all the daytime talk shows and late night programs. In fairness, she didn't look too eager or comfortable in the spotlight, but the reporters and the cameras worshipped her. Her fifteen minutes of fame had exploded into infinity and beyond. The talking heads couldn't stop talking about her and fussing over her, flashing on every gory detail of the crash.

He didn't bring that plane down. Hell, it was probably already in the air by the time she called. Jack downed the rest of his Jack Daniels and mentally kicked himself in the ass. He could justify his actions all he wanted, but what if he could have saved that child? What if the disaster could have been averted?

Sarge thought so. He had reamed him out in front of the whole squad for not following the rules and reporting Katherine Crystal's call. And he'd had a mouthful to say about the Midtown Strangler and Jack's failure to make any progress on that case.

To make matters worse, Sarge had hired Katherine Crystal to consult with him on the strangler case. That is, when she wasn't flying around the country making television appearances.

Jack passed by his bathroom mirror and pulled up short. Jesus, he looked like a werewolf. He had to get rid of all this hair. But a pact was a pact, and he still hadn't caught the strangler. He scratched his chin. His head was beginning to itch. Or maybe it was the mind games Katherine was playing with him. Maybe she was into voodoo magic.

She'd come into the precinct last week to discuss the case. She certainly didn't dress like any cop he knew. She stuck out like a sore thumb walking around Midtown in her tight, low-cut red designer dress, dripping in jewelry and tripping in her high-heeled shoes. He'd had to catch her twice when the heel of her shoe got stuck in a sewer grate. She felt good in his arms. But she had no law enforcement experience to speak of. She was just a drag on the investigation. Nothing more than eye candy—window dressing.

"He's not here," Kate had insisted on their walk-around.

"What do you mean, he's not here? He's not in Midtown? Not in Atlanta?"

"Not in this country."

"How do you know that?"

"I've had a vision."

Jack was exasperated. "Are you frigging kidding me?"

Kate had gone quiet, completely clammed up.

"Well?" Jack demanded. "What did you see?"

Kate crossed her arms and stood on the sidewalk outside the precinct. "You won't believe me."

Sometimes he wanted to kick her in her well-rounded butt. Sometimes he wanted to grab her butt and kiss the breath out of her. Working with her these past few weeks had done a number on him.

"He's gone home," Kate said.

"Okay, I'll bite. Where is home?"

"Australia," Kate said simply.

Jack shook his head and walked into the precinct

16

with Kate on his heels. He was not working with this nut job. She was pulling things out of the air.

Sarge signaled them over to his desk.

"Jack, Kate, there's been another murder. Scumbag with the same MO as our Midtown Strangler. A copycat."

"He's not a copycat," Katherine insisted softly. "He's the same killer."

"Impossible," stated Sarge. "Sydney, Australia, is his new killing field."

Jack choked. "Australia?" He looked at Katherine.

"Yep. He's gone Down Under."

Jack turned to Katherine. "How did you know? Did Sarge tell you?"

"This is the first time I've mentioned it to anyone," Sarge said. "We've been asked by the police to fly to Sydney to see if we can be of assistance."

"We?" Jack asked warily.

"You and Kate."

Jack shook his head. "Not going to happen."

"Listen to me, Jack. They didn't ask for you. They asked for Crystal Ball Kate. I'm sending you along as her escort."

Jack bristled.

"They've seen her on TV and they feel she could help them break the case."

"They don't need a pseudo-psychic who couldn't see the future if she tripped over it. She doesn't know the first thing about murder. I'm the legitimate law enforcement professional, the one familiar with the case."

"Sour grapes," Kate mumbled.

Sarge's eyes narrowed and skewered Jack's. "Your

vast knowledge about the subject hasn't done you much good in solving your case, has it? You *will* go with her and make sure she gets anything she needs to solve this case."

"You mean like her assistant?"

"Whatever she needs."

Katherine smothered a smile. She was mocking him. In front of Sarge and all the guys standing around doing a lousy job of pretending they weren't listening. He didn't find it the least bit amusing, but apparently everyone else thought it was hilarious.

"I'll go home and pack, Sergeant," Katherine said pleasantly.

After she left the precinct, Jack gritted his teeth and faced the captain.

"She sells art for a living," Jack said. "The kind of art with lines and shapes and colors that don't look like anything."

"I don't care if she's a dog walker. Her track record speaks for itself. Now you go to Sydney and keep close tabs on her. Don't let her out of your sight. You got a problem with that, take it up with the lieutenant or the captain. The orders come from higher up. My hands are tied. But if anything happens to her, I'm holding you personally responsible. Make sure the department looks good. Don't screw this up."

Jack stewed all the way home. He didn't need this aggravation. He wasn't going to be a cop the rest of his life. He was going to law school at night, and he was close to graduation. As soon as he got his degree and passed the bar, he was going to be a lawyer. Maybe it was time to quit. His father had loved being a cop. Jack didn't. But he wanted to catch the serial killer who had terrorized Midtown. That was a matter of personal pride.

He was sure the murderer in Sydney was not the same man, despite what Crystal Ball Kate had said. But what choice did he have? He could either go to Sydney with the wacko psychic or quit the force. It would be so easy to call in his resignation.

Jack walked into his condo and looked around at the clutter. What kind of a mess had he gotten himself into? He wanted to give Crystal Ball Kate a piece of his mind.

Frowning, he picked up the phone and started to dial.

Chapter Three

En route to Sydney, Australia

"Miss, are you all right?" The flight attendant spoke in hushed tones. Katherine felt Jack's arms reach over and gently shake her shoulders.

"It's just another bad dream," Jack assured her. "She'll be okay."

"Take your hands off me," Katherine said, jolting forward until the tug of her seatbelt yanked her back against the uncomfortably stiff seatback. Agitated, she gripped Jack's wrists and hung on for dear life.

"You were having that dream about the plane crash again. You're scaring the other passengers. Go back to sleep," he ordered.

Easy for him to say. Within minutes, the man was snoring like he didn't have a care in the world, although in sleep Jack fidgeted as much as when awake, adjusting his hulking frame to find a comfortable position. Katherine almost felt sorry for him. *Almost.* The seats were too cramped even for someone of her size, and he had almost a foot on her. Her thighs rested in an awkward position on the hard seat cushion. She looked over at Jack. They'd been sitting next to each other on this plane for almost twenty hours. And he'd been stuffing his face for most of that time.

Whenever Jack stood, his head bumped into the

overhead luggage compartment. He was probably a bed hog, too. As if she'd ever share a bed with a man with all that body hair. She didn't care much for cavemen. He had probably been a linebacker in college. A linebacker who'd gotten his head bashed in one too many times. He didn't seem too bright.

He was also a total pig, or else he had a tapeworm. When he wasn't sleeping, he was eating. The man was perpetually hungry. Every time she came back from the lavatory, the flight attendant had delivered another snack. For someone his size, there was not an ounce of fat on the man, but he was so damn big, he was constantly crossing over into her personal space.

Katherine didn't tell Jack that the subject of her latest dream was not Rivers' plane crash. She had started flashing on the Sydney strangler again, the same man who had gone on a killing spree in Midtown Atlanta, then abruptly changed continents without changing his MO.

The Down Under dream episode had exhausted her, drained her so completely she could hardly keep her mind focused. It wasn't easy for her to fall back asleep. But the flight attendant had appeared unflustered. This plane wasn't going down.

"Now I know where I've seen you before," announced Perky Patty. Correction, Shelby was the name on her badge. Sexy Shelby, then. "You're Crystal Ball Kate, that psychic on TV, the one who predicted Ocean Rivers would die in the plane crash."

Katherine frowned. She hated her new moniker.

"How do you do that?" Shelby asked.

"Do what?"

"Make those predictions. Have you always had

magical psychic powers?"

"They're not magical powers," Katherine objected, rolling her eyes and picking up a magazine, pretending to read it. "I just see things."

"Your magazine is upside down," Shelby persisted.

Katherine turned the magazine around and shoved it into the seat pocket in front of her.

"If you can read my mind, then what am I thinking?" Shelby challenged.

Was she wearing an invisible sign that read Free Readings on Board? Katherine reached up and pressed the button to turn off her overhead light. She knew exactly what Shelby was thinking. The woman was easy to read, since her mind was as porous as a sieve, with silly thoughts leaking out of it at a steady rate. She was hovering, probably hoping Jack would wake up. She didn't have to be a mind reader to know Shelby had been coming on to Jack the whole flight. The flight attendant was a shamelessly transparent bubblehead. *Is there anything I can do for you, Detective Hale? Anything I can get for you? Can I freshen your drink? Show you around Sydney after we land? Show you what's under my uniform?* Well, she hadn't said that, exactly. But she was undoubtedly thinking it.

Shelby knew Jack was a police detective because he'd had to inform the airline he was carrying a weapon onto the plane. A cop with a weapon was a total turn-on to some women. And why should she care? They weren't a couple. But Sexy Shelby didn't know that.

Katherine yawned, hoping Shelby would get the hint and start paying attention to passengers in another row.

As the cut-rate Koala Blue jet streaked across the

sky, rattling like an enormous wash bucket, Katherine had the chilling feeling the Sydney serial killer was about to strike again. She could sense him stalking his next victim. She wasn't sure they would arrive in Sydney in time for her to prevent the senseless death of yet another young woman.

Since the New South Wales Police Force in Sydney had contacted the Atlanta Police Department inquiring about Katherine's ability to help in their case, she had seen the Sydney strangler in a number of visions. He was young and handsome, blond, and innocent-looking. His victims were, too.

She had described the man to Sydney police over the phone, but they wanted her in Australia, in person, to wring every bit of knowledge out of her, to bleed her mind dry.

In the past, the closer she came to a crime scene, the stronger her visions were. So perhaps it was better for her to be on the strangler's turf where the action was. But she needed to detach herself. She worked better if she could clear her mind of all emotions.

Katherine grabbed her bottle of water and swallowed two more aspirin. The more powerful the visions, the more painful the headaches. That's the way it worked. Pharmaceuticals never seemed to help. She dug the heel of her hand into her forehead to blunt the total terror she was channeling from the victims.

Katherine had the urge to call ahead and alert the authorities, but what exactly could she tell them? What clues could she give them she hadn't already shared? She desperately tried to remember details of the images she'd seen. Where the strangler was holding his prey, something, anything that would help the Sydney police locate the latest victim before her fate was sealed. When he did strike, Katherine would blame herself. Because she wasn't fast enough, perceptive enough, good enough, to keep it from happening again.

Still groggy, she tried her best to relax and wondered how long she had been out. Her watch was still on Atlanta time.

She unbuckled her seatbelt, shifting her gaze to the right. She was virtually trapped between Jack in the aisle seat on her left and the woman wearing a face mask, who had been coughing her brains out in the window seat during most of the flight. She probably had the swine flu. Why hadn't Silly Shelby isolated her and contacted the CDC?

The cabin was dark. A movie was running, some frivolous comedy she hadn't been in the mood for since she'd already seen seven movies on this never-ending flight from Atlanta to Sydney.

Beauregard Lee Jackson Hale was a mouth breather. Was it possible for a sleeping man to look smug? Somehow he managed it. His beard seemed to be sprouting tufts. She didn't trust men with beards. Beards could hide a lot of secrets.

At the moment, Jack's head was pressing like a granite boulder against her bare shoulder, and his beard was scratching her flesh. She had half a mind to snap his picture and upload it to Facebook. Either that or wake Rip Van Winkle up with a baseball bat.

Katherine shifted her body away from Jack's thick head, allowing it to drop down to rest on his own shoulder. What did she care if he woke up with a stiff neck? She wobbled out of her seat. Her legs were cramping and she was dying to stretch them, but first she had to slip past The Incredible Hulk and into the aisle. She eased around Jack, careful not to wake the sleeping giant.

The captain's melodious voice wafted over the loudspeaker. "We're making our final approach into Sydney."

"Kate?" Jack groused. "Where are you going? Get back to your seat. You heard the captain. We're about to land."

Darn. Jack was awake. Did the man sleep with one eye open? Maybe all cops hovered in a perpetual state of alert. Why was he acting like an annoying big brother, like she was some kind of irresponsible child he was stuck babysitting? He was treating her like she was under house arrest, *which* she wasn't. She was a civilian consultant and should be treated accordingly.

The man was unbelievable. His captain must have given him specific instructions not to let her out of his sight, and he had taken his marching orders literally. Jack's boss had no doubt charged Jack with keeping her on a tight leash to make sure she didn't cause any more embarrassment to the department. She might as well be wearing an ankle monitor. He'd hardly taken his eyes off her, when he wasn't sleeping or eating, except when she had to use the bathroom, and even then the permanent scowl on his face made it clear he was pissed because he was left to cool his heels outside the lavatory.

"I'm just going to the restroom. Stop following me. Give it a rest, Bobo."

"Why don't you try calling me by my real name for a change?" said Jack, unfastening his seatbelt.

"Beauregard Lee Jackson Hale?" Katherine

snickered. "You have more names than the Prince of Wales. Bobo is easier to swallow." That made her think of the story about Jonah and the whale. Beauregard was as big as a whale, and he looked big enough to swallow her whole.

"Just call me Jack. I hate Beauregard. My mother calls me Beauregard. I let her get away with it because, well, she's my mother."

And we all know how Southern boys feel about their mamas, Katherine thought.

"Okay, jackass, I mean Jack, I don't want you to have to chain me to the seat with those handcuffs." Katherine's eyes sparkled as she reached out to lift the restraints from Jack's pants pocket when he attempted to get up from his seat.

He grabbed for her, but she slipped through his fingers.

"You're not my boss, and you don't scare me," Katherine said, power walking to the restroom, jangling the cuffs for effect, a wide grin breaking out on her face, feeling the best she'd felt in twenty-four hours.

Jack rushed after her and grabbed her arm. "That's police property. You're asking for it."

"Asking for what?" she teased.

She thought she could outrun him, but the very moment she thought she was home free, she felt his fingertips on her back. He was going for her T-shirt, her favorite Michael Kors T-shirt. It was already too tight. She didn't need him to stretch it. She zipped down the aisle, but he was closing in fast.

Breathless, she ducked into a vacant lavatory, locked it behind her, and splashed some frigid tap water on her face.

Jack knocked on the door.

He had seen her go into the restroom. Did the man think she was Houdini? They were at a cruising altitude of 36,000 feet. Where did he think she was going?

"Look, I need to take a leak before we land."

"Who's stopping you?" Katherine called out. "Do you need my permission? Or do you want me to stand guard while you relieve yourself? Use another restroom or hold it. I'll be out in a minute."

"Don't wander off. I want you in your seat when I get back."

"Where do you think I'm going to be, idiot? In an overhead luggage bin?"

Katherine shook her head and stared full on into the mirror, bummed when she came face-to-face with a pair of bleary eyes, a rat's nest on top of her bed head, and a mouth full of cotton behind her faded lips.

"Kate." More knocking.

"Get a grip. I'm still in here," she shouted.

Jack might be a police detective, but he had no rights over her here in the air or anywhere. Even if he did have a ginormous gun. She'd seen it up close and personal, even stroked—and was mesmerized by—the gleaming metal while he was asleep. Was it true what they said about men packing big guns? That got her to thinking about stroking something else... Don't even go there, she thought, banishing those naughty thoughts.

Katherine flushed the toilet, ran a brush through her dark ringlets, touched up her lipstick, and tried her best to smooth the wrinkles from her jeans. She looked like Dracula's wife. What a mess. Why did she even care how she looked? Jack was the most irritating man she'd ever met. She certainly wasn't interested in him.

He did have a certain animal magnetism. Okay, he was sexy as hell, but she didn't traditionally go in for the all-brawn-no-brains type. Her ideal mate-meter was malfunctioning. It must be the long flight and the dangerous proximity.

Picking up her purse from the filthy floor, she pulled the knob toward her, unfolding the door, and caught Jack leaning into Shameless Shelby, his flushed face inches from hers.

As Katherine narrowed her eyes, they sprang apart, evidently guilty of some major indiscretion.

"The captain has turned on the Fasten Seatbelt sign," Shelby said abruptly. "We're in our final descent, so you two need to get back to your seats." Then, "See you in Sydney, Jack," Shelby purred in her irritatingly bubbly voice. She tilted her head and gave Jack a final sultry glance, brushing against him possessively on her way down the aisle.

"Looks like I interrupted something," Katherine said, allowing her eyes to scan Jack's body from top to bottom, à la Shelby, and finally returning her gaze to his piercing blue eyes.

"Shelby was...um...interested in my weapon," explained Jack.

"I'll bet she was," Katherine said, smirking. She shook her head, reached into her purse, and tossed Jack his cuffs. Jack caught them easily.

"You and Shelby may need these later," she said, tightlipped.

"Damn prima donna. If you're so clairvoyant, then guess what I'm thinking right this minute."

Jack was more difficult to read, since his head was as thick as a cement block, but she imagined he and

Shelby were planning an intimate rendezvous in Sydney. Maybe he'd already copped a feel from the flighty flight attendant, taken a taste of her lips. Who cared if he had? She wasn't usually the jealous type. Jack apparently found Shelby attractive, in a blonde-bimbo sort of way. Most men would.

Katherine smiled mischievously and spoke slowly, and loud enough for Shelby to overhear. "You're wondering if we have enough time for a quickie before we land?"

"You are so off base."

"Am I?" she drawled wickedly, in the sassiest tone she could muster. Katherine tried to negotiate her way around Jack, but he was as big as a brick house, and he grabbed her arm roughly.

Somebody was mad.

"Did anyone ever tell you you're a major pain in the butt?" Jack said.

"No, you're the first."

"Is seeing things that aren't there part of your psychic talent?"

"Very funny," Katherine said, continuing to stare at Jack.

"You are more trouble than you're worth, you know that?"

Unfortunately, most men she'd dated had come to the same conclusion. She wished that just once she would meet a man who could understand her and appreciate her for who she was, psychic baggage and all. It hadn't happened yet in thirty years.

She had to admit that somewhere under all that shaggy underbrush the guy could be a major hottie. If he would just spring for a haircut.

"The bathroom's free, if you want to shave. Or you might ask Shelby if she has a pair of hedge clippers."

Katherine flashed a smile and waved before purposely sashaying down the aisle and settling into her seat, making sure he got a good look at her booty, which she considered one of her best features. If she had to be stuck with this bozo, then she was damn well going to enjoy herself at his expense.

Minutes later, Beauregard—and she would be calling him that as often as possible—slid into his seat and glared into her eyes with his dangerous baby blues.

"I foresee a tirade coming on in the very near future," she said lightly.

"Don't give me any of your extrasensory shit."

"You're crass."

"And you're a quack."

Katherine pursed her lips and turned away toward the coughaholic in the seat next to her. She covered her mouth and felt her teeth tighten. She was not a quack, and she resented him saying so. His attitude was grating on her already frayed nerves.

"You were saying something about my beard?"

"You look like a Civil War reenactor," she said, fastening her seatbelt and giving him a cursory glance. "No, one of the seven dwarfs. Goofy."

"Goofy's a dog," remarked Jack as he buckled up next to her, bumping her with his elbow.

"Then Scraggly."

Jack lowered his voice. "As you well know, I was on an undercover assignment, which is why I grew this beard, before the department sent us to follow our serial killer—or a damn good copycat—to Sydney."

"It's definitely him," she insisted. "He's not a

copycat. The same man who killed those girls in Atlanta is the one murdering them now in Australia."

"Do we have to have this conversation in front of all the passengers?" Jack whispered. "This is official police business."

"I think the less we say to each other the better," Katherine warned. "Just let me do my job so we can go home."

"To Mr. Psychic?"

Katherine blew out a breath. "There is no Mr. Psychic." And probably never would be.

"Why not? How come a perfectly presentable thirty-something woman like you is not attached?"

"Gee, you're generous with the compliments," Katherine said, brushing back a loose curl from her face. "And I'm not thirty yet. But I'm sure you already knew that. I'm sure you *think* you know everything there is to know about me."

"I'm an investigator. Investigators investigate." Jack paused, dipping his eyes down to Katherine's painted toes and then raising them to take in her breasts.

Her heart stuttered.

"Anyway, I'm curious to find out what kind of man does it for you."

Katherine sighed, lifting her shoulders. "Something about me seems to scare off the men I date. Maybe I should stop predicting they're not going to get laid." She glanced at Jack to gauge his reaction. "Most guys are surprised to learn that my head doesn't spin around on its axis when I go into a trance. That I'm not possessed."

"It probably freaks guys out when you tell them you're a mind reader."

31

"I'm not a mind reader, exactly," Katherine objected and sat back in her seat, pretending to read her magazine. Why should she reveal all her secrets to this Neanderthal? Sure, she could read moods, like anyone in a serious relationship. It was hard to take a guy at his word, though, when, more often than not, she could intuit what he was really thinking, the good along with the bad. But Jack was an enigma. Was he interested in her or wasn't he? She couldn't tell.

That was probably just one of the reasons she was the biggest loser in the relationship game. Add Beauregard to the growing list of people, including her parents and her former fiancé, who were mystified by Katherine Crystal. Too bad she didn't come with an operating manual.

The fact that she could see the future with such horrifying clarity, in such devastating detail, day after day and nightmare after nightmare, meant she could never rest easy and was rarely easy to be around. She accepted that she was different, dateless and lonely, but that didn't mean she liked it.

She turned to look at Jack. "I'd give anything to be able to walk on a beach and watch the waves crash, and not see a car crashing around a hazardous curve. To feel the warm sand between my toes instead of the fear on the face of a drowning swimmer."

She wiped the tears from her face and closed her eyes, as she recalled those horrific moments. She held her head and rubbed her eyes as she felt another headache coming on.

Jack looked at her with sympathy in his eyes. His concern seemed genuine. How much should she reveal? Could she take a chance that he was beginning to take her seriously?

"To see a white gull swooping down for his daily catch, instead of a metal bird falling out of the sky, which is exactly how I ended up in this predicament in the first place."

"Well, you're the one who called the media," Jack reasoned. "If you hadn't, you'd still be anonymous, just another poor little rich girl."

Katherine held back the urge to slap his face.

The Ocean Rivers case had been her debut onto the national stage. Now she was hunted by the media. Word of her "paranormal powers" had gone viral. Local police departments around the country wanted to hire her. Politicians wanted her to assess their chances with the voters. Who needed pollsters or public opinion polls when they had the "all-powerful, all-knowing" Katherine Crystal?

Katherine felt anything but powerful. In fact, she felt like a failure. Even if she got it right and no one listened, it was a matter of life and death. The truth was, she just wanted to be left alone. No one would guess she'd trade all that notoriety for just a few moments of peace. There were no beautiful sunsets in her world, only tragedies in the making.

****

How could Kate be so sure of herself? She may have the whole world fooled, but he knew, and soon the New South Wales Police Force would know, that Ocean Rivers was just a lucky guess. *Crystal Ball Kate, my ass.*

"You're nothing but a charlatan," Jack accused. And he intended to prove it.

"A charlatan? Really? Who talks like that?"

Katherine flipped her hand as if to dismiss his accusations.

"Would you prefer 'fake' or 'fraud'? Same difference."

"I don't want to be here anymore than you do," Katherine seethed. "I didn't ask for you, especially not you. If you had listened to me in the first place, Ocean Rivers might still be alive. I don't need you watching my every move and second-guessing me. There are lives at stake."

"I know that." Jack turned to face her. He looked down into her eyes and a lock of unruly hair fell across her forehead, making her seem younger, more vulnerable. He studied her intently.

"Honestly, just between the two of us, up here in the stratosphere, no reporters, no cameras..." Jack lowered his face and his eyes bore into hers, trying to capture the visions floating through her consciousness. "Can you really see things before they happen?"

She shrugged. "Sometimes I get only flashes, brief visions of disasters." She closed her eyes and looked away. "Earthquakes, floods, drownings. But the plane crash that killed Ocean Rivers plays over and over in my mind even now, and it's trapped in my head in Technicolor. I relive it every day." *With the choking clockwork of the Groundhog Day movie.* "I've learned to take my premonitions seriously."

"I wish I had," Jack admitted, genuinely sorry. "So, how does this psychic thing of yours work? Do you read tea leaves? Tarot cards? Palms? Inquiring minds want to know." He grew serious. "Humor me."

Katherine hesitated. "Everyone is psychic. We all have a second sight or sixth sense. You know, the hunches and intuitive feelings we sometimes get. I just happen to be able to channel or tap into a universal spiritual energy field."

Jack placed his hand on Kate's face and tipped it toward his. "Can you really see into the future?"

Katherine nodded, letting the warmth of his fingers seep into her soul. "I see into a possible future. If you know what lies ahead, there's always that chance you could change the outcome."

Jack dropped his hand. "Like you think I could have done if I'd listened to you about the plane crash."

"Exactly."

"How can you be so sure you're right?"

"Some things I just know. Some things I don't want to know. But one thing I know for sure. Absolutely everything that is wrong in my life now is your fault."

****

Jack shifted in his seat and their legs touched, sending shock waves down her body. Katherine feigned disinterest as Beauregard blustered around next to her. His legs were too long, and he was too bulky to fit into his seat comfortably. Understandable, since he was the size of an ox. Of course, he had insisted on the aisle seat, even though that was her seat of preference.

Her real preference had been to sit in first-class, like she was used to, but she was working for the government now—actually two governments, the Cities of Atlanta and Sydney—so the roomy seats, solicitous service, and white tablecloth dinners were just a dream. If this airline even *had* a first-class section.

Katherine buckled up as the plane began its descent into Sydney. She was absolutely beat, out of sorts, and tired of tasteless airplane food, flirty flight attendants, and the stale smell in the cabin. And she was tired of being locked in, of sitting in this same tight spot for almost twenty-four hours, tired of being watched constantly by her own personal guard dog.

Katherine couldn't wait to get to the hotel. She was dying for a hot shower and the opportunity to relax for a while in her cozy (she hoped) hotel room and enjoy a good seafood dinner from room service. She was up for some tasty Balmain bugs, which Beauregard's travel guidebook defined as butterfly fan lobsters that thrived in the waters around Australia. Then she was going to hibernate for the evening so she could be refreshed before their morning appointment with the commander of the New South Wales Police Force.

She and Beauregard were definitely not on the same page of the guidebook, or any other book. She sensed he had no intention of lounging around the hotel. Right now, he was probably mentally outlining all the things he wanted to do when he got into the city—starting with a bus tour of Sydney to get acclimated and a stop at Bondi Beach. For a guy who went strictly by the book, that didn't sound like proper police procedure. How could his mind be on sightseeing when a serial killer was on the loose? She was willing to wager that Beauregard was a country bumpkin, a mama's boy who had never traveled out of his comfort zone.

"We could visit the Sydney Opera House," Jack said, leafing through the Sydney guidebook he'd had his nose buried in since they'd taken off from Atlanta, when he wasn't tailing her or sleeping or eating. He'd probably memorized it by now.

"The guidebook says the Shangri-La Hotel is conveniently located in the historic Rocks district, right in the heart of Sydney's City Centre," he told her. "That's very close to the Central Sydney police station where our meeting is. The Shangri-La is supposed to have killer views of the Opera House and Sydney Harbour Bridge."

"You should be less concerned with killer views and more worried about the serial killer." Jack didn't have to see the faces of the victims or feel their suffering. If he did, he wouldn't be making such idiotic suggestions.

"You've never really been involved in a serial killer case, have you?" Jack asked pointedly.

Katherine didn't want to admit she was scared or unsure of herself, but there was no way around the fact that she was out of her element. She sold artwork for a living, serious artwork, to buyers with serious money, but she had no experience with serial killers or the seamier side of life.

"No, this will be my first time."

"Well, I have, and it's not pleasant," said Jack, kicking his legs out. "We will find this guy, but I think we need some downtime before our ordeal, to get our bearings. It's always a good idea to immerse yourself in the city, get the lay of the land."

Downtime sounded good to Katherine. Lack of sleep and the constant barrage of visions had her head pounding. But her idea of downtime was not sightseeing.

"There's even something called a Sydney Harbour Bridge Climb that starts right around the corner from our hotel," Jack said.

"You want to climb a bridge after an exhausting plane trip?"

"Why not? It will get the blood flowing. After the climb, we can relax and hang out at Circular Quay, maybe take a commuter ferry to the Taronga Zoo, see some koalas, some kangaroos. I understand they have some great kangaroo on the menu Down Under, too. Our appointment isn't until tomorrow, so we've got the whole day ahead of us to do whatever we want."

"Hold on there, Beauregard." Katherine bristled. "Besides the fact that you are gross and disgusting to even mention *seeing* kangaroos and *eating* them in the same breath, we are not going anywhere together. For one thing, we're not here on a sightseeing trip. This is all about police business."

"Then why don't we go straight to police headquarters? Why did you insist on waiting a day?"

"Because I knew I'd be exhausted after our twenty-four-hour flight," Katherine complained. "I can't see straight or think straight. And my brain is turning to mush. My internal time clock is all out of whack. In order to do what I have to do, I have to be rested so I can concentrate, open myself up to feel things, focus. How can you even think of sightseeing when there's a serial killer on the loose?"

"The guidebook says the best way to overcome jet lag is to get on with your day, eat your meals, and stay awake," said Jack, openly thumbing through the guidebook to find the passage he was citing.

"Do you believe everything you read in there?" Katherine retorted, reaching over to grab the guidebook from him. "What if the guidebook told you it would be a bigger thrill to jump off the Sydney Harbour Bridge than to climb it? Would you jump?"

"Maybe, with a parachute or a bungee cord."

"You like to live dangerously. I prefer to get my adventure fix watching TV from the safety of my hotel room."

"If the psychic prima donna needs her beauty rest..."

"Take that back," Katherine said irritably.

"I'm only speaking the truth. Admit it. You have no idea who the killer is, what he looks like, or where he is. This whole trip is a big boondoggle to you, but as long as we're here—"

"If you really believe that, then you're even more of a jerk than I thought."

Jack shrugged.

"What time is it?" Katherine asked.

"You're the psychic. You tell me."

"You know what I mean. Sydney time."

"How should I know?"

As if on cue, a voice came over the loudspeaker.

"This is Captain Hayes. We're about to land in Sydney. It is currently eight a.m. Sydney time. Thunderstorms are predicted for later this afternoon. On behalf of your Sydney flight crew, we'd like to thank you for flying with Koala Blue Airlines today. We hope you enjoyed your flight and that you enjoy your stay in Sydney. It was a pleasure serving you, and we hope to see you back again soon on Koala Blue."

Thunderstorms. Perfect. She should have predicted that. The weather fit her mood exactly.

Jack Hale had made no secret of the fact he thought she was bizarre. He'd pitched a hell of a fit when his superiors ordered him to accompany her to Sydney. He wasn't a babysitter. She was a quack. She knew nothing about police procedure. *Blah, blah, blah.* He had bordered on insubordination and had almost been fired over it. He'd definitely gotten his ass handed to him. That had been fun to watch. For a giant, he didn't have such a big brain, and he wasn't very flexible.

Finally, his sergeant had settled it.

"Young Jack, I'm making allowances for you because I knew your father," said Sarge at the end of the upbraiding. "Everything isn't always black-and-white. I'll admit this is a little unorthodox, but what choice do we have? The media is watching every move we make. We're out of options, and we need all the help we can get. You will either accompany Miss Crystal to Sydney or you can walk out this door now and leave your shield behind." He hesitated, offering a last piece of advice. "Your father was not a quitter."

Jack had grumbled, but in the end he had caved. Katherine smiled at the memory, did a little victory dance in her mind. She was determined to be taken seriously.

From what she could tell, Beauregard was as rigid as a stone, a play-by-the-rules kind of guy who wasn't bothered by shades of gray or nuances. You were either right or you were wrong. He had obviously already written her off as irrational, and his goal was to make sure the police in Sydney got the same impression of her.

Well, she had a goal, too. To help the NSW Police Force catch their serial monster in record time so she could get out of there and as far away from Beauregard Lee Jackson Hale as possible.

Chapter Four

Sydney, Australia

Jack stepped up to the registration desk at the Shangri-La Hotel while Katherine soaked in the soothing décor of what was obviously a first-class hotel. Impressive setup. Now this was more like it.

"Reservations for Hale and Crystal."

The woman behind the counter typed their names into her computer and frowned. "Is that Catherine Crystal with a C or Katherine Krystal with a K?"

"Katherine with a K and Crystal with a C," Katherine answered, relieved that at least one person in the world hadn't heard of her.

"Here it is. The gentleman who made the reservation requested one room."

Katherine stepped up to the counter, elbowing Jack out of the way. "There must be some mistake," Katherine insisted. "I don't want to be anywhere near this man."

"I have a lovely suite with a king bed reserved for Detective Jack Hale and guest."

"Well, I'd like a room on a separate floor," Katherine replied. "Preferably a separate property."

The desk clerk's hands flew over the computer keys, searching for a vacant room. "I'm sorry, Ms. Crystal, but we're all booked up. We have three conferences and a wedding going on at the hotel." The clerk made some notations and handed her an envelope. "Detective Hale's suite has a spectacular view. You won't be disappointed. But I'd like to offer you and Detective Hale a free breakfast to compensate for the mix-up."

"I don't care how many conferences you have going on or how magnificent the view is. And I can assure you I *will* be disappointed if you can't find me another room."

"Again, I'm terribly sorry," said the desk clerk, who sounded apologetic but whose impatient tone reflected a woman who was obviously experienced at handling difficult guests. "But Detective Hale's suite is very spacious. I think you'll be quite comfortable there. It's one of our best rooms."

"I don't care if it's the Taj Mahal. Who made these reservations?" Katherine demanded, staring ominously at Jack. *"Detective* Hale?"

"The room was booked by the New South Wales Police Force at their special rate," answered the desk clerk.

"Maybe the police department couldn't spring for two rooms at these prices," Jack said, looking sheepish. "But they really splurged on this hotel."

"I don't need a fancy hotel."

"Somehow I doubt that, Miss I-Always-Travel-First-Class. But it's important that we're near the police station."

"The closer you get to Sydney Harbour, the more expensive the rooms are," explained the clerk. "If you want mid-range rooms, you'll have to head inland."

To Katherine, with utter exhaustion in every bone

of her body, inland sounded like another planet. She doubted she could make it upstairs, even on the elevator. "This has nothing to do with cost and everything to do with the fact that you plan to keep me under surveillance. There's no way we're going to sleep in the same room."

"It's not a room, it's a suite," Jack shot back. "My orders are not to let you out of my sight." Jack fidgeted with his wallet.

"I thought so," Katherine stated impatiently, lifting the oversized Michael Kors purse from its perch over the handle of the suitcase and sliding it over her shoulder. It felt like a lead weight. "Do you always take your orders so literally?"

"Following the rules keeps you safe. So does being together 24-7, and if that means sharing a room, then so be it. You're my responsibility while we're in Sydney."

"Oh, so you did tell them we only needed one room?" she challenged, emphatically shaking her head. "I am not shacking up with you. I hardly even know you. And I don't *want* to know you. This is ridiculous." Katherine turned to the clerk. "Can you please book me a room at another hotel?"

"I can try, Ms. Crystal, but all the hotels in The Rocks district are full. This is the most popular time of the year in Sydney."

"Just my luck," Katherine muttered, turning back to Jack. "I'm dead on my feet. I'm ready to fall asleep right here in this lobby, and I don't think I can make it as far as another hotel anyway. So there'd better be a separate place for me to sleep in your *suite*."

"Live with it, sister. You, me, Sydney—the possibilities are endless."

"You are just trying to rile me, and it's not going to work," she said, trying unsuccessfully to remain calm. "All right, if I have to stay in the same suite, I am going to make your life a living hell. By the time I'm through with you, you will regret the day you met me."

"Too late," he seethed. "I already do."

****

Katherine drew back the floor-to-ceiling blackout curtains and the wispy white sheers in the suite at the Shangri-La and gawked at the jaw-dropping view. She'd traveled all over the world with her parents, seen some pretty awesome scenery, but of all the hotel rooms, in all the places she'd ever visited, this view was the most magnificent. If it wasn't one of the Seven Wonders of the World, it should be.

Even through the settling mist, the sight of the city took her breath away with its panoramic view of Sydney Harbour, Sydney Harbour Bridge, the Sydney Opera House, and the coves beyond. Boats dotting the harbor breezed in a dynamic watercolor come to life, their gentle wakes trailing like shooting stars across the sun-sparkled water.

The hotel website promised spectacular, but spectacular didn't even begin to do justice to the scenic feast laid out before her. Tired as she was, she'd love to browse through some of the local art galleries and buy a painting of just this scene, or at least a postcard.

Katherine turned and took in the spacious room with its larger-than-life king-sized bed and a royal purple quilted floral headboard that stretched nearly to the ceiling. The room was washed in a welcoming warm yellow paint. There was a huge comfortable-looking tufted couch, two flower-patterned wingback chairs, a desk, and a ginormous flat-screen TV.

Before she could scope out the sleeping arrangements, the toilet flushed and Jack sauntered out, like a male dog marking his territory, apparently proud of the way he'd done his business. Actually, she'd been sauntering too after communing with the luxurious bathroom facilities in their suite. The bathroom even had a crystal chandelier.

"Are we ready?" he said.

"Ready for what?"

"To see some of Sydney."

"First of all, I don't think I can tear myself away from this view."

"It is pretty sweet," he said, joining her at the window. "But the real thing is out there."

"You go ahead. I'm whipped. I think I'll just take a cat nap."

"Then you'll zone out for the rest of the afternoon. I told you, we need to stay up all day and then we'll be back on our regular sleeping pattern and eating schedule. Come on, I'm starving."

"Why am I not surprised?" she said, folding her arms across her chest. She sighed. "Actually, I could eat something light. Maybe some broth. I think I'll order from room service."

Jack ambled over to the bed. "Quite a bed," he said.

Was he insinuating something? "Quite a couch," Katherine countered. "That's where you'll be sleeping."

"Hey, this bed is big enough for Kate Plus Eight."

"It was your idea to get one room, Papa Bear. You're not sleeping in my bed, no matter how many bowls of porridge you try to ply me with."

"Why, do you snore?"

"How would I know?"

"I know you have nightmares," Jack stated, lowering his voice to barely a whisper, "when you dream. I mean at least you did a lot on the flight over."

Of course she had nightmares. The world was a scary place, and there were a lot of scary thoughts tumbling around in her brain, thoughts she couldn't control. Sometimes her mind was a freaking horror show.

"Okay, let's run down to Circular Quay and have a snack while we watch the ferries take off," Jack suggested. "My treat. It's supposed to have a great view of the bridge."

"What's wrong with the view from our room?"

"Nothing, I just want to be up close and personal."

Up close and personal. Katherine felt her face flush and her legs start to give way. "Oh, God, no," she whispered, reaching for purchase and grabbing air.

She felt Jack's hand on hers just before she crumpled to the ground.

****

Jack rushed to her side, catching the swaying woman in his arms just in time. He carried her to the bed and shook her. She was starting to scare him.

"Kate, are you okay?"

She wasn't responding. He was trained in CPR. Should he try that, or call the hotel operator? One minute she was admiring the view, and the next she was unconscious. What had just happened?

"What's wrong?" he said, checking her pulse. Maybe her clothes were constricting her. She hadn't eaten. Maybe she was dehydrated. He reached over to the end table for some bottled water.

Still nothing. Why were her lips blue? He started CPR. Breathed into her mouth, pressed against her chest.

Kate's eyes flew open and her arms flailed against him.

"What are you doing?" she said, sitting up against the headboard. "You were trying to suffocate me."

"I was trying to save your life," Jack said, breathing easy again. She was okay.

"You had your hands on my boobs."

Jack sighed and smiled. "I was doing CPR."

He twisted off the lid and handed her the bottle of water. "Here, drink this."

She took a drink from the bottle.

"You had some kind of episode. Does this happen often? What triggered it?"

"It-it's what you said. 'Up close and personal.' " Katherine's eyes widened in horror. "He says that."

"Who says what?" *Was she delirious?*

"The Sydney strangler, right before he kills the girls," said Katherine, pressing the heel of her hand to her head.

"Do you have another headache? I can get you a cold washcloth. How about an aspirin?" Jack laid his hand on Katherine's forehead and he felt helpless. She didn't have a fever. "What about the strangler?"

"He's close. He's somewhere right around here. I don't want to go out. Please."

She struggled against him, and he held her close until she quieted. She turned pale and her breathing was irregular. She had him worried. He didn't know what she needed from him. Food, water, sleep? A hug?

Jack expelled a breath and relented. "Okay, we'll order up room service."

She was shaking. Something was frightening her.

"You don't have to be afraid, Kate. I'm here." Jack pulled back the bedspread.

"Under the covers, now. You're shivering." He rubbed her shoulders. "We'll do whatever you want to do. You need to eat something, rest. You said so yourself. You're totally exhausted. What would you like to eat?"

"I can't eat anything now," Katherine said, biting her lip. "We need to get to the police station, right away. I'm afraid something is going to happen."

Jack frowned and studied Kate. "What do you think is going to happen?"

"Something bad, to the girl."

"You're not making any sense. A minute ago you said you wanted to stay in," Jack reasoned. "Now you want to go out to the police station. Why?"

"We're running out of time."

Chapter Five

"Can you give us something more concrete to go on?" asked Homicide Squad Commander Michael Jones, his skepticism evident by the pessimistic arch of his brows.

"He's blond," replied Katherine.

"That describes most of the population of Sydney," said Jack, standing sphinx-like, mouth pursed, arms folded across his chest, leaning against the wall in the commander's office.

The New South Wales Police had accepted her assistance because they were out of answers and a young girl was in trouble and needed help. And she wanted to help. But they wanted answers fast. She couldn't turn her abilities on and off like a spigot. Her visions often came unbidden. She couldn't control them any more than she could control the weather or the stock market.

"She can't give you anything because she doesn't know anything," Jack said. "This is a major waste of everyone's time. Now if you want my help—"

"I can see him," Katherine hesitated, screwing her eyes shut, desperately wanting to help, furious at Jack for sabotaging her and calling her abilities into question before she even got started.

"Well, then maybe you can work with our sketch artist," suggested Commander Jones.

"I'd be happy to."

"You're an artist, why don't you just draw him yourself?" Jack suggested.

"I sell art. I don't paint it."

"Can you at least be a little more specific about what you're seeing?" Commander Jones urged hopefully.

Katherine bit her lip. "He's very handsome, sexy, smooth, and brash. And he's a sharp dresser. They—the girls he's stalking—go with him willingly," Katherine continued. "He's charming. He flatters them. He makes them want him, want to be with him. He's charismatic, but normal looking enough to blend in, like a chameleon," Katherine added. "But there's nothing normal about him. He has a dark, evil streak."

"One look at the crime scene photos will tell you that. Anything else?" asked Commander Jones, frustration etched on his tired face.

"Can we see the crime scene photos?" Jack asked. "Maybe that will trigger something."

The commander handed Jack a thick file. Jack spread out the color photos on the commander's desk, so Kate could get a good look at them.

"How many girls has he strangled?" Katherine asked, bile rising in her throat. She'd already seen flashes, brief snatches of what was in these pictures in her mind, but seeing them so brutally close—murder in Technicolor—was a different matter.

"Five, that we know of," answered the commander. "Kylee Wilson has been missing for two days now. He usually dumps the bodies of his victims after three days. If he sticks to his pattern, Kylee doesn't have much time left, that is, if she's still alive."

"May I see a picture of Kylee?" Katherine asked.

The Commander slid her a picture of the girl—a winning smile, dressed for a prom, her sheer white gown offsetting her white-blond hair, flawless complexion, a white orchid adorning her hand. She was the picture of purity and innocence.

The girl in this picture was most definitely still alive. But she was fighting the battle of her life. Katherine could feel her terror, hear the hitch of her shallow breaths.

"He wants them to taste fear," Katherine said, slipping into a trance-like state. She squeezed her eyes shut, trying to visualize Kylee, get into her mind.

The room went dark.

"I just want to get to know you, Kylee," the strangler whispered, "up close and personal." He slid the muzzle of his gun against her cheek, then down her neck to her naked breasts. Kylee was shaking, shivering like a frightened bird, trapped in the cage of a cold, dungeon-like room. Bound uncomfortably in a vertical position to a post. The rope chafed against her delicate skin, now raw, every time she moved. The man followed his weapon's movement, his fingertips nuzzling Kylee's face, caressing her neck and then winding their way lower.

Kylee moaned.

"Now don't move or make a sound. You know what happens to naughty girls who make me mad. I really don't want to have to hurt you."

Kylee's eyes glazed over. He had drugged her, but only slightly, so that she was responsive, still aware of her surroundings, still frozen with fear.

The strangler put down the gun and wrapped his

huge hands roughly around Kylee's throat as she tried to wriggle free. Her jerky movements only excited him. He squeezed until he almost shut off the flow of air from her windpipe.

Almost, but not quite.

The fun was just beginning. He was going to take it slower this time around. He had all the time in the world. It was loud upstairs. The party was in full swing. No one could hear her screams.

Kylee was fragile, very small. He'd played with small birds like Kylee before. His mother said he didn't realize his own strength. He played too hard and, sometimes, the tiny birds died before he was finished with them. That made him sad when the birds died before their time. And then it made him mad. That had happened with the last girl. She'd left him before he was through with her. He wasn't going to let that happen with Kylee. They had the whole night ahead of them.

Kylee was a virgin. He had picked her for that particular reason. He'd tested her to make sure. She was pure and he would initiate her. He could have any girl he wanted, any time he wanted. But there was no challenge when things came too easily.

The strangler picked up a can of cold beer and took a swig. He already had a nice buzz going. His tuxedo jacket was folded neatly on the couch. He'd had to put on a heavy wool sweater. It was cold down here. Kylee's nipples were straining for his touch. Against her will. It was more fun that way.

The strangler laughed. He loved a good struggle. Despite the drugs, Kylee was feisty, and she had a lot of fight left. He had chosen well. Maybe he should untie her and see what she could do. See how far she could get. It wasn't exactly a fair fight. He had all the advantages.

"Untie my hands, please," Katherine pleaded. "I need to sit down."

Kate was already seated and her hands were unrestrained. She was obviously in the throes of a nightmare or one of her visions. The tears flowing down her face wrenched Jack's gut. He didn't know why he suddenly felt so protective of her.

"Kate," Jack whispered softly.

Katherine's eyes fluttered open.

"Kate, what's happening?"

Katherine's body strained against the invisible bonds. She continued to whimper.

"We need to wake her up, now," Jack insisted, alarmed.

"No," argued the commander. "She might have more to give us."

"Stand back," Jack threatened. Grabbing Kate by the shoulders, he gently shook her. "Kate, Kate, open your eyes. You're safe now. You're with me."

"I was there. I saw them."

Jack looked into Kate's violet eyes. He could get lost in those eyes. "I know." He wouldn't have believed her if he hadn't witnessed Kate's visceral reaction first hand.

"Look, you don't have to be afraid. I'm packing. It's my job to protect you."

"Have you ever used that thing?" Kate was staring at the bulge in his breast jacket pocket which hid his holster and gun. He'd screwed up once when he'd ignored her warning call about Ocean Rivers. He wanted to be sure she had no illusions about his ability to perform in a crisis.

"If you mean have I ever killed anyone, no, not yet. But I'm perfectly capable of using deadly force." Just thinking about guns always made Jack think of his father. Officer Jackson Hale had been shot and killed in the line of duty and had been branded a hero. His father had also used deadly force, yet he'd still gotten himself killed. Ever since then, ever since Jack had decided to become a cop, he knew that an officer in or out of uniform had to be prepared to draw a line in the sand, to lay hands on. Even if that meant taking away someone else's father, someone else's husband.

"Do all cops have such big egos?" Katherine asked.

Jack ignored her remark. Cops had to have inner confidence. Most of the cops he knew had it. His father had had it, in spades. Would he be as brave as his father if the time came?

Dredging up unhappy memories suddenly made him tired, almost too tired to move. But he wasn't going to let Kate or Commander Jones see it.

"What did you see?" the commander wanted to know. "Could you tell where he was holding her? Did you hear any noises, buses, church bells—anything that would give their location away? Were they near the water?"

Jack turned his anger on the commander. "Can't you see she's upset?" Jack accused, his eyes narrowing. "She hasn't eaten anything since we landed. Get her something to eat and drink while she composes herself." Jack looked around the room for a couch or something more comfortable than the straight-backed chair Kate was sitting in. "Is there somewhere she can rest for a while? She's been through a lot."

Katherine sat mutely on the chair, pressing a hand against her forehead.

Jack wondered how he had suddenly transformed into Kate's knight in shining armor.

"We're wasting time," the commander railed, pacing around the room, flexing his right hand like he was ready to punch someone. "I'm going to get my sketch artist in here while everything is still fresh in her mind."

Jack stood solidly between Katherine and the commander. "Now you listen to me. This woman is my responsibility. And we're going to do this my way or not at all."

Shrugging his shoulders, Commander Jones picked up the phone and barked out some orders. After he hung up the receiver, he led Jack and Katherine into a dimly lit reception area with an overstuffed green leather couch.

"She can rest here until the sketch artist comes. My secretary will bring up some food and something to drink."

"Okay," Jack said, flexing his shoulders. "Okay. How are you feeling, Kate?"

"It was horrible." Katherine turned her pale face up to his. "Jack, we need to catch that man and lock him away before he can hurt anybody else. He's sadistic."

Jack rested a hand firmly on her shoulder. "We will. We will, don't worry. I promise." He knew his promise to her hadn't been worth much in the past. This time it would be different.

"I'm afraid it might be too late for Kylee," she stated.

Jack looked up when a young officer with a sketch pad followed the commander into the room.

"Kate cannot start until she's had something to eat," Jack insisted angrily.

Katherine placed her hand over Jack's. "That can wait. This is too important."

Jack frowned. He didn't like it one bit. The woman had been through a lot. She had been on the verge of hysteria and now she was calm. Too calm. Highs and lows. Her mood swings had him worried. She needed to eat something. But he'd go along with her, for now.

The commander approached Katherine. "Miss Crystal, this is our sketch artist. He'll work with you to help you flesh out any details you can remember about the man you saw."

Katherine stood up and shook hands with the artist. Then Jack put his hands on her shoulders and guided her back into her seat.

She covered her eyes with her hands and began talking. She described in detail the exact shade of blond and the texture of the man's hair, his magnetic blue eyes, his deceptively sweet dimples, his broad build, and his hands. His large, strong, bone-crushing hands.

"Was his nose about like this?" the artist queried.

Katherine opened her eyes and nodded.

"What about the room where he kept her?" the commander prompted. Can you describe it?"

After about half an hour, the sketch artist held out his sketch pad.

"That's him," Katherine said, pointing to the drawing, agitated.

Commander Jones walked around the table, took one look and exclaimed, "Miss Crystal, you've made a terrible mistake."

"That's the man in my vision," Katherine insisted.

"I know that's the man you *think* you saw, Miss Crystal, but Lucas Taylor is not the strangler."

"Who's Lucas Taylor?" Katherine asked.

"He's the son of the Lord Mayor of the City of Sydney," said the commander.

"Kate seems certain," said Jack. "How do you know it's not Taylor?"

"Because I know the Lord Mayor personally, and I know Lucas, and he's not—"

"Not what?" Jack demanded.

"Not smart enough for one thing, sad to say. Handsome bloke, for sure, has a way with the ladies, but he's not quite right in the head. Ever since his motorcycle crash. He was driving without a helmet. Well, he couldn't pull it off. Wouldn't."

"Are you saying he's not capable of doing something like this?" Jack nearly shouted, his irritation evident. He'd been around all types of killers and he knew with certainty that anyone was capable of murder. "Do you really think that all serial killers are geniuses? That serial killers have to be smart to be sadistic?"

Commander Jones frowned at Jack, fidgeted, and rubbed his chin. "That's not it at all. Certainly he's capable, physically. He's strong as an ox, like yourself, but he's privileged. He wouldn't get his hands dirty. He could have any woman in town, if he wanted. He's Sydney's most eligible bachelor."

"Just because a person is rich doesn't mean he can't be a sick bastard," Jack countered. "Maybe if we paid the Lord Mayor a visit, we could let Kate meet this Taylor person and see for herself if she gets any kind of vibe or strange feeling."

"I'm afraid that would be quite out of the question," Commander Jones objected, raising his voice. "We can't just walk into the Lord Mayor's home and arrest his son on a *feeling.* We need hard evidence."

"How can we gather evidence if we can't see where the suspect lives?" Jack said.

"He's not the suspect," the Commander repeated.

"Yet," said Jack. "I'm not telling you how to do your job, but—"

"It certainly sounds that way."

"Where does the Lord Mayor live?" Jack asked.

"The Lord Mayor and his son live in inner-city Redfern in a converted warehouse. Very upscale. In fact, they're having a party there right now. My boss is one of the guests."

"Then get him on the phone," Jack pressed.

"That's out of the question."

"Just find out if the son's at the party. Kate and I could go over there. He doesn't know either of us."

"On what pretense?"

"You could get us invited."

"On a fishing expedition?"

Jack pulled on his beard. "We'd need a warrant to search the place."

"That's harassment. We don't know that the boy is even involved." Commander Jones pulled a handkerchief out of his pants pocket and wiped the beads of perspiration from his forehead. "It could cost me my job if we're wrong."

"And it could cost a girl her life if Kate's right."

"We'd be getting a search warrant based on a hunch," the commander argued.

Jack pulled the commander aside, out of Katherine's hearing range. "Look, I was the first one to think Crystal Ball Kate was a fake. But you saw her in there. What if she's right? Are you willing to gamble on a young girl's life? The papers will crucify you if we lose another one." *Like they did to me.*

Commander Jones appeared to consider Jack's position. "I suppose I could get a warrant to keep in my back pocket and drive to his house on an urgent matter I need to discuss with the boss. Then you and Miss Crystal can have a look around. If you find something, don't be a hero. I'll send some squad cars over for backup."

"How far away is this warehouse?" Jack inquired.

"Not far from here. We'll take my car," Commander Jones said, barking orders as he flew into action, alerting his team, calling the judge about a warrant.

"Come on Kate," Jack said, taking her hand and leading her out of the station as they followed the commander to his car. "Let's go catch a killer."

Chapter Six

Catch a killer? The reality of what she was up against hit her like a sharp slap in the face. She had no experience with crime or criminals. Jack Hale was right. She was out of her league. She wished she were anywhere but in the back seat of an unmarked squad car, sitting next to the macho cop who had absolutely no confidence in her abilities, hurtling her way into the dead of night to hunt down a serial killer.

"No sirens," instructed Commander Jones to his team over the radio, slowing the unmarked car as he approached the vicinity of the Lord Mayor's home. He pulled into the driveway and ordered the valet to make sure his car was accessible.

Jack, Katherine, and the commander got out of the car and approached a woman holding a clipboard in front of an open door.

"Michael Jones to see Chief Commissioner Williams on urgent business," said Commander Jones.

The woman glanced over her shoulder inside the living room to where the commissioner was standing with a drink in his hand, chatting with the Lord Mayor. She shook her head and clicked and unclicked her pen, clearly unhappy about the unscheduled intrusion of unexpected guests.

"May I have your names again, please?"

"Commander Michael Jones and these are my

associates, Detective Jack Hale and Ms. Katherine Crystal."

"That's Katherine with a K and Crystal with a C," Katherine noted, stepping into the porch light.

Jack rolled his eyes. "Who cares how you spell your name? We're wasting precious time." He slung the reprimand like he was dressing down an underling, not a colleague.

"You're not on the list," the woman persisted. "Do you have some identification?"

"Is this a party or an interrogation?" the commander hissed, jerking his badge from his pocket and flashing it in the gatekeeper's face. He pulled back his jacket to give her a bird's-eye-view of his .357 Smith & Wesson revolver. "Allow me to introduce my good friends Mr. Smith & Mr. Wesson. I don't leave home without them. Why don't you check again? I'm sure we're on the list."

Flustered, the woman stepped back. "I don't like to interrupt The Lord Mayor, but I'll get Chief Commissioner Williams."

"I would appreciate that." The commander turned back to them and whispered, "Katherine, you and Jack get busy. Have a look around. Be inconspicuous."

Jack and Katherine followed the commander into the house and had started to disappear into the crowd when Jack placed his hand on Kate's shoulder to stop her.

"I'd like to hear this conversation," Jack whispered.

Commissioner Williams walked over to the commander. "What are you doing here, Jones?"

"We're looking into the possibility that the, uh,

Lord Mayor's son, that is, Lucas Taylor, may somehow be involved in the Sydney Strangler case."

The commissioner's face flared in anger. "Involved? In what way?"

"The psychic we brought over from Atlanta had a vision. She identified Taylor as the Strangler."

"She had a *vision*? Is this some kind of a joke? And you thought you'd come to the Lord Mayor's house, interrupt his party, and question him about his son? That's outrageous! You don't have a suspect and you're grasping at straws."

Jack nudged Katherine, herded her in with a cluster of guests, and planted her squarely behind an indoor ornamental tree to hide them from the commander's view.

"I have a woman, the psychic, here, and she's trying to see if she gets any—"

"Vibes? Is that the word you're looking for, Jones? I know I authorized this psychic thing as a last ditch resort because you and your people have absolutely nothing to go on, but I will not allow anyone from my staff to insult the Lord Mayor this way. I think you'd better find this psychic person and go."

"Yes, sir," Commander Jones said, looking perplexed as he glanced around the room. The commander cleared his throat. "I...uh...seem to have lost them, sir."

"Well, you'd bloody well better find them, then, Commander, if you fancy your job." Commissioner Williams scanned the room, then straightened his tie. "I'm going to smooth things over with the Lord Mayor, and when I look up, I don't want to see you here."

Commander Jones surveyed the room and spotted

Jack and Katherine behind the potted plant. The crowd was restless. Apparently everyone in the room had heard the argument. The Lord Mayor confronted the commander.

"Problem?" the Lord Mayor said.

"Just a routine police matter," Commissioner Williams assured his host.

"Do you sense anything yet?" Jack asked, grabbing Katherine's hand and ushering her into the next room and out of sight of the Lord Mayor.

"I'm not a crime-sniffing dog, for heaven's sake," Katherine barked.

"I know, but are you getting a feeling or whatever it is you woo-woo types get?"

"Woo-woo types? Katherine bristled. "Really?" She cleared her head, ignored the *jack*ass next to her, the blare of the music, the smells wafting in the air, the jumble of conversations, and focused. That's when she heard the scream.

She turned to Jack and grabbed his arm. "Did you hear that?"

"Hear what?"

Katherine closed her eyes again and concentrated. He was so close. He was here. Right here. Her skin crawled as she watched the strangler touch his latest victim.

"Kate, what's wrong," Jack asked, rubbing her hand. "You're as pale as a statue and you're as cold as stone."

"Don't hurt me again. Are you going to cut me?"

"Sssh. We're just getting started. It's going to be a long night, Kylee. Just relax and enjoy." The strangler massaged Kylee's neck. Kylee struggled against her

63

bonds.

"Just practicing," he said.

"I'm cold," Kylee whimpered.

"Don't fight me," the strangler murmured as he stroked Kylee's breasts and trailed his hand down to her thigh.

"Are you in a trance? Kate, Kate, wake up."

Kate shivered and looked up into Jack's face.

"What happened to you? Where did you just go?"

"I saw him. I felt his evil presence. He's definitely here. We've got to find him before—"

Commander Jones was heading toward them.

Jack squeezed Kate's hand.

"I've been looking all over for you two," said the commander. "We've got to get out of here."

"We can't leave," Jack said. "Kate is onto something. She says he's here."

"I've looked everywhere, at all the guests, and there's no sign of the Lord Mayor's son."

Jack faced the commander. "Did you ask the Lord Mayor about him?"

"That's one thing I *can't* do. Chief Commissioner Williams instructed me to get off the property. He'll have my job if we stay here any longer."

"Commander, I know he's here." Katherine groaned. "We've got to stop him."

"Does this house have a basement?" Jack asked.

Commander Jones shook his head and shrugged his shoulders. "Let me call the station and see if we can track down the schematics or blueprints for the house. Maybe there is a basement or a safe room of some kind. Meanwhile, I'll alert my people to stand by at the back entrance."

Commander Jones turned to look at Katherine. "Are you sure about this? Or is this just a hunch?"

"I bet against her once," Jack interrupted. "I won't make that mistake again."

"All right. I'm going to call and see what's holding up our search warrant."

****

The backbeat of a band pulsed in Katherine's ears, in contrast to a chorus of cicadas, singing in the Sydney spring night.

Commander Jones shone the flashlight onto the blueprints he had stretched out on his squad car in the darkness.

"Bastard's soundproofed the basement, according to these plans, but there's no extra security," reported the Commander. "Bugger is confident no one will suspect him or find him in The Lord Mayor's house."

"*His* own house," Jack asserted.

"You'd better be right, Kate," Commander Jones muttered, casting a sideways glance at her before issuing the order to break down the basement door.

"I pray I am," Katherine whispered. Her heart tripped as the door splintered and a small uniformed force blustered into the room, weapons drawn. She wanted the strangler to be there, but she was afraid of what else they'd find.

"Lucas Taylor," the commander shouted. "This is The New South Wales Police Force. We have a warrant to search your basement."

"Keep back, Kate," ordered Jack, who had also drawn his weapon.

"I'm coming in," Katherine argued, trailing Jack.

"Then stay behind me." Jack moved her forcibly

out of the line of fire.

Katherine stepped over the threshold into a scene out of a horror movie. This basement bachelor pad was definitely the killer's playground. Bloodstained sheets, shackles on the wall, and a limp, naked Kylee sagging against a steel pole, tools of torture spread out on a nearby table. Women's clothing and underthings—frilly, fragile, and bloody—were scattered on the floor.

Jack checked the young girl's pulse. "She's alive, but barely," as he used a Swiss Army knife to tenderly cut the ties that bound Kylee's hands and feet.

"Christ," sputtered a sickened commander, breathing deep to keep from heaving. "Where's the sick bastard who did this?"

The SWAT team spread out and checked each room in the basement.

The toilet flushed. Lucas Taylor sauntered out of the bathroom, half-dressed, blond hair mussed and pale skin gleaming with sweat, singing, "Kylee, time to wake up again." He froze when he saw the officers.

A second later Lucas sprinted into action and ran for cover in the bathroom, but Commander Jones was quicker. He stuck his booted foot in the door and pushed against the force on the other side before Lucas could lock it and barricade himself in.

"It's over, Taylor. Come out or I'll blow your fuckin' head off."

"Do you know who I am? My father—"

"I know just who and what you are, and I don't care who your bloody father is, you're going down. No more hiding behind Daddy."

Together the commander and his team broke the serial killer's hold on the door and pulled the bug out of his hidey hole.

Jack carried Kylee over to the couch and placed her head in Kate's waiting lap. Kate covered the girl with a blanket she'd found tossed carelessly over a throw pillow and wrapped a protective arm around her shoulder.

"You're safe now, Kylee. You're going home."

Kylee wept a stream of silent tears. When she looked over at her captor, she started trembling uncontrollably and she couldn't stop.

The commander read the Lord Mayor's son his rights, jerked his hands behind his back, and cuffed him roughly.

"How do you like it now? You like it rough? I can do rough."

"Commander, we'll take him out the back," Jones' second-in-command said.

"No, we'll be making a little detour through the house, to give Daddy and his party guests a good look at his freak of a son."

"You can't do this," shouted Lucas. "I have my rights."

"Let's talk about your rights down at the station. I want this whole damn place swept for evidence. Make sure he doesn't have anyone else down here."

The commander walked over to where Katherine was sitting. "Great job, Kate." He pressed her shoulder emphatically. "You should feel good about what you did here today. You saved this girl's life."

"You're going to be okay now," Commander Jones assured the girl gently. "We've got him. He can't hurt you anymore."

Katherine held Kylee closer, both of them shaking.

Nothing about this place made her feel good. She couldn't wait to get home, away from this house of horrors. She'd never been so scared in her life. Scared for Kylee. Scared for herself. Her parents had been right about predicting the future. She had no business tampering with other people's lives, messing with the unknown.

Chapter Seven

Aboard a Koala Blue jet en route to Atlanta

Katherine pretended to sleep while she squinted at Jack, who was half-hidden behind a newspaper, trying to get comfortable in his cramped airline seat. Turned out Jack wasn't as big a jerk as she'd originally thought. In fact, he had been very protective of her in Sydney, and he'd been there when she needed him. He hadn't apologized, but he wasn't cracking any more "woo-woo" jokes or mocking her "magical powers." So that was a step in the right direction. The fact that Flight Attendant Barbie wasn't on the return flight was another plus.

"Kate," he nudged her shoulder. "Are you awake?"

Kate smiled. The man wasn't exactly subtle. She'd hardly had enough time to admire him surreptitiously or finish her in-flight fantasy about being tangled up in the satin sheets on the king-sized bed at the Shangri-La Hotel in Sydney, wishing Jack had not agreed so readily to sleep on the couch. She was vulnerable and thoroughly shaken up by the whole experience. She needed to be comforted. Hell, she wanted to do more than talk to Jack, as macho and insufferable as he had been. Maybe it was just the adrenalin, but she'd been having naughty thoughts about Jack throughout the flight.

"I guess," she said. "What's up?"

"You're famous."

"What do you mean?" Kate straightened in her seat.

"You're all over the *Sydney Morning Herald* and *The Daily Telegraph*."

Kate grabbed the newspapers from Jack's hand. "Why did they have to mention me?" Katherine said, lips pursed when she saw her picture splashed all over the front page of the newspaper. Her parents had repeatedly warned her not to make headlines. She read a few paragraphs about her role in the Sydney Strangler case and the recounted story of how she had predicted the death of the son of Vince Rivers.

"What are you so steamed about? You're the new 'It' girl. Apparently you single-handedly caught the Sydney Strangler."

"I didn't catch him. You and the commander did."

"Information you provided led to his arrest."

"Just a technicality."

Jack took her chin in his hands and tipped her face up to him. "Kate, look at me. We couldn't have done this without you. That's a fact. So face it."

"I don't want to ever have to go back there," she said.

"Hopefully, you won't have to. But if we have to go to Sydney to testify at the trial, that's a small price to pay to get that sick psycho off the streets. He won't ever see the light of day, and if justice is finally done, we'll execute him."

"I thought the commander said Australia had abolished the death penalty."

"We're trying to get him extradited to Georgia,

where we do have it. My team is busy trying to tie him to the Atlanta killings, refute his alibis. We have our people checking the Lord Mayor's travel records. If we can match Junior's DNA to the evidence we found on the dead girls at Atlanta College, and if the Lord Mayor was in Atlanta during the time of the killings and his son was traveling with him, then we've got him dead to rights."

Katherine was still looking at the newspapers with a frown on her face.

"So what's bothering you?"

"I just hope the Atlanta papers don't run anything. I don't want my name associated with another case."

"Why not?"

"My parents don't want me doing this kind of thing."

"Saving lives? Isn't your mother an attorney and your dad a federal judge?"

"Yes, but she and my father shun publicity. They'll be furious if this gets out. They haven't recovered from the swirl of publicity surrounding the Vince Rivers crash. They think this sort of stuff is somehow less than respectable."

"Well, normally I'd have to say I agree with them. But in this case, I can't discount what I saw or what you did. How do *you* feel about it?"

"Conflicted, I guess. I've had these dreams, feelings, welling up inside of me ever since I can remember, and I can't go to my parents. My mother used to call my visions headaches. 'KC, dear, are you having one of your headaches again?' she used to say before she dismissed them. The Vince Rivers case was the first time I acted on my instincts. It felt…good, right."

"Better than selling paintings to socialites?" Jack said, barely hiding his amusement. "Do you plan to work at an art gallery selling somebody else's work the rest of your life?"

Katherine looked up at Jack in disbelief. He was the most exasperating man. One minute he was signaling his approval and the next, dismissing her abilities. She was good at her job. Intuitively, she knew which paintings should go home with which patrons. But that knowledge was useless now, because no one except the super rich was buying paintings anymore, not in this economy, and they preferred dealing with Sotheby's or Christie's rather than a local gallery.

"Apparently not, since I just lost my job at the Freyer Gallery. I haven't even told my parents yet."

"You got fired?"

"Laid off. Nobody has any money to buy fine art anymore. I was the top salesperson, *when* people were in the market for my product. To answer your question, no, that's not what I pictured myself doing for the rest of my life, but right now, that's all I've got going. What about you? Planning to be a cop forever?"

"I've got a degree in criminal justice and I've almost graduated law school."

"My mother says there are already too many lawyers," Katherine said, snorting.

"But how many lawyers have police backgrounds? I know the justice system from the ground up. One day, I want to have my own detective agency. I'm covering all the bases."

"Sounds like you know just what you want. I envy you."

"I guess with your parents' connections and money, you really don't even need to work. Must be nice to have a safety net. Parents who believe in you."

Jack fixed her with his searching blue eyes, and she flinched under his frank appraisal.

Jack didn't know how wrong he was. Her parents were both realists who believed only in proven facts. They were both methodical and reserved, so it was frowned upon to show emotions in the Crystal Palace, otherwise known as her family home in Buckhead, the toniest section of Atlanta.

Wasn't Jack listening? Hadn't he heard her mention that neither of her parents knew what to make of her psychic abilities? They usually chose to ignore her random visions of inconsequential future events, such as consistently predicting winning lottery numbers. They chalked it up to coincidence when she knew someone was at the door before the doorbell rang or a lucky guess that she knew the phone was going to ring before it did. Or when she had a dream that usually came true. But they found her serious visions of disastrous events, over which she had no control, more worrisome. Katherine considered her special abilities natural, but to her parents they were unnatural, supernatural, an embarrassment, and the less said about them the better.

Worse, she sometimes felt like she didn't even belong in her family. Both her parents were successful overachievers. She was a failure, by any standard. No job now, no means of support, and she didn't want to continue to freeload off her parents. She wasn't exactly living in their basement. She had her own suite in the Crystal Palace. But she was still wandering on an unknown future path, trying to find her way.

If she were truly successful, would she still be living at home? And would the gallery have terminated her because they no longer needed her services? She had been embarrassed when she had to admit to Jack that she was unemployed. But she wasn't about to back down.

"And what if I did want to sell paintings for the rest of my life?" she challenged. "There's nothing wrong with that. I appreciate beauty."

Jack stared at her intently, then looked away, leaving her to scan the papers and wonder what she did to put the latest scowl on his face.

****

If he didn't know better, and she wasn't always so damn angry all the time, he'd think *Crystal Ball Kate* had cast a spell on him, a love spell. He'd been watching her sleep, taking cover behind a newspaper to hide the fact that he couldn't take his eyes off her. She was having a hell of a dream if that smug smile on her face was any indication. Probably about some guy— some lucky guy.

All he could think about since they left Sydney was kissing her. He'd come so close in the hotel room as they were packing up and preparing to fly back to Atlanta. They were both ginned up after catching the Sydney Strangler. For all his bluster, and the control he wielded over innocent, helpless young girls, Lucas Taylor was just a sniveling little creep who had broken down like a crybaby when Commander Jones perp-walked him by his father in front of all the Lord Mayor's distinguished party guests. The commander had caught hell from Chief Commissioner Williams for doing it so publicly, but he still admitted it had been worth it.

They'd finished up all the paperwork and said their goodbyes to Commander Jones at the station, and then Jack had taken her out for a big dinner to celebrate the fact that his long-term losing streak was finally over.

Back at their hotel suite, he could still see Kate perched in the window seat, sunlight streaming in, highlighting the golden streaks in her hair, sprinkling sunshine like fairy dust. She was marveling over the view, and he was thinking the view from inside the hotel room was pretty great, too. He'd walked up behind her and placed his hands squarely on her shoulders. She'd startled and turned around, and at that moment, as he gazed into her bottomless violet eyes in that stunning face, he'd wanted nothing more than to take her in his arms and find out what it would be like to kiss a psychic, to be part of her future.

He'd resisted the urge and the moment was lost. But his desire for Kate was still alive and kicking. The look she'd given him then made him think she really could read his mind. It was uncanny.

He hoped she didn't know what he was thinking right now, sitting so close to her, winging their way back to Atlanta. She hadn't given him a clue as to what was going on in that complicated, messy mind of hers. Or whether she'd want to see him again when they got back to Atlanta.

"So, what do you plan to do when you get back to Atlanta?" Jack asked, testing the waters. "With all this publicity, you have an open ticket to travel around the world solving mysteries and problems."

"You wouldn't believe the endless parade of

reporters knocking on my parents' door looking for a scoop since the Vince Rivers prediction," Katherine said. "Inquiring minds want to know: Who is *Crystal Ball Kate*? Where did she come from? What's going to happen next?

"It's all about the road not taken, and everyone thinks I can point them in the right direction. How can I point anyone in the right direction when I don't know where I'm going myself?"

"Well, I'm not a psychic, but I can pretty much predict where we're going now," Jack said. "Back to Atlanta."

"Very funny." Katherine shifted in her seat, trying to get comfortable.

"But seriously, are you going to continue doing police work?" He was crowding Kate in her seat. His arm was touching hers as they fought for purchase on the armrest between them. He was winning. He enjoyed the electric shock sensation whenever they came in contact. Kate, not so much. She was grabbing her left shoulder and twisting her body in an effort to angle away from him. He couldn't help his bulk or his muscles. He was a big guy. He turned his head to face her.

"Not if my parents have anything to do with it. As of now, the 'Crystal Ball Kate,' franchise is closed for business."

He didn't know how he felt about that. He didn't want her on his turf on a regular basis, but she had been a big help on the strangler case in Sydney.

"But, Kate, you have a true gift. You can help people. You already have."

"Jack, my parents were right," said Katherine. "I'm

not cut out for this. I'll answer the dozens of messages on my cell phone from agencies who want me to solve a police case or people who want me to predict their futures, let them know I'm not interested. My phone's still ringing off the hook. I was finally forced to change my number. But somehow they've managed to track me down."

"Who exactly is calling you?"

"Friends of Vince Rivers—fellow actors and the beautiful people—calling incessantly, looking for stock tips, advice for the lovelorn, and career recommendations. Should they accept this movie role or turn it down? Could I contact the spirits of their loved ones from beyond the grave? I'm not a medium, for heaven's sake. I mean, I've dabbled in tarot cards, but I don't read palms to predict the future."

"Thank goodness for that," Jack said vehemently.

****

Don't go soft on me now, Jacko, he cautioned himself. Just because she's the most beautiful woman you've seen in a long time. Maybe ever. A man could get lost in that oh-so-touchable, temptingly soft, dark fall of ringlets and those compelling violet eyes and that smile. God, Kate's smile could light up the night sky. The moon would pale in comparison. You're falling for that melodramatic act she just put on, and she's luring you in with her feminine wiles. She's just like all the rest of the frauds.

He should know. He'd had experience with mediums. He had been just ten years old when his father was killed. Desperate and distraught, his mother brought a parade of nut jobs into their home and into their lives and finally settled on her medium of the

77

moment, a cunning woman named Heddy Henrietta Grainger, or Madame Hydrangea, as she instructed her clients to call her. Looking back on that time in his life, he knew he should have sized Madame Hydrangea up as a fake from the start, and, like all mediums, Crystal Ball Kate deserved to be painted with the same brush.

The interloper summoned spirits for a fee, a very hefty fee, and claimed she could contact Jack's dead father. So two nights a week, for almost a year, he'd sat at their second-hand dining room table holding hands with his mother and Madame Hydrangea, futilely watching his mother suffer the false hope of catching a last glimpse of her departed husband.

Furniture had moved, lights had flashed, candles had flickered. He didn't know it back then, but today he saw those special effects for what they were—parlor tricks—and he recognized the medium as a fraud, perpetrating a bunch of hokum to take advantage of a grieving widow's loneliness. Even at ten Jack knew he didn't like the woman and that she was lying. He had learned a valuable life lesson. His mother believed love could last beyond the grave. If that was where being in love got you, then he wanted no part of it.

Jack's elbow accidentally bumped into Kate's. They both retreated to their respective spaces, crowded as they were. There was definitely something there. A spark. An attraction whenever they were together, which they pretty much had been, 24/7, in the past week. He couldn't be developing feelings for Kate. That was impossible. Not just because he didn't believe in love but because she was who she was. A psychic. In his mind, it was a dirty word.

Jack shut his eyes and tried not to think about the

tempting sprite in the seat next to him. That was hard to do. Mainly because he was getting hard imagining what it might be like to press his lips against hers, feel her body—her naked body—under his. Touch those magnificent breasts, do more than touch them. They'd slept in the same room, but not in the same bed. And he'd had trouble maintaining pure thoughts and keeping his hands from roaming.

He grabbed the magazine in the seat pocket in front of him and held it strategically on his lap. Hopefully Kate hadn't noticed the bulge.

Maybe, when they got back to Atlanta, they'd trade emails and phone numbers. He'd call her, sleep with her once, get rid of the restless explosion of energy he felt whenever he was around her. Then it would be on to the next one-night stand. He had no qualms about sleeping with a psychic, unleashing his pent-up anger about Madame Hydrangea on Kate, but long-term love wasn't in the cards for them.

Chapter Eight

Atlanta

Jack drove to Kate's family estate on West Paces Ferry Road in Buckhead. The Crystal Palace, as the media called it, was almost as big as the Governor's Mansion down the block. A far cry from the three-bedroom brick house he'd grown up in. After his father died, his mom had refused to give up the house—and the mortgage—she'd shared with her husband and son. So she'd taken a job to cover the house payment and to put food on the table for herself and Jack.

Jack put the car in Park and shut off the engine. He turned toward Katherine and put his arm over the back of her seat.

Katherine smiled, then involuntarily yawned, clapping a hand over her mouth. "Sorry, I'm exhausted." She dropped her hand and fiddled with the clasp of her purse. "I'd invite you in, but I really need to get some sleep."

"No problem." Jack would have loved to go in and take a look around. He'd never been in a house like hers before and never would, not on a cop's salary.

More reason to buckle down on his studies, keep up his grades.

Jack removed his hand and dropped it to the gear shift. He let the car idle, staring at Katherine awkwardly in the dark. Was this it, after all they'd been through together? He hadn't even kissed her. Unless he counted the mouth-to-mouth he'd performed when she passed out in the hotel room. They hadn't talked about the take down, diced it and sliced it, which is what they liked to say around the station. Would they ever see each other again? The thought of never again laying eyes on her unforgettable face, never being near enough to touch her, to watch her sleep, to hear her laugh, was agonizing.

Katherine took in a deep breath, let it out. "Well, I guess this is it." She opened the car door as Jack got out of the driver's side to help her with her luggage.

"You don't have to do that," she said. "I'll be fine. Thanks for the ride from the airport, and, um, everything."

Jack just stood there, glued to the asphalt. His mind and body were at odds. His body wanted to pull her into his arms, kiss her senseless, take her home to his bed, or hers. Hers was closer. His mind reminded him that he'd sworn off long-term relationships with women and this one could break him.

A laugh broke through. Who was he kidding? A class act like Katherine and a rookie cop? She would never waste her time with someone like him.

And what could come of it? There was no such thing as love. This was something else. Lust, maybe, but it wasn't permanent, so probably cutting off all ties was the best course of action.

****

This was awkward, Katherine thought. The big dope was just standing there, immobile. She was a psychic, for heaven's sake, and she wasn't misreading the signs. She may not be able to read his mind, but she could tell he was interested. Maybe her sixth sense had jet lag.

There was chemistry on both sides. He had wanted to kiss her in their hotel room in Sydney. But something had stopped him. So this was it? They were never going to see each other again? Resigned, she turned away from the car, swung her handbag over her shoulder and started rolling her suitcase up the driveway.

She looked back at Jack, who was still standing there staring at her, and she shook her head. Men. What was the big jerk waiting for? An engraved invitation?

Oh, what the hell. She was a liberated woman. If she wanted to kiss him, and she was dying to, then she would have to make it happen. She dropped her luggage and ran back to the car.

"Jack," she said, staring at him. "I'll probably regret this, but I wanted to thank you for everything in Sydney."

"I should be the one thanking you," Jack said, looking oxlike just standing there.

She reached up, wound her arms around his neck, and pressed herself against him, seeking the warmth and comfort she knew she'd find there. God, he felt good. And then she stood on her tiptoes and kissed him. Not a peck on the lips but an amorous kiss. She put everything she had into it, her whole body, including her tongue.

She felt something, a big something, and she ground against his erection. Jack grabbed her butt to keep her pressed against him, right where he wanted her, and responded in kind by kissing her back. Wow, he was a good kisser. Very experienced. She wanted more, and she could tell he did too. Should she ask him in? Was that too forward? No, not with her parents there. But she'd given him a signal that she was interested. The next step was up to him, if there was going to be a next step. She had a good feeling about it.

Suddenly, she felt tired. She pulled her lips away from his and hugged him one last time, almost fell asleep against him.

"Well, Beauregard, that wasn't half bad," she murmured.

Jack adjusted his jeans. "Kate, I don't know what to say."

She laughed. "Then say goodnight."

He pulled her back into his arms and hugged her tight. "I don't want to leave you. You feel so good."

"You feel pretty good yourself, but I'm beat. I really need to go."

"Could I call you?" Jack asked, shifting from one foot to the other.

"I'd like that," she answered. "Do you want my number?"

"I'm a detective. I could probably find it."

"Right," said Katherine, nodding.

He took both of her hands in his. "Goodnight, Kate, sleep tight," he said, planting another sexy kiss on her lips, leaving her wanting more. "Sweet dreams, now."

Oh, yes. She'd definitely be dreaming about Jack Hale tonight.

Chapter Nine

The house was silent and as eerie as an empty crypt. There was no sign of her parents. Katherine wheeled the luggage into the foyer and removed her cell phone from her purse. She'd forgotten to turn it back on after the plane landed. She'd probably only missed some more messages from Vince Rivers' hangers-on. Maybe someone wanted to locate a missing puppy. She was up for something easy for a change.

She missed her parents. She wanted to discuss the next chapter in her life. She may as well tell them she'd been let go by the gallery. Opportunities to help people with her psychic gift were piling up. But she wasn't going to make a move in that direction without their approval. If she could just talk to them, she knew they would help her find an answer. This might be the path to a new and exciting future. As horrible as the serial killer episode was, she had found working with Jack exciting.

The last message was from her parents.

We read about what you did in Australia, "Crystal Ball Kate," and your father and I are anxious to talk to you about it. You're all over the news. I think this kind of exposure is dangerous. We've gone to the cabin at the lake to get away from all the reporters. We'll be back Sunday afternoon. Love you, darling.

Sunday afternoon. That was today. Actually, it was

getting dark outside. They should have been home by now. Maybe they'd stopped somewhere for a romantic dinner. They were still a couple of lovebirds, even after so many years of marriage. She wanted a loving marriage like her parents had found. She hoped to have it one day. She called her mother's cell phone but it went straight to voice mail. The same thing happened when she called her father.

What did her mother mean by dangerous? She wasn't in any danger. And she wasn't getting any strange vibes, no prickle at the back of her neck, if you didn't count the chills she felt when she thought of Jack. She knew everything was all right. She was just anxious to see her parents, especially her mother. She wanted to talk to her mom about things…Jack, mostly, and the way she felt about him, how her heart was beginning to open up to him.

She lugged the suitcase and her carry-on up the curved staircase. She could have taken the elevator, but she didn't like to use it when nobody else was home. The idea of getting stuck in an elevator was not her idea of fun. She'd had too many visions about what could befall a person in an elevator to take her misgivings lightly. Daddy would have carried her bags up, but he wasn't here.

She left the suitcases on the floor near her closet. She could unpack tomorrow. Then she undressed, went into the bathroom, and took a long, steamy shower. That felt good. If she had known she would be alone in this big house, she would have invited Jack up. No doubt they would have ended up naked in the shower and then in bed. They had both wanted that. But then she might have fallen asleep before they made love.

85

She pulled her favorite nightgown from the drawer—a flowered flannel—grabbed her pink Ugg slippers, covered herself with a fluffy bathrobe, and flopped down on the bed to take a short nap until her parents got home. When she dreamed, she dreamed of Jack.

She woke up to a ringing phone. Her head was foggy. She couldn't see the clock. She still had jet lag. Maybe she should let the call go to voice mail. But it wouldn't stop ringing. She decided to answer it. It might be her parents. They hadn't come home yet or they would have woken her up.

"Mom?"

"Is this Katherine Crystal? Are you the daughter of Judge Tyler and Jessica Crystal?"

Katherine's mind shifted into focus. She sat up and swung her legs over the bed. "Yes, I'm Katherine Crystal."

"This is Doctor Malek at Midtown Memorial Hospital. I'm sorry to have to tell you this, but your parents have been in an auto accident."

Katherine's heart hammered in her chest. This must be some kind of a trick or a nightmare. Someone was playing a prank on Crystal Ball Kate. If her parents were hurt, she'd know it. If she could predict that a stranger's plane was going to crash, it stood to reason she could predict that her own parents were in trouble. "There must be some mistake."

"I'm sorry, Miss Crystal. Their car went off the road. There was an explosion. The police were called to the scene and an ambulance brought them to the hospital, but we couldn't save them. Is there someone you'd like me to call?"

Katherine was numb. She refused to accept that her parents were no longer in this world.

"Where did it happen?" Katherine demanded, powering herself out of her fog. "When?"

"I don't have any of the details. I just—I know—I knew your parents, and that's why I called you."

Of course. The trauma wing at the hospital was named after her parents. She'd attended the dedication. Her parents were personal friends with many of the physicians. She was sure the hospital had taken the best care of them. It was undoubtedly out of the scope of their job to call the next of kin. They were doing her a favor.

Were her parents lying on cold slabs in the Tyler and Jessica Crystal Trauma Center, waiting to be transferred to the hospital morgue? How had the accident happened? Had it been raining? They'd driven to the lake hundreds of times since she was a girl. Her father was a cautious driver. The route was mapped in his brain. He could have driven it on autopilot.

Katherine shivered and pulled the robe tighter around her. *"Is there someone you'd like me to call?"* The doctor's words jumbled in her mind. *Car crash, explosion. Police. Jack.*

Jack. When she hung up with the doctor, she called Jack's cell phone. She'd programmed his number into her phone in Sydney. *Please, let him be home.*

"Jack Hale." His voice sounded hoarse and faraway, like it was coming from the bottom of a bottle. She'd obviously woken him up from a jetlagged sleep.

"Jack, it's Katherine." Her chest heaved and a soft cry escaped her lips.

"Kate?" he asked, sounding more alert.

Tears streamed down her face. She was frozen, unable to go on.

"Kate, are you still there? Did you get another flash?"

"Nothing," she whispered. "No warning. I didn't feel anything."

"What's wrong? I don't like the way you sound."

"Jack," she whispered, clutching the phone, afraid to release the words into the atmosphere. If she didn't say them out loud, maybe the whole thing would be some horrible nightmare. Maybe she just needed more time to process what was happening. Maybe things would go back to the way they were before she got the call, before she got home, before her parents had left the cabin.

But this wasn't someone else's nightmare. It was hers, and she had to face it. But she didn't want to face it alone. "It's my parents. There's been an accident. They didn't make it. But I think it's a mistake. I'm their daughter. I would know if something was wrong, right? I mean, I would feel it. I know I would."

Jack's voice broke in. "Where are you now?"

Kate looked around her room, feeling as if her body were detached from her mind. "At home, of course." She leaped out of bed and started rummaging through her drawers. "Can you pick me up and take me to Midtown Memorial? I'm sorry to bother you, but I didn't know who else to call."

"Just wait. I'll be there in fifteen minutes." The phone line clicked off.

Katherine hung up the phone. She had to get to the closet, pick out something to wear. Jack would be here soon. But her legs felt rigid, like they were stuck in cement.

She needed to be downstairs to let Jack in. Still numb, she managed to step into a pair of blue jeans and a sweater. Shoes and socks. Slow and easy. One foot at a time.

She tried to remember the last thing she'd said to her mother. They had been arguing about the trip to Australia.

"You can talk to the police from Atlanta," she'd said. "There's no need to go all the way to Sydney."

"But Mom, I have to go. Those girls need me."

"It will be dangerous." Her mother's usually laughing lips had pursed into a slash of disapproval. Jessica Crystal was a first-rate trial lawyer. Katherine rarely won an argument with her mother.

"I'll be accompanied by a detective and surrounded by police," she had countered.

"Your name is all over the papers, dear." She'd patted Kate's hand. "That man knows you're going to be there. What's to stop him from getting to you before you help the police get to him?"

Katherine hadn't thought of that. Hadn't been worried about herself. All she could see were pictures of dead bodies in her head. Young girls, helpless, the strangler's hands around their throats, squeezing the last ounce of life out of them. She didn't have a choice. She had to go.

"Promise me you'll be careful," her mother had said, finally.

Why had it happened? Her parents had gone to the lake to avoid publicity, publicity she had generated. It was all her fault they were dead. And why hadn't she warned them? She could flash on the future of a perfect stranger, but she couldn't even save her own parents.

The doctor had said the police were on the scene. Did they suspect foul play? It wasn't uncommon for judges to be targeted.

Katherine heard a loud knock on the door and jumped.

"Kate," Jack bellowed. "Kate, are you in there?"

Kate forced herself to walk downstairs to the front door and unlock it. "Jack, you're here," she said, feeling faint, trying hard to focus on his face before everything went black.

Jack had imagined Kate in his arms dozens of times in the last two weeks, just not like this. He had made a call to the station before he arrived, inquiring into the accident. Apparently, the accident was under investigation. All eyes were on it. When an accident involved a federal judge, the department wasn't taking any chances. They'd even called in the FBI.

Jack lifted Katherine up, saw the key in the door, and locked it behind them. He gently deposited her in his car and put the seat belt around her. God, she was tiny and vulnerable and light as a feather. Then he got into the driver's seat and took off for the hospital, using his emergency siren.

Katherine was obviously in shock. Getting her checked out was his first priority.

He pulled up to the emergency entrance, handed his keys to the valet, and went around to the passenger side of the car.

"Kate," he nudged her gently. "We're here. We're at the hospital."

She stirred. "Jack." She looked up at him but didn't move.

"I'm here, sweetheart." He lifted her and walked into the hospital and over to the ER desk clerk. "I'm Detective Jack Hale. This woman is in shock. She needs to be examined."

The woman handed him some forms, and he grimaced.

"I don't have time to fill out any damn forms. Didn't I make myself clear? This woman needs to see a doctor. Now."

"Sir, I realize you're upset, but we have our rules."

"Fuck your rules. Find me a doctor, right now."

"If you don't calm down, sir, I'm going to have to call the police."

Jack bared his teeth and growled at the receptionist. "I *am* the police. I'm here about the two dead bodies."

The receptionist's mouth opened and her eyes widened in alarm. "Two dead bodies?"

Jack eyed her menacingly. "And if you don't get me a doctor right this minute, there's going to be a third," Jack threatened. He looked down at Kate in alarm. God, she wasn't moving, and she was so pale. Was she even breathing? What if—? He couldn't let anything happen to her. He hadn't known her for very long, but he didn't understand until this very minute how important she had become to him.

Chapter Ten

Jack took Kate's hand and helped her out of the emergency room bed.

The doctor had given Kate the okay to leave. She had been in shock, and he'd instructed her to go home and rest. But Jack knew she wasn't going to be able to rest, given the fresh nightmare of her parents' death.

She was going to need him now, and he would be there for her. "Kate, honey, I know you're still in shock. This is very difficult, but I will be with you every step of the way."

Kate squeezed her eyes shut and tears spilled out of the corners, soft sobs overtaking her.

Jack remembered when he had seen his father's body in the coffin at the visitation. He had been only ten at the time. But he didn't imagine the hurt got any easier with age. And he still had his mother. To lose both parents at once must be unbearable. He ached for Kate.

He pulled her into his arms and let her cry. After a few minutes, she pulled away and wiped her nose with a tissue she pulled from her purse.

"Sorry," she whispered, her eyes avoiding his. She took a deep breath, let it out slowly. "Thanks."

"I'm glad you called," he replied, putting his arm around her shoulder. "If you're not ready to see..." He swallowed the rest of his sentence when he felt Kate's shoulders tense.

She shook her head. "No, I'm ready. Please, I want to see them."

Leading the way, he directed her to where her parents' bodies were. He was intimately familiar with the morgue at this hospital. He'd seen enough of the Midtown Strangler's victims. Knowledge he'd rather not have.

"Are you ready?" Jack repeated, wrapping his arm around Kate and walking her slowly to the elevator.

"How can you ever get ready for something like this?"

"We don't have to do this now, if you don't want." Jack pulled Kate closer and kissed the top of her head. She was shaking. He rubbed her shoulder and she folded into him.

"I'm glad you're here," she whispered.

"So am I, sweetheart," Jack said, thinking Kate looked tinier and more vulnerable than he'd ever seen her. God, he wished they were anywhere but here, but if she had to go through this, he was going to make sure she wasn't alone. He was going to protect her, even knowing there was nothing he could do to fix this.

The surgeon who had operated on Kate's parents, the one who told Jack he'd meet them in the hospital morgue, walked up and extended his hand.

"Katherine, I'm Dr. Malek," he said, clasping her hand. "We spoke on the phone."

"Yes," she said flatly, her voice barely a whisper.

Jack took Katherine's other hand and she gripped it tightly. He reached out to shake the doctor's hand. "I'm Detective Jack Hale of the APD. I'm with Kate."

"Glad to meet you, Detective. If you'll both follow

me."

Kate and Jack followed him into a dimly lit area. Two bodies lay on separate tables, draped in white sheets.

Dr. Malek walked to the tables and, one by one, slipped the sheet down to uncover her parents' faces.

Kate trembled and squeezed Jack's hand. For a minute he thought she was going to faint again. Jack put his arm over her shoulders and held her up as they walked toward the tables.

From a distance, lying in peaceful repose the way they were, their bodies so still, it looked to Katherine like they weren't dead at all but might just be under the covers, sleeping. They had been pried from the wreckage. There had been an explosion, but yet, from where she stood, they were almost untouched. But no less dead.

They had been alive when they were brought in. What had their final thoughts been? Had they called out her name? Had they been in pain? If so, why hadn't she felt their pain, heard their cries for help?

She inched closer to the bodies, and when she saw them she flinched in horror, her body shaking.

Katherine turned to Jack. "These are not my parents."

Jack turned back to the doctor, puzzled. "Doctor, has there been some mistake?"

The doctor shook his head. "Look closer. There's no mistake."

Jack coaxed Katherine back toward the bodies.

Katherine shook her head. "My mother's face. That's not..." Katherine keened loudly. "There's nothing left of..." She went limp in Jack's arms.

"Kate," Jack said firmly, holding her up so she could get a better look.

She reached out hesitantly to touch her mother's hand and smooth it over the ring her mother wore.

"It's her wedding ring," Katherine acknowledged flatly. "Her clothes." Her hand hovered over her mother's mangled face that she could not bring herself to touch, and then she kissed her mother's cool forehead. This was what was left of her parents, once so vital and full of life, their faces once so expressive. She touched her father's shirt, then his pants, and rubbed his shoes. "It's him," Katherine acknowledged.

She would never see her mother smile again or hear her father's booming laughter. Never hear her mother's voice or see her lovely face. Never hear them tell her how much they loved her, which they always did. Never be able to tell them how much she treasured them.

An unbidden picture of her mother standing in front of a mirror in the dressing room of their favorite department store, trying on clothes during one of their frequent mother-daughter shopping trips popped into her mind. Her mother looking beautiful, graceful, alive. A fleeting glimpse of her handsome father, sitting in his chair in the den reading the paper, commenting on a particular article, keeping her updated on the news of the day. Then the images were gone. Nothing was left and she was alone. Cold and alone.

"Dr. Malek?" Katherine gulped. "Did they suffer?"

"It was over pretty quickly," Dr. Malek assured Katherine. "In the end, they didn't feel anything. I'll leave you alone now. I'll be waiting outside when you're finished."

Tears slipped down her face as sorrow shook her body uncontrollably. She dropped Jack's hand and wrapped herself around her mother, laid her head on her mother's breast and cried.

"I'll be outside with the doctor," Jack said, releasing Kate.

"No, stay," Katherine insisted, tugging at Jack's hand. "Please." She didn't want him to leave her, not for a minute. She couldn't get through this ordeal without him. It was premature, but she had already imagined introducing Jack to her parents. Under different circumstances, he would have been invited to dinner to meet them. Her mother would have welcomed him openly, warmly. Her father would have scrutinized him and grilled him, but not judged him. This was not how she wanted their first meeting to go.

Jack nodded, bleary-eyed, standing ramrod straight, staring first at Kate and then at her lifeless parents. "I know I never met your parents, but death is part of my world. It's always a shock and it's never easy." He rubbed his now clean-shaven chin. "I wish I knew the right thing to say to you."

Kate looked up at Jack. "Your beard is gone. When did you have time to shave?"

Jack smiled ruefully. "The minute I got home." They shouldn't be talking about such mundane things as beards, he knew, but he guessed Kate didn't want to face reality yet. "What do you think?"

"I can see you now," Katherine said softly. "What will happen next?" she wondered aloud, looking up at Jack and away from her parents. "I mean, where will they go?"

"Someone will need to pick up the bodies—I mean

your parents. You'll have to tell them where you want them delivered." Jack shifted uncomfortably when he saw the look of confusion in Kate's eyes.

"Delivered?"

"The funeral home," Jack replied in a gentle voice.

"I don't know what they would have wanted. We never talked about it." Kate started to sag and Jack held her up. Her parents were so self-sufficient. They had always taken care of everything.

"I'm sure you have a family attorney who might have instructions about their wishes."

"Of course. Judge Bamberger." Kate nodded as the adrenalin kicked in. She needed a plan. The judge would help her. "Judge Bamberger and his wife were my parents' best friends. He's like family. He almost was family." Jack looked puzzled, but she didn't have time to explain. "I need to call him. I need to notify everyone in my mother's firm. My parents had a lot of friends. People need to know. I have to make arrangements."

Jack put his arm around Kate and pulled her close. "Let me help you. Why don't I take you home now, and we can get started."

"But who will stay with them? They shouldn't be alone."

Jack stared at Kate, his brows furrowed in concern. Her parents were dead. Did she truly understand that? Obviously, it hadn't sunk in yet. In Kate's mind, she needed to watch over them. "Of course. We can wait until the people from the funeral home get here."

Kate walked over into a corner and made a phone call, and then she came back to Jack.

"I just talked to Judge Bamberger. He will contact

the funeral home. He's going to meet me here, and then he and his wife will go with my parents to the funeral home to make arrangements."

She glanced back at her parents' bodies. "You probably see this all the time," Kate commented, swinging her purse strap over her shoulder.

"Like I said, death is part of the job, but it's not something you ever get used to." He still hadn't gotten used to his own father's death, twenty years later. Being so close to death just brought all the memories rushing back. "I was just ten when my father was killed, shot. I don't think I'll ever get over it," Jack admitted, shaking his head.

"I'm sorry, Jack," said Kate, squeezing his hand.

Jack rubbed her hand with his thumb. Kate was amazing. To have endured what she did, yet still have the capacity to comfort him. "I understand the pain you're feeling. I wish there was something more I could do for you." He hated to see Kate hurting. It was a pain that never healed. He couldn't leave her to face the void alone. He would see her through this dark time.

"You're here. That's enough." Kate clung to Jack's hand.

"Let's wait somewhere more comfortable so you can rest a while," Jack suggested. Kate took one last look at her parents, found Jack's hand, and followed him out.

Doctor Malek was waiting outside.

"There's an FBI agent here who wants to ask Katherine a few questions," said the doctor. "I asked him to wait in that room," he said, indicating a door across the hall. "Katherine, when you're ready to talk, I can answer any of your questions."

Katherine clasped the doctor's hand. "Thank you, Doctor, I really appreciate all you've done."

"Your parents have done so much for this hospital over the years. I wish I could have done more." Doctor Malek ushered Jack and Katherine into the room across the hall and said his goodbyes.

A tall man in a dark, tailored suit came toward them. "Are you Katherine Crystal?"

Katherine nodded, then turned toward Jack. "And this is my friend, Jack Hale, from the Atlanta Police Department."

The agent shook Jack's hand. "I'm Agent Terrance Spaulding, with the FBI." He turned to Kate. "I'm here to investigate your parents' case. I'm sorry for your loss, Miss Crystal." He motioned to a couch behind him. "I'd like to ask you a few questions, if I may."

Jack sat Katherine on the couch and whispered in her ear. "Are you up for this now?"

"I want to do this," she answered. "I need to find out what happened to my parents."

Jack nodded, kissed her on the forehead and sat down next to her.

"Thank you," said Agent Spaulding, taking out a pen and a small notebook. "Miss Crystal, do you know anyone who might have wanted to hurt your parents?"

"Hurt them?" Katherine folded her hands together and looked up at Jack.

Jack placed his hand over Kate's folded ones. "What Agent Spaulding wants to know is if any of the cases your father handled might have resulted in any dissatisfied clients or if, as a judge, a verdict he issued might have angered one of the parties."

Katherine blew out a breath and concentrated. "I

don't know any specifics about my father's cases."

"Miss Crystal, it's very common for a judge, especially a federal judge, to have enemies," explained Agent Spaulding. "We have to look into all the angles, all possibilities."

"Everyone loved my parents," Katherine countered. "They were the most wonderful people in the world. I don't know anyone who would want to hurt them."

"Of course, we'll be checking recent court records, interviewing your parents' colleagues, ruling out suspects, and we've already had investigators at the scene of the crime, checking out the car for sabotage."

"Suspects? Crime? Sabotage?" Katherine asked, frowning, turning to Jack. "Wasn't this an accident?"

"No, Miss Crystal," announced Agent Spaulding. "Your parents were murdered. And until we find out who is responsible and why, your life might be in danger too."

Chapter Eleven

The day was much too beautiful for a funeral. The Atlanta air was crisp and clear. The trees were just beginning to lose their leaves as she was being forced to shed her parents. Her parents loved fall, so maybe it was fitting that they were being lowered into the ground in their favorite season. Watching their caskets disappear into the earth was the hardest to bear. Katherine choked and almost lost her composure.

The minister was speaking, and Katherine nodded appropriately, but she barely heard a word. She had remained numb throughout the service. Hundreds of people had viewed her parents' bodies during the visitation the previous evening and dropped by the house to pay their respects. Many more had shown up for the funeral. It seemed like the whole town had turned out, including the Mayor of Atlanta, many dignitaries, judges, colleagues from her mother's firm, and lifelong friends. That was comforting, but it didn't change the fact that she was all alone now.

She'd had some friends from the gallery, but now that she didn't work there, they'd lost touch. There were no relatives left on either side of the family. She was the last remaining Crystal.

Katherine grappled with the shovel and sent a spray of dirt into each of the cavernous holes in the ground. The cemetery workers would finish up.

Jack had been correct in assuming her parents had expressed their wishes in advance of their deaths. Her parents' attorney had handled every detail according to the Crystals' very specific directives, which was a good thing, because there were a lot of decisions to make. Determining the burial place, picking out the caskets—down to the type of wood and the lining—deciding what type of service to conduct, prayers and hymns, readings and remembrances. Her parents had chosen a Celebration of Life service. Their friends had handled the catering arrangements so she could receive guests at the house after the funeral.

Judge Tyler and Jessica Crystal had even written their own eulogies. Her only consolation was that they had died together and would go on to the next chapter of their lives as one. Of that she was certain. A love that strong didn't die when the body shut down. Her parents weren't going to remain buried in a box in the cold ground. They weren't even here now. Perhaps they were hovering temporarily, watching the graveside service, watching her now, but their spirits had been filled with so much life she was sure they would soon move on to the next challenge, spreading their light throughout the universe, trying to right wrongs somewhere in the great beyond. That brought a slight smile to Katherine's lips. But they could never have imagined that she'd have to bury both her parents at the same time.

At the conclusion of the service, Katherine wandered away from the crowd and sat on a cold stone bench dedicated to someone in another family. She felt a swell of sympathy and a crowd of concerned eyes tracking and registering her every movement, searing her from a respectful distance.

Katherine crossed her arms and looked up at the wispy clouds in wonder. She was aware of a host of spirits all about this place of death—newly unleashed spirits, fleeting, floating, some visible, some evil, some benign, some barely there, but she was connected to them and they to her. They whispered to her, enveloped her. She drew a deep breath, sighed, and let them in, finally.

When she was feeling better, she would try to contact her parents on the other side. She was sure she could. A groundswell of untapped powers waited within her, ready to emerge. Tendencies she'd tamped down while her parents had been alive now cascaded out of her like a waterfall. She wasn't exactly sure what they were or how to control them, but something was definitely different, and she was open to learning more.

She had shaken countless hands, hugged and kissed a lot of her parents' friends, and she was worn out. Even Justin Bamberger, the son of her parents' best friends, made an obligatory appearance and, before he left, he followed her over to the bench to offer his condolences. She and Justin had grown up together. Both sets of parents had expected them to get married, and they had been engaged briefly, but Katherine had broken it off, dashing everyone's hopes, especially Justin's.

Justin kissed her, a less than discreet, more than passing kiss. She could tell he was trying to make her feel something, but she felt nothing but emptiness.

"Little Cat in the Hat." Justin always opened with the same line whenever he saw her. He'd started calling her that at his Bar Mitzvah, when she and her mother had worn matching hats to the synagogue to watch him become a man.

"When are you going to stop calling me that?" Katherine said, pursing her lips.

Justin just laughed, patted her head where a hat should have been, and took hold of her hand. He looked down at her, his blue eyes twinkling mischievously. "Probably never."

She was aware of his towering height, his dark, tousled hair, his perfectly chiseled face, and the muscular, athletic body she knew rippled beneath his stylishly tailored but appropriate suit.

"You look good," Katherine admitted. "How have you been?" Inclining her head, Katherine made room for him beside her on the bench, for old time's sake. He would always hold his place as her mother's favorite suitor, after all.

"Been reading about my favorite psychic," he answered, crowding her just a bit too close. "You're all over the news. I can't turn on the TV without reading about Crystal Ball Kate. Do you think that's advisable?"

"I can't control what people write or say, and I don't really want to talk about that," Katherine objected. "Especially not today."

"Cat, I'm really sorry. Is there anything I can do for you?" Justin flashed his puppy-dog eyes, then broke out into a boyish grin. He was always trying to insinuate himself back into her life, when she'd made it perfectly clear it was over between them. He couldn't accept her the way she was, visions and all, was freaked out by them, in fact. His solution was for her to ignore them. He thought her visions were something she could suppress or cover up at will. Something she would outgrow. He wanted to mold her into her mother. She didn't fit the mold, would never have made him the proper corporate wife, and she knew it, even if he didn't.

He still had hold of her hand, and she tried to extricate herself, but he wasn't having any of it.

"Justin," she admonished, yanking her hand away.

"Still don't like to be touched in public, I see," he shot back in a huff.

"Not by you, and not at my parents' funeral," she answered dryly. She wished he would just disappear. Wished, at that moment, she had the power to make him vanish.

Justin folded his arms across his chest. "Someone's gotten cranky since we broke up."

"Yes, I'm cranky. I haven't really slept since I arrived home from Sydney. And I'm not in the mood for your inappropriate sense of humor or your drama." She turned away from him and stood up. "Thank you for coming. I appreciate it, really, but I need to go back to the house." Home would be a strange and lonely place without Mom and Dad.

Leaving him on the bench, she walked over and took a final look at the gravesite. Then she turned to step into the limousine the funeral home had provided.

She felt a hand on her shoulder.

"Kate."

She turned around. Of course she'd known Jack would come. He had barely left her side since that night at the hospital. There had been some photographers waiting when he'd dropped her off at her house after the visit to the hospital. Jack had flashed his badge,

105

firmly grabbed their cameras, and chased them away. They wanted to know what was next for Crystal Ball Kate. How could she tell them if she didn't know herself?

"Who's the asshole?" Jack asked, glaring at Justin, who got up from the bench, smoothed the crease on his suit jacket, and walked toward the paved road to his car.

"Just an old friend," Katherine sighed. She couldn't wait for this day to be over.

"An old friend who can't seem to keep his hands off you? Or his mouth?"

"Okay, we were engaged once." Katherine looked up to gauge Jack's reaction.

Jack frowned and looked to be on the verge of sulking. Men were so predictable.

"Please don't tell me you're going to go all jealous on me at my parents' funeral."

Jack's expression turned contrite, but he increased the pressure on her shoulder. "I came to offer you a ride home."

"No, but thank you," she said, gently lifting his hand from her shoulder. His sympathy was cloying. Everyone's was. "The limousine from the funeral home will take me home. I need to go back and at least show my face at the house, and then I'm going to crawl into bed and never get out. You've done a lot already. You've done enough." She hoped that didn't sound like a brush-off. She hadn't intended it to be. But she just wanted to be alone.

"If that's what you want, then, okay." Jack shrugged.

"It's what I need right now," Katherine assured him.

The light had gone out in Jack's eyes, but she was too exhausted to worry about hurting his feelings. She needed to rest her tired body and her restless mind. The night headaches were back in full force. Her doctor had called in a prescription for sleeping pills, and she was going to take them to shut off the incessant voices in her head. She imagined herself as the princess in the Sleeping Beauty story, drifting off to an enchanted sleep. Maybe after she was rested she could face the handsome prince. Right now, she couldn't deal with Jack's pity and concern, or his possessiveness. And she couldn't depend on him forever. She had to learn to stand on her own two feet. She was, after all, alone.

She knew she was pushing him away, but she wasn't sure what to make of their on-again-off-again relationship, if it could even be labeled a relationship. Since they'd met, they'd only been together during a crisis. She didn't even know what a normal life was anymore.

She'd call Jack in the next few days to see if he'd learned anything new from the police about her parents' murder. Agent Spaulding from the FBI had given her his card and promised to follow up, but Jack spoke his language. He would help her sort through all the jargon and get to the bottom of the crime. She couldn't imagine who would want to kill her parents. But whoever was responsible for their deaths was going to pay.

In the hospital, Agent Spaulding had warned her that her life might be in danger, but her safety was not really a concern to her. Jack, on the other hand, had hardly let her out of his sight. He was the overprotective type and she knew he was only being cautious, but she wasn't his responsibility. He'd probably stick with her 24/7 if he had his way. So she had to be the one to make the break. It was better for both of them.

Chapter Twelve

Katherine wasn't ready to let them go. She knew she should go through her parents' things. Donate their clothes to a deserving charity. But she wasn't up to it. She didn't know how much more of this she could take. There had been the reading of the will, which now left her independently wealthy, but she'd rather be dirt poor than have to live without her parents. Rambling around in this empty mansion, which now seemed stone cold and lifeless without her parents in it, she was lost, bereft.

She'd left the safe till last. That's where she hoped to find more intimate traces of her parents. Keepsakes, papers, pictures. Maybe a letter—for her?

Katherine hoisted herself out of the comfortable, apple-green wingback chair and walked over to the safe. She knew the combination but had never used it. Never had to.

She swung open the safe, brought out the contents, and placed them on the coffee table. Her mother's favorite necklace, a wedding present from her father—priceless not only in terms of dollars but in sentimental value. Katherine handled the stones, the last tangible vestige of her mother. Some bonds, stock certificates, property deeds, gold coins, pretty much the kinds of things you expected to find in a safe.

Rummaging through the papers, which she would

have to discuss with her parents' lawyer, now *her* lawyer, she came across a yellowed document.

What was this? Looked like some kind of contract or, no, it was an adoption certificate. Adoption certificate? That made no sense at all. She picked it up and examined it more closely.

Then it dawned on her. It was probably some kind of private adoption her father had handled for one of his clients when he had his own practice. Did she need to return this to its rightful owner? Well, her attorney would know what to do with it. She started to toss it aside when she noticed the date of the adoption. May 19, 1983. Her birthdate. That was too much of a coincidence, and she didn't believe in them. She read further.

Birthplace: Casa Spirito, Florida.

Birth mother: Juliette Spencer.

Birth father: Rev. Carter Coulter.

Who were these people and why was this document in her parents' safe? And why was the baby on the contract born on *her* birthday?

Katherine rubbed her eyes. She'd been born right here in Atlanta at the hospital on Peachtree Street, the same place her parents had died. Baby Girl Coulter had been born in Florida, a home birth, in a town she'd never heard of. No connection, except for the date and the fact that Baby Girl Coulter's papers were in her parents' safe, almost thirty years later.

Katherine picked up the phone to dial her attorney. This was really none of her business. It was a private matter between Juliette Spencer and Reverend Carter Coulter, but there was her father's signature on the document. Her father's lawyer would know the answers, or at least where to go to look for them.

She quickly hung up the phone. What if this was one of those illegal adoptions? You read about those all the time, the ones done under the table, for outrageous amounts of money, where couples who couldn't conceive bought a baby on the open market. What if this was such a case? She didn't want to involve the attorney at the risk of sullying her father's reputation. You never knew who you could trust these days.

Without realizing it, she had subconsciously dialed Jack's number. It had been on the card he pressed into her hands at the cemetery. She'd had his number on speed dial, but she hadn't bothered to call him since that day. She wasn't ready to face Jack again or think about what was happening between them. And he hadn't called her. She could hardly blame him. Since the funeral, she had pretty much shut him out of her life.

"Hale here."

"Jack—" Katherine looked down at the adoption document and coughed.

"Kate, are you all right?"

"I'm fine. I'm—I had a question. There's something I'd like you to take a look at. Something…unofficially. Could you come over?"

"Now?" His voice sounded froggy.

"Did I wake you?" Of course she had, because she had lost track of time.

"I had a late shift last night, but I'm off today, so I'll be right over."

"Thank you."

Katherine heaved a sigh of relief as she realized she trusted Jack, implicitly.

In the kitchen she poured herself a glass of lemonade while she waited. There was a lot of food left over from after the funeral service. She set out some cheese and crackers and some cookies, two plates, napkins and glasses. Jack had a big appetite and he might be hungry. She felt bad that she hadn't invited him back to the house after the burial, but she'd wanted to be left alone, and he had respected her wishes. But now she needed to see him.

He must have flown over, because he materialized at her front door in record time. That made sense. He lived in Midtown, and Buckhead wasn't that far away.

"Come in," she said, and he stepped through the door. She led him into the dining room. Katherine couldn't stop staring at his face and felt an almost overpowering longing. She was so glad to see him. She hadn't realized how much she missed him.

"How are you holding up?" Jack considered her to be as fragile as a china doll, she knew.

"Okay, I guess. I'm still numb. I can't believe this happened, that I'm never going to see my parents again. And I can't get my mind around the fact that someone tampered with their car. Do the FBI have any leads yet? They won't tell me anything." Katherine smoothed her hands down her green velour running suit. It was wrinkled because she'd slept in it. Jack must think she was a mess. Her mother wouldn't have approved of her state of complete disarray.

"Nothing definitive to report yet," Jack said, still staring at her sympathetically. "Things like this take time."

Was he referring to the investigation into her parents' murder or the time necessary to get over their deaths?

"I don't know how you're coping. When I lost my father, well, I'm still not over that, and to lose both parents at the same time... I can't even imagine what you're feeling."

It was comfortable being around Jack again. She'd missed their closeness. When she could bear thinking about anything. She didn't really know much of anything about him. Maybe it was time to learn more.

"What's your mother like?" Katherine asked, as she offered Jack a chair and placed a dessert plate and a glass of lemonade on the end table, within easy reach. One thing she did know about him. He was perpetually hungry. "You still have her, don't you?"

"Yes. Mom is great," Jack answered, attacking the food with a vengeance. "A little too trusting. I mean, she's open to anything. After my father died, she, um, brought a medium into our house who claimed she could contact my father."

"Did she?" Katherine asked, moving closer.

"Are you serious?" Jack said. "She was a fraud. My dad was dead, and that was the end of it. You don't actually believe you can contact the spirits of the dead, do you?"

Katherine bit her lip. That's exactly what she believed. And she was determined to try it.

Jack shook his head and pursed his lips. "You're not considering doing that, are you, Kate?" But he could see plainly that she was.

Katherine lowered her head. "I don't believe they're just gone. Don't you believe that love survives—?"

"You and my mom are so gullible. Like two peas

in a pod. When will you ever learn that love is not that powerful?"

Katherine lifted her chin. "My parents' love was. I-I really think they're together right now."

Jack rolled his eyes. "Sorry to disappoint you, Kate, but you're not thinking rationally. You have to look at it from a scientific point of view. When the body goes into the ground—"

"Stop!" Kate shouted, stomping her foot, then covering her face with her hands and sobbing as she sank into the wing chair opposite Jack's. "I don't want to hear it!" She wanted to shut off her brain. Some things didn't bear thinking about.

Jack bolted out of his chair, crossed the distance between them, and gathered her into his arms. "I'm sorry. You're not ready to hear it. It's okay, baby," he said, trying to soothe her by rubbing her back.

Kate finally stopped crying and pulled out of his arms. "You're just trying to placate me. And you are so wrong about the power of love." She gestured toward the ceiling. "Somewhere out there…I know they're still together. You'll never convince me they're not."

Jack was overcompensating. He was all for getting her to talk about her tragedy, but he staunchly refused to confide in her about his. He'd built up an emotional barrier between them as big as a boulder.

"When your father died," Katherine began tentatively. "Could you tell me about that?"

Jack stiffened and began pacing the room. "I don't want to talk about it," he said. "Let's just say this medium should have been arrested."

"For what crime? Peddling false hope?"

"It went way beyond that." Jack struggled with his

anger in his desire to be supportive of Kate.

"I'm a psychic, too," she challenged. "Are you going to arrest me?"

Jack narrowed his eyes and he regarded her quizzically. "That depends. Have you done anything illegal?"

Katherine bit her lip. "Not that I know of, but there is something that might be, well, not quite kosher. I don't know what to make of it, but you have to promise me that if you look at it, you won't report it."

"You know I can't promise you anything like that if a crime is involved."

"Still going strictly by the book, Beauregard? I don't think it's anything that sinister, but I've asked you here as a friend, not as a detective. I don't want the police involved in this."

Jack turned to face her. "Kate, you can trust me. I'm not going to do anything that would get you into trouble."

"That's why I called you." She walked around the coffee table and pushed the adoption document toward Jack.

He examined the piece of paper for a few minutes. Then he looked her squarely in the eyes.

"Where did you get this?" he demanded.

Katherine blinked. "Is this an interrogation?"

"Well?" Jack tapped the paper with his index finger and stood waiting for an answer.

"Are you going to make me take a lie detector test?" Katherine bristled and finally relented under the pressure of his gaze. "I found it in my parents' home safe. What is it?"

Jack rubbed his chin. "It looks like an adoption of

some kind, but not a legal one. This is not an official certificate. What does this have to do with you?"

Kate shrugged her shoulders. "Well, I'm not sure. But look at the date."

"May 19, 1983," Jack read.

"That's the day I was born."

"Could be a coincidence," Jack said, half-heartedly.

"I don't believe in them."

"Neither do I." Jack looked at the names on the certificate. "Have you ever heard of these people? Juliette Spencer and Reverend Carter Coulter?"

Katherine shook her head. "Never. And I never heard my parents talk about anyone by those names. Maybe it was a private adoption."

"Where the parents pay through the nose to buy a baby?" Jack accused.

Katherine shrank back. "That's pretty cynical."

"Yes, and it's also illegal. I doubt if your father was involved in anything like that. He was a respected judge."

"And he was just an attorney at the time I was born," she noted.

Jack scratched his head and reviewed the document again. "This Baby Girl Coulter was born in Florida. Where were you born?"

"In Atlanta, as far as I know. That's what it says on my birth certificate."

Jack fixed her with a knowing glance. "Birth certificates can be forged."

Katherine stuck her chin out. "I don't think my father would be involved in anything illegal."

"Desperate people do desperate things every day,

Kate," Jack reasoned, softening his glare.

"My parents weren't desperate."

"You're an only child, right?"

"Yes."

"Didn't your parents ever want more children?"

"My mother told me she couldn't have any more children, that I was enough. I always wanted a brother or a sister."

Jack glanced at the document, trying to piece together the clues, to determine what was missing.

"Maybe you already have one."

Katherine held up a hand. "You mean I might be a twin, that this Baby Girl Coulter is somehow related to me?"

"I didn't say that. What if you *are* Baby Girl Coulter?"

Katherine looked up at Jack. "Are you saying that my parents bought me?"

"I'm not saying anything, but it does raise suspicions. Your parents certainly could have afforded to buy a baby, judging by this house. But this document doesn't prove anything, and we can't exactly ask them now. There's no dollar amount written on here. This isn't a bill of sale, but it's worth looking into."

Kate hesitated. "How would you do that?"

"First, by conducting some research on the Internet. Making a few calls, possibly taking a trip to this place, Casa Spirito. Are you up for that?" Jack considered the prospect of another trip with Kate with promise. He missed her, and the thought of spending all that time alone with her on a car trip was tantalizing.

"But not in an official capacity." Katherine shot Jack a warning glare.

"No, I've got some time coming. Why don't we take a little trip to Florida?"

Kate seemed to weigh the idea. "Well, okay. I don't want anything coming out that would reflect negatively on my parents. And the media—those vultures would love to get their hands on something nefarious about me or my family."

"Do you have a computer here?" Jack asked, looking around the room.

"Yes, in my bedroom."

"Your bedroom?" Jack's voice rose an octave and his eyes twinkled.

"Yes, but don't get any ideas."

"Me?" Jack threw his hands up. "Furthest thing from my mind. The only thing I'll be turning on around here is your computer." *Unfortunately.*

"I could have predicted you'd say that. It's already on. Follow me." Katherine led the way.

Jack followed her up a winding staircase worthy of a *Gone with the Wind* movie set. "Sorry. I'll stop making stupid comments, if you'll forgive me."

Katherine took a right turn and ushered Jack into a spacious bedroom on the left that overlooked an Olympic-size swimming pool, a tennis court, and some woods, with a jaw-dropping view of the Atlanta skyline. "You live like a princess."

"A lonely princess," Katherine lamented.

"You're not alone now, are you? I'm here."

Katherine smiled and pointed to her workspace. "Have a seat, Detective."

Jack sat down in Kate's chair and began entering data. His hands flew across the keys. "Hmm," he said, after about fifteen minutes of surfing the net.

"Tell me what you found?" Katherine's hand flew to her heart.

"Well, a cursory search brings up several entries about this Juliette Spencer. Says she's a first-class scam artist."

"Jack, you're teasing me. I know you're just making that up," Katherine said.

Jack smiled and turned his attention back to the computer. "Apparently she's a strong psychic and spiritual healer in a small community called Casa Spirito, Florida. She's known as Psychic Juliette. Her ad says she's a gifted psychic intuitive and a medium specializing in love, relationships, careers, and other passions." Jack took Kate's hand and pulled her around to give her a closer view of the screen. It felt good to have her so near again. He squeezed her hand reassuringly and she squeezed back.

Jack smiled and felt his heart stutter. He turned toward the screen and back to the business at hand. "As far as the old reverend, he's the founder of a secret spiritualist society in Casa Spirito, a federally tax-exempt church governed by a board of trustees, which he heads." Jack's fingers flew across the keys. "It looks like he was booted out of another spiritual community in central Florida. No reason given. He has his finger in a lot of pies down there," Jack observed. "He's a certified trance medium and spiritualist healer who claims to be a descendant of one of the world's most illustrious mediums. He is known throughout the community as a spiritualistic seer who can communicate and channel through spirit guides. Sounds to me like he's a first-class crook."

"How can you be so certain? You don't even know

the man."

Jack frowned. "I know enough to know I don't like him already. He's about twice this Juliette woman's age, and he's married and was married at the time this child was conceived. He must be a very randy reverend. And I can't find any official record of any child born in that community on that date. I say we go down there."

Katherine nodded her approval of his plan. "When can we leave?"

"Let me clear it with the department, and I'll pick you up tomorrow morning. I'll drive."

Katherine placed her hand on Jack's arm. "Thanks, I really appreciate this."

"No problem. This is a mystery, and I want to get to the bottom of it."

Katherine closed the files and they walked downstairs.

"What is your sign?" Katherine asked as they stood in the living room.

"My sign?"

"Yes, what month were you born?"

"What difference does that make?"

"All the difference in the world. I study the position of the sun, the moon, the planetary rising signs, and other astrologic aspects."

"Are you a palm reader?"

Katherine lifted her hands, palms up toward Jack. "I've studied palm reading. Astrology is a hobby of mine. I can consult an astrology chart to determine romantic compatibility, among other things."

Jack took one of Kate's hands into his, inched closer, and softly traced imaginary lines on her palms. Kate shivered. "I thought your parents didn't like you dabbling in the occult."

Kate tried to pull away, but Jack just took her other hand. "They didn't know. It was something I hid and experimented with when they weren't around. Like you probably hid *Playboy*s under your bed. I hid tarot cards."

"Caught me," Jack chuckled and pulled Kate's body in to his.

"For example, I'm a Taurus," Katherine said, trying to extricate herself from Jack's hold, unsuccessfully.

"What am I?" Jack asked, lowering his voice to a whisper, his lips dangerously close to hers. He was breathing heavily. "I was born on January twenty-third." He felt Kate move restlessly against his body.

"Then, you're an Aquarius, so your Zodiac element is air," she said softly. "Taurus is the earth sign. Taurus and Aquarius are considered potential soul mates. Aquarius embodies traits that are missing and needed to fulfill Taurus. But the attraction between air and earth can't last too long, if you ask the stars."

"I'm asking you, sweet Kate," Jack whispered against her ear. Kate tried to twist out of his grasp, but he pulled her harder against him.

Kate licked her lips, and if she didn't stop wriggling, he was going to kiss her until she quieted. She had already invaded his senses and if he wasn't careful, she was going to creep into his heart. And love was definitely not on his agenda.

"Aquarius has a special charm. He's mysterious and seductive," Katherine sighed, snuggling against him. "Aquarius will be instantly attracted to Taurus. But Taurus and Aquarius don't make the best bed mates."

She gave him a challenging look, as if she were drilling straight down into his mind.

Well she got that right, Jack thought. The instant attraction part, anyway. She was dead wrong about the bed mates. And damn it to hell, he couldn't wait to prove it to her.

Chapter Thirteen

Casa Spirito, Florida

Katherine could hear the ocean from her room at the quaint Victorian bed-and-breakfast in the pretty seaside town of Casa Spirito on the Florida coast. After an exhausting seven-hour drive from Atlanta, she'd had a restless night. Once she'd thrown back the white chintz curtains, the sun came streaming in and she could see the ocean, and smell it too. She was mesmerized by the relentless rhythm of the waves in their unceasing roll to the shore, and for the first time in weeks she felt a sense of well-being, of comfort, of peace. She ran a brush through her hair, applied her lipstick, took a last look in the oval mirror in the bathroom, and went downstairs to meet Jack for breakfast.

She hoped Jack wouldn't continue the litany of psychic jokes and disparaging remarks he had regaled her with on the trip to Florida.

"This place is out in the boondocks," he'd complained at dusk, when they'd finally arrived in Casa Spirito, past fields of cows and horses, a row of towering pine trees, and oaks trimmed in Spanish moss. Each of the homes, some brick, some ramshackle wooden ones, flew flags proudly in their front yards beside covered carports.

After a delicious meal of scrambled eggs, bacon, and biscuits and a fresh-squeezed glass of Florida orange juice, she and Jack took a leisurely stroll through the tiny town.

They walked along a quiet, shady street lined with pine trees, past the grand, two-story stucco Casa Spirito Hotel, a large church with a tall wooden cross, art galleries, walking paths, and parks.

The tempting smells of a bakery and a coffee shop wafted through the air. There were souvenir shops, a bookshop, a gift store, and a row of gaily-painted Victorian houses, with swinging wooden signs advertising the names and businesses of the owners. Psychic-mediums, handwriting experts, spiritualist healers, spiritual counselors. Each house was unique. Most had wind chimes, tinkling in the ocean breeze. One had orange trees full of ripe, fragrant fruit. Many had Chinese ornamentation—a pond, a spiritual garden, benches, private sanctuaries.

For a moment, Katherine pretended she and Jack were really a couple. She breathed in the sweet smell of orange blossoms and felt true contentment. She imagined this was what it would feel like if she belonged to Jack, if they were on their honeymoon—starting a new life—exploring the unknown together.

A well-fed gray cat sauntered over and sidled up to Katherine.

Jack grinned. "A kindred spirit?"

"No, just a friendly feline."

"At least it's not a black cat," Jack observed.

"Jack, you're seriously misinformed. Black magic is not part of spiritualism."

Jack threw his hands in the air. "Excuse me if I

don't know the rules of witchcraft."

Katherine punched Jack's arm and reached down to stroke the cat.

Jack shook his head. "I feel like I'm in Oz. Maybe this cat was Toto in another life. I know one thing, Dorothy, we're not in Georgia anymore." As they continued their walk, they watched a white-haired gentleman in an old-fashioned suit and tie greet a client before ushering her into his house for a reading. "And there's the wizard."

Katherine sighed.

The cat trailed behind her and Jack glanced back at it, as though debating whether to try shooing it away, before he gave Katherine a quizzical look. "Hey, Miss Pied Piper, you seem to have picked up a follower."

"Jack, you're a nut."

"I've been called worse."

As they passed another cemetery, two giant black ravens perched on a Celtic cross grave marker took flight.

"I think those big-ass crows are following us," Jack remarked.

"They're not crows. They're ravens."

"Isn't that a bad omen or something?"

"The raven is a symbol of magic."

"Black magic," Jack joked. "Maybe they're just fat homing pigeons."

They stopped at the entrance to the Casa Spirito Bookstore and Welcome Center in the scenic town square, and Jack took her hand. It was a casual gesture for him, but his hand felt warm and right in hers.

Overwhelmed with sensory possibilities as they entered the store, she dropped Jack's hand and ran around the shop touching the crystals, colored stones, and quartzes—pink, white, purple, and green, in all shapes and sizes. Then she browsed through the chakra charts and the books about healing. There were tarot cards, and T-shirts with the messages such as "Lift Your Spirits" and "Don't Touch My Spirit" emblazoned across the chest in an array of colors. She wanted one of everything.

"If you have any questions, I'd be happy to answer them," said a middle-aged sales clerk in a flowered muumuu, her glasses dangling from a gold chain around her neck.

Some style of electronic, mood-lifting music played, hopefully not designed to put someone in a buying trance.

"I feel like I'm on an acid trip," Jack whispered. "Maybe I'd better check my chakra at the door."

Katherine elbowed him. "Be quiet. She can hear you."

"Where are you from?" the woman asked, unruffled.

"You're a psychic. You should know the answer to that question," Jack said.

Katherine turned to Jack. "Don't be an idiot." Then she looked apologetically at the sales clerk. "My boyfriend thinks he's being funny."

Jack grinned. "If she can read my mind, then she knows I'm just kidding. I'm sure she gets that all the time. Actually, we're here for a reading," Jack announced. "What's the procedure?"

Katherine laughed. Jack was going to give himself away with his no-nonsense cop talk about procedures.

The clerk led them up some wooden steps into a

separate room, decorated with two comfortable flowered couches and a display of flyers. There were flyers about auras, spirit activities, mini readings, healing services, spiritual teachings, the science of spiritualism, and historic tours. There were announcements about mediumship development, encouraging students to "step into their power," and lectures on a variety of topics, including the basics of spiritual development and balancing out your energies.

A number of the workshops and seminars looked appealing. She would love to get a chance to learn more about developing some mediumistic skills. Imagine a place where everyone was enlightened. Where she wouldn't be an object of curiosity. The people who lived in this community were kindred spirits.

Jack picked up a green flyer. "Hey, Kate, I like the sound of this class. "Self-Exploration. Get in touch with your body, emotions, and spirit. Be sure to bring a pillow and a blanket." He wiggled his eyebrows suggestively. "I wouldn't mind getting in touch with *your* body."

Katherine shook her head. "You're acting like a horny sixteen-year-old."

Jack smiled and reached out to grab Kate, but she maneuvered her way toward a club chair next to a wooden table with a white telephone. Next to the chair was a large white-board with names and phone numbers of certified mediums who were available for readings that day, along with racks of business cards. The names were written in cursive in different handwriting styles and in blue, purple, and hot pink magic marker, obviously by the individual mediums.

The clerk pointed to the names. "We don't

recommend which one you should call," she explained. "See which name speaks to you. Use your intuition to see if you're drawn to someone, if you're in tune with them. Then use the phone on the table by the white-board to call the medium and set up an appointment."

"How much is this going to cost me?" Jack asked gruffly.

"The readings range from fifty to seventy-five dollars for the standard thirty-five-to-forty-minute session," reported the clerk. "More if you get a CD. You can go longer."

"I see you accept credit cards," Jack noted, reading the sign on the table.

"Yes," said the clerk, "And all of our mediums are SCSCMA-certified."

"Did you say Scammers Certified?" Jack repeated, feigning innocence.

Katherine kicked Jack and whispered, "Behave yourself."

The long-suffering clerk just smiled wearily and walked away as if she were used to non-believers.

"Couldn't help myself," said Jack, breaking out in a wide grin.

"These people are serious," Katherine said. "Please don't insult them."

"I hope this Psychic Juliette woman is working today, or we came all this way for nothing."

"Jack, you are giving off some negative vibes. I wish you would try to be open to the possibilities."

Jack feigned a wounded look. "I'm an open book."

Katherine rolled her eyes and looked up at the white-board. There were about ten names listed in various colors of magic marker.

Jack scanned the board and threw up his hands. "Wait. I'm getting a message. One of these names is speaking to me. Bingo, Psychic Juliette. This is our lucky day. All we do is pick up that bat phone over there and make an appointment." Jack walked over to the wooden table, picked up the receiver and dialed.

Katherine's heart fluttered. Was she ready to meet Juliette Spencer? The plan had sounded good when she and Jack discussed it on the drive to Florida, but the prospect of finding out she might be adopted and coming face-to-face with a woman who might be her birth mother was unsettling. She leaned into Jack and held her hand over his so she could hear the voice at the other end.

"Is this Psychic Juliette?" Jack asked.

"This is Juliette Spencer."

"Yes, um, Psychic Juliette, my fiancée and I would like to get a reading as soon as possible this afternoon. Do you have any openings?"

"How did you hear about me?" the voice asked.

"I saw your ad on the Internet. It um, spoke to me. We were in the area and thought we'd stop by. We're at the Welcome Center."

"I have some time now, if you'd like to come for a reading. I'm right on the main street, the fourth house on the right, past the post office. How much time do you need?"

"About an hour. We're on our way."

"Fiancée?" Katherine asked.

"Just play along. We can't just barge in there and ask her about a baby she may or may not have given up for adoption thirty years ago. That would freak her out. We'll see what we can learn, get to know her a little first."

Katherine's stomach was doing flip-flops.

Jack squeezed Kate's hand as they walked toward the house number listed on the board for Psychic Juliette.

Kate frowned and looked down at their joined hands.

Jack followed her glance. "Look, we need to practice. We're supposed to be engaged. Make it look real. Play along, like we're in *love*."

Katherine pursed her lips. "You don't even believe in love."

"Don't have to," Jack said. "We're undercover. This is just another assignment."

"Right," Katherine said, thinking how good it felt to have Jack's hand in hers. But it was all a pretense on his part. Katherine bit her bottom lip.

"Don't be nervous," Jack said. "I'll do the talking. Just follow my lead and improvise."

A moment later, Jack's bravado seemed to have evaporated.

"What exactly do you think will happen in this so-called reading?" Jack asked.

Katherine shook her head. So much for Jack taking the lead. "Well, I picked up this sheet at the Welcome Center that gives suggestions for a good reading." She reviewed the flyer as they walked toward Psychic Juliette's house.

"First," Katherine began, "it says you have to put your mind at ease and relax. It creates a better atmosphere for the reading. Then let the medium proceed at her own pace and in her own way. Don't expect her to discuss your most pressing problems at once. Let the medium know when she is correct. Don't try to confuse her. And this one is tailor-made for you, Beauregard. 'Don't argue with the medium.' "

Jack threw up his hands, letting Katherine's hand drop. "Me, argue? What other sage advice does that flyer offer?"

"It says some things may make more sense by the end of the reading and that you may not understand the message until after you've had a chance to think about it," Katherine read.

"That sounds vague, like fortune-telling."

"Mediumship is not fortune-telling," Katherine corrected. "She's going to provide guidance. She may or may not make a prediction, but even if she does, you have the power to change future events."

Jack looked doubtful. "How exactly do you think this thing will work? Do we just start asking her questions?"

Katherine glanced down at the sheet and read as she walked beside Jack. "It says here if you want to ask a question, meditate on it in advance of the meeting. Give the spirit ample time to give an answer. Spirits don't claim to have answers on the spur of the moment."

"Do you know how silly that sounds?"

"Maybe to you, Jack. That's how it works for me. I can't just predict things at will either. A vision has to come to me. When the forces aren't there, they're not there."

"The forces?" Jack scoffed. "You mean like in Star Wars?"

"Spirits are mysterious," Katherine stated, refusing to take the bait. "These mediums are supposed to be able to communicate with angels, spirit guides, and the collective consciousness."

Jack snorted. "Just so you know, I think this whole idea is wacko and that this Juliette person is a fake. I hope you're not going to believe anything she tells us."

"I appreciate your offering to drive down here with me," said Katherine. "I know you don't think anything positive is going to come of this, but I want you to at least keep an open mind."

They walked a few blocks—past a health food store, an ice cream shop, an Indian restaurant, the Casa Spirito, Florida, U.S. Post Office, and another row of brightly painted wooden houses with cars parked along the road and American flags at the entrances.

"Patriotic bunch," Jack noted, as they stopped by an old-fashioned lamp post and the sign and house number they were looking for. "The corner of Psychic Street and Aura Avenue?" Jack read the street sign and snorted. "Really?"

"Stop it, Jack. I'm warning you," Katherine groused. "I've had it up to here with your lame psychic humor. It's not very funny."

Jack apologized. "Sorry. I'll try to behave." His barely smothered smile communicated that he had no intention of behaving.

Katherine looked up at the two-story Victorian— the largest and nicest house on the block. She smelled fresh paint—cheery yellow and powder blue—and the scent of the roses climbing up the white lattice work on the front and sides of the house.

She noticed the neat boxes of violets, a patch of sunflowers, and the antique woven rockers on the wide, inviting front porch that virtually shouted, "Relax and stay awhile." Attached to the house was a gift shop called "KARMA," sporting a green and white sign emblazoned with yellow moon and star designs. The church bells chimed the start of a new hour. Water flowed from a fountain decorated with a bronze statue of a fairy with a wand, in a tiny meditation garden at the side of the house. The scene was something out of a storybook, and it looked somehow familiar.

Jack looked at the house and then at Katherine. "This looks like a gingerbread house, and I feel like we're Hansel and Gretel about to have a close encounter with the wicked witch."

Katherine rolled her eyes, but she was too nervous to spar with him.

"Looks like we're at the right place," said Jack, stopping to read the sign at the entrance. "*Psychic Juliette's, Certified Medium, Spiritual Counselor and Healer. Readings. Unique Gifts. Walk-Ins Welcome.* Her rates are pretty steep. I signed us up for a one-hour session. She's probably some kind of a quack—an expensive quack."

"Jack, not all psychics are quacks. At least give her a chance."

Jack shook his head. "Well, what could it hurt? We're only out a hundred bucks. Money means nothing to you."

Katherine scowled. "That's unfair. If we find a lead about my birth, then it's worth all the money in the world to me."

At the entrance to the shop, which displayed some large and beautiful pink, green, and blue quartz stones in the window, Katherine stopped and grabbed Jack's hand.

"What is it?" Jack asked. "Is something wrong?"

"I don't know. I feel some kind of strong pull."

"A bad vibe?" Jack wondered, patting the .40-caliber Glock 27 in its leather Galco Miami Classic holster tucked away under his jacket.

"No, actually, it's not menacing. I have a feeling that things are going to change for me, maybe forever," Katherine whispered, biting her bottom lip.

"Well, we'll never know if we don't go in." Jack opened the front door, and they entered a tiny reception area, which opened onto a gift store.

Katherine and Jack walked around the shop. She noticed shelves of beautiful stones and small black-and-white labels advertising that they were from China. Farther into the store, Katherine saw a very finely crafted collection of silver and gold handmade jewelry—featuring colorful stones set in rings, bracelets, and necklaces—enclosed in a glass case near the register.

Jack picked up a large white crystal with a pointed edge. "Very New Age," he pronounced, wielding the crystal like a sword.

Katherine peeked behind a deep blue velvet curtain into a small anteroom with a plush loveseat and some matching chairs. She motioned Jack over.

She and Jack were about to walk into the room, when they heard a noise behind them.

"I'm out here in the shop," said a very attractive woman who came out to greet them. Jack had a feeling he'd seen her somewhere before. "You must be…"

When she saw Katherine, she hesitated, staring at her visitor open-mouthed.

Katherine was used to stares. By now she was a

household name on TV. It wasn't unusual for strangers to stop her on the street and point, saying, "You're Crystal Ball Kate. You're that psychic on TV." She'd smile, wouldn't deny it, but never acknowledged it. She was still uncomfortable in the spotlight.

Jack stepped toward the woman. "I'm Jack Hale, and this is my fiancée Katherine Crystal." Jack hugged her to his side possessively. "Are you Psychic Juliette?"

"I'm Juliette Spencer. Just call me Juliette. Come in, please," she said, directing them to the room behind the curtain. She addressed a girl behind the counter. "Jasmine, would you please take over in the shop while I'm in session?" Jasmine nodded. As they followed Juliette, the psychic's shoe caught on the oval sisal rug, but she kept her balance and pointed to two identical chairs. "Have a seat, please."

Evidently the psychic was as nervous as they were. Katherine and Jack sat down across from Juliette. "You have a lovely shop," Katherine said sincerely, offering a bright smile. "Some beautiful things. Do you also live here?"

"Yes, I live upstairs above the shop."

Katherine clasped her hands in her lap. "We're new at this. We're not sure exactly what to do or say. Do you ask us questions? Do we ask you questions? What kind of things can we find out?"

"Well, I do séance circles by appointment, communications with deceased loved ones on the 'other side,' private psychic readings, numerology, psychometry, energy and spiritual healing, and regressions."

"Regressions?" Katherine asked.

"Yes, death is just a transition. We don't typically

135

condone hypnotism. But I can take you back through your past lives and do a Past Lives Reading."

"Past lives?" Jack asked skeptically. "You mean like reincarnation?"

"Yes, and karma. I can help you find those vital spiritual connections that explain many things in your current life. Perhaps you've been together in a past life."

Katherine's eyes widened.

Jack shook his head. "Seriously? You actually believe in that stuff?"

"Oh, yes," said Juliette, studying the couple intensely. "And in your case, most definitely. This is not your first time around."

****

As Kate babbled on nervously, Jack took the opportunity to study the medium. It hit him like a punch in the gut. Something strange was going on. Or he was seeing double. Psychic Juliette was the mirror image of Kate, just an older version. They could be sisters. The medium was a knockout, sensual, with fiery amethyst eyes and velvet black hair, falling in loose ringlets, like Kate's. She had a very compelling face, like Kate's.

Psychic Juliette looked at Jack. "First, do you have any questions?"

"Are you a medium or a psychic?" Jack asked.

Juliette smiled warmly. "I get that question a lot. Everyone is psychic in some way; everyone has a sixth sense of sorts, thought waves alerting them to what the universal spirit is trying to tell them. Mediums have a natural energy and ability to capture those thoughts from a higher power—a merging of the mind and the spiritual world around us."

Jack massaged his chin. She was spouting the same nonsense as Kate did.

"You look as if you are expecting a razzle-dazzle act," said Juliette. "I want this to be a positive experience for you."

Jack frowned. "Just what is supposed to happen in a reading?"

"Think of me as your spiritual counselor. I facilitate communications between you and people who have made the transition to the next world. It may not even be with someone you've known. I can't promise you contact with a specific spirit. My abilities enable me to be receptive to messages from a higher power so I can process and deliver those messages to you. I'm a mental medium. I also work as a healing medium. If in the first ten minutes you feel there is no connection, then you will walk away and no money will change hands."

"That sounds fair," Jack conceded.

"Could you tell me again the primary purpose of your visit?" Juliette asked, hugging her elbows.

Jack stopped staring at her and spoke. "Um, my fiancée and I are trying to determine if we're compatible, and if we have a future together. We're afraid we might be rushing into marriage, and we wouldn't want to make the wrong decision. Your ad says you specialize in love and relationships. Well, we're in love, but what I—what we—want to know is, will the relationship last?"

"Are you going to do a tarot reading? Or a palm reading?" Katherine interrupted excitedly. "I've always been interested in tarot cards."

Juliette smothered a smile. "If you'd like. I keep a

tarot deck on hand because people expect it. And the cards are pretty." She reached into a drawer and pulled out a deck of The Goddess Tarot cards. "But those are just the psychic trappings of the trade everyone is familiar with. So I may use these tools to more easily convey my message or make what I have to say more digestible. But I don't traditionally use them. I don't need them. My abilities aren't written in the cards." Juliette paused and placed her hands on the tarot deck on the table and looked knowingly at Katherine. "And neither are yours."

Kate looked at Jack and nudged him.

"I can start with a tarot reading and answer your questions about love and your future," stuttered Juliette, who continued to stare at Kate. Did Kate notice the resemblance, too?

"I'm shuffling this tarot deck of seventy-eight cards and turning over the card Venus," explained Juliette. "Venus is the Roman goddess of love." She smiled at Katherine and Jack. "She's also the queen of pleasure and passion."

Jack's interest perked up when he heard those words. He could be passionate.

"Your love is very strong and so will your passion be, when you finally come together."

Jack couldn't help but notice the flushed look on Kate's face. Maybe this Juliette woman did have some kind of gift, Jack thought. She obviously knew he and Kate hadn't been to bed together yet.

"Now I'm turning over the Magic card, representing Isis, the great Egyptian fertility goddess," Juliette continued. "Isis is a very potent symbol of magic, loss, and redemption."

Katherine looked at Juliette. "What does it mean?"

"It means there's a growing awareness of the magic within yourself, a yearning to grow beyond your perceived limitations."

Katherine stared meaningfully at Jack, and then back at Juliette. "That's right."

****

Katherine searched Juliette's violet eyes, the same unusual color as her own eyes, and she felt a tangible, almost electric connection to the woman. Compounded by the fact that she could have been looking into a mirror. People always said she looked like a gypsy. So what if the woman had dark hair and violet eyes, just like hers. A coincidence, perhaps? Didn't someone say that everyone had a twin somewhere?

Juliette pushed the tarot cards to the side and folded her hands in front of her. "Now then, is there anyone you want to contact? There are some strong spirits surrounding you both."

Jack frowned doubtfully.

"What do you see?" Katherine asked excitedly. "Can our loved ones check in on us? What are they doing on the other side?"

"I can answer those questions," the psychic responded. She turned to Jack and fixed him with her unusual eyes. "There's an amazing aura around you," Juliette said.

Jack looked like he was about to spit.

"Did you bring a picture of your departed loved one?"

Jack shook his head in denial. "I never said anything about a departed loved one."

Juliette sighed heavily.

"Okay, if that makes you uncomfortable, then let's move in a different direction. Let me start with a palm reading with the young lady, with Katherine," the psychic said softly.

She took Katherine's hand and held it, igniting another spark of recognition, a palpable connection within her.

"Is there anything you want to know?" Juliette asked Katherine.

Katherine stared into the air thoughtfully. "Will I have children?"

Juliette smiled and answered, "Of course. You are very fertile."

"Will they look like me?" Jack asked snidely.

Katherine slapped his arm. "Please behave."

Juliette coughed and tried to conceal a pained expression. "The young lady has just suffered a tragic loss."

Kate looked at Jack in amazement.

Lucky guess, he mouthed.

Juliette turned Kate's hand over gently and traced the path of her life lines and love lines. Tears glistened in her eyes.

"But I feel the presence of your loved ones. It is very strong."

"Are they together?" Katherine asked hopefully.

"Of course," said Juliette. "The bonds of love cannot be broken."

Katherine smiled and looked at Jack.

"I knew you would come one day," Psychic Juliette added.

The air in the room crackled. "How could you know that?" Katherine asked warily.

"You have the gift, too," Juliette noted.

Katherine looked up at Jack. He shrugged. *Another lucky guess?*

"I'd like to know more," Katherine demanded. "You said you knew I'd come one day. What did you mean by that? What do you know about me?"

****

Without answering the question, Juliette released Kate's hand, raised Jack's hand, and turned it over, studying it carefully, then tracing her finger across his palm.

"You have also suffered a tragedy, lost a loved one, but your loss occurred many years ago," Juliette said.

Jack frowned. "Everyone has lost someone," he said angrily. "That's an easy guess."

"You don't trust me," Juliette stated calmly. "You don't have faith."

"Let's just say I've been burned by your type before."

"Jack, back off," Kate said, kicking Jack's foot under the table.

Juliette laughed, and her laugh was warm and genuine.

Jack flinched. What was so funny? It was almost as if this woman could drill down into his mind and read his thoughts, his *unflattering* thoughts, about Madame Hydrangea.

"Most people are skeptical when they first come to me." Juliette brought Jack closer and whispered to him. "You are surrounded by love here."

"That's vague," said Jack, trying to mask his emotions.

"Your father is very proud of you, of the man

you've become, that you followed in his footsteps, and of how you protected your mother."

Jack leapt out of the loveseat.

"All right, this charade is over. I don't know how you found out all this stuff about me, or what you think you know, but I'm not buying what you're selling."

Jack reached into his pocket and slapped a $100 bill on the table in front of Juliette. "Keep the change." Then he started to walk away.

Kate jumped up and grabbed Jack's arm, pulling him aside.

"She's not a prostitute," Kate argued in a fierce whisper.

"I call it as I see it," Jack said. This whole thing has been a big mistake."

Kate pulled Jack back down to the couch. "Let's finish our reading," she coaxed, prompting, "Remember why we're here. Our future?"

Jack plopped back onto the loveseat, next to Kate, grabbed the $100 bill from the table, folded his hands, and started a slow and silent burn.

Juliette spoke. "When you're ready to communicate with your loved one, Jack, I can make that happen. His spirit is close. It's always with you."

Jack looked around the room. He didn't see any spirits. The woman was a looker, but she was also a charlatan. She was obviously weaving a spell on him. Next thing he knew, Juliette would try to levitate the loveseat. She was no better than Madame Hydrangea. A first-class fake. They were all fakes. With the exception of Kate. She was the genuine article.

"I'll take a rain check on that," Jack said, tapping his foot in an attempt to tamp down his temper.

Juliette turned her attention back to Kate.

"You also have a strong aura, the strongest I've seen since, well for a long time. And your love lines, both of them, are powerful and intertwined. You asked if you belonged together. And the answer is yes, you are soul mates. You were destined to find each other, again, and you have. You're both very lucky. You will have a long and happy life."

Okay, the first good news of the day, Jack thought, although it sounded like a fortune prediction of the cookie-cutter variety. If Kate believed they were meant to be together, maybe she'd be open to taking the relationship to the next level—the bedmate level.

Then Juliette frowned. "But there will be trouble. Very bad trouble, and soon. You will have obstacles to overcome," she warned the couple.

"Juliette, I'd like to show you something, and I was hoping you could answer a few questions." Kate glanced at Jack, who nodded his head, signaling his assent to broach the real reason for their visit.

"If I can."

"Have you ever heard of a man named Reverend Carter Coulter?"

The psychic shuddered. Her eyes grew cold, and she drew back.

To Jack, the room seemed to darken.

"He is the spiritual leader of this community," Juliette said simply, her face now inscrutable.

Kate handed Juliette the piece of paper she'd removed from her purse. "Please look at this. Are you the Juliette Spencer mentioned in this document?"

Juliette lifted the piece of paper and looked at it, her face contorting in pain and then surprise. Her hand flew to her heart. "Where did you get this?"

"That's not important now. Is this your signature?"

Juliette studied the signature on the paper, and her eyes blurred with tears. "Yes, but—"

"Where is the reverend now?" Jack interrupted.

Juliette's hand flew to her heart. "The reverend keeps his own counsel. You can find him at the church or at his estate. Anybody can give you directions."

Katherine was growing impatient. She needed answers and she needed them now. "Did you give birth to a baby girl on this date?" Katherine pointed to the year listed on the document.

Juliette didn't answer.

"Was Reverend Carter Coulter the father of your child?" Jack accused.

Juliette appeared frozen with fear. Then, seconds later, she lifted her hands and the pack of Goddess tarot cards scattered to the floor. Facing up was Isis, goddess of loss. "This session is over unless you tell me what is going on. I must know."

Jack pointed a finger at the psychic. "What's going on, Juliette Spencer, is that you gave up a baby for adoption, an illegal adoption, thirty years ago." He continued to grill her, though she appeared shaken. "Do you know what happened to that baby, where she is today? Did you have twins?"

Juliette didn't answer. She hugged her arms across her chest in a defensive position.

Jack pulled a card out of his pocket and placed it on the table along with the $100 bill. "Here's my card. If you remember anything, give me a call."

Juliette looked at Katherine with tears in her eyes. Jack took Katherine by the shoulders before she could respond and marched her out, up the street, past the row of miniature Victorian houses, and back to the bed-and-breakfast.

Jack was rattled. "Imagine, telling me she could communicate with my father. You believe all that crap about the bonds of love?"

"Do you think that woman is my real mother?" Katherine asked, biting her bottom lip until it bled.

"I don't know, but she definitely knows more than she's telling us," Jack said. "She's afraid, but of whom or what I don't know. Probably that reverend. Did you see how she reacted when we mentioned his name? We're going to pay Reverend Carter Coulter a visit after lunch. I'm sure the woman at the bed-and-breakfast will know where to find him." Jack turned to Katherine and framed her face in his hands. "You know, Kate, you *could* be related to that woman. It's uncanny how much you two look alike. Did you see it?"

Katherine said nothing. But the connection to the woman was growing stronger, and it didn't fade the farther away she walked. She paused at the entrance to the Casa Spirito Bed & Breakfast and took a last look back toward the town. In the distance she saw Juliette standing outside her shop staring back at her.

Chapter Fourteen

Katherine and Jack were enjoying a fresh fried seafood lunch on the patio of the Casa Spirito Bed & Breakfast, at a table facing the ocean. It was a beautiful day. A warm breeze blew up from the water, while gulls swooped lazily and dragonflies dashed by against a cloudless sky. Several fishing trawlers moved slowly across the horizon. Dolphins surfaced and played on the smooth surface of the sea. A silver shadow crossed the water, an airliner taking off for unknown places. Katherine lifted her face toward the sun, closed her eyes, and smiled. Despite the task at hand, she was relaxed, perhaps for the first time in days. What a peaceful place this was. She felt at home here.

"Jack, what was that episode back at Psychic Juliette's about?"

Jack chewed a bite of his grouper sandwich and wiped his mouth. "What episode?"

"I understand if you don't believe in psychics, but your attitude and animosity toward her went way beyond hostile."

Jack shrugged.

"Why don't you tell me what you have against sensitives?"

Jack took another bite of his sandwich and picked up a few French fries. "You wouldn't be interested."

Katherine swallowed a spoonful of her She Crab

soup. "I am interested. You're being irrational, and I want to know why. A while ago, you mentioned something about your mother and a medium. I think there must be more to the story than you've told me."

"Okay," Jack began, slapping his napkin on the table. "I can see you're not going to quit until you pry it out of me."

"I'm not prying," Katherine objected.

Jack tapped his forefinger repeatedly and began talking. "I've already told you part of the story. It was right after my dad was killed. My mother was devastated. There was nothing I could do to raise her spirits. But then she talked to a friend who suggested she call in a psychic. Can you believe that? My mother brought in this gypsy-looking woman, a so-called psychic, named Heddy Henrietta Grainger. She called herself Madame Hydrangea. For the next two years, she came to the house two or three times a week to 'raise my father's spirit.' "

Katherine put down her soup spoon. "Did that give your mother any comfort? You said they never contacted him, not even once?"

"You really think people can contact the departed?" Jack raised his voice and unbuttoned the collar of his polo shirt. "My father was dead. I saw him in the casket. There's no way he was ever coming back. I knew that, but my mother was convinced she would see him again, could see him again, that their 'love' could survive and thrive beyond the grave. The only thing that thrived was Madame Hydrangea's bank account. Besides what she was paid for those fruitless sessions, she recommended several bogus investment schemes, and she took my mother for almost everything

147

she had, including my dad's police pension, which was supposed to support us, and it was all for nothing."

Katherine blew out a breath. "You were only ten years old, Jack. You wished she could. You wished with everything you had that Madame Hydrangea could bring your father back, didn't you?" Katherine stared knowingly into his eyes. Kate could see she was right. Jack had been hopeful, but when his hopes were dashed, he'd turned angry.

****

Jack picked up the remainder of his fried fish sandwich and finished it in one swallow. Damn woman was perceptive as hell, and it was making him uncomfortable. It was like she had a window into his soul. It went beyond spooky and bordered on irritating.

"Jack, talk to me."

"Why do I even have to talk, when you can read my mind?" Jack took a drink of his iced tea and then set down the glass. "I was the man of the family. I was supposed to take care of my mother. That woman took advantage of her, and I let it happen."

"Be reasonable, Jack. You were just a boy. No one would have blamed you. And so to you, all psychics are fakes?"

"Aren't they?"

"Do you think I am?" Katherine looked at him directly.

"No, not you. I've seen you in action. I can't explain whatever it is you've got, but you have something powerful. I don't know what it is, but your gift is real. You're nothing like Madame Hydrangea."

Kate bit her lip, reached across the table, and placed her cool hand on his warm one. She smiled and felt Jack's body relax.

"It's nice to finally know the source of your distrust of mediums."

Jack looked apologetic. "I didn't mean anything personal."

"I told you before, I'm not a medium," said Kate. "I don't do séances. Although I don't discount them. But Madame Hydrangea? She does sound like a kook."

"She was more than a kook. She was a crook. And a lecherous old lady who preyed on vulnerable widows and children. She gave me the creeps, too. Her hands were always cold and clammy."

"She put her hands on you?" Katherine sounded shocked and disgusted.

"More than once," Jack admitted. "I never told my mom. Her heart was already broken."

"So you let her think—?"

"That maybe she really was communicating with ghosts. But I guarantee my father would have turned over in his grave if he thought that woman was anywhere near my mother. He wouldn't have fallen for her black magic. And neither did I."

Kate choked. "You think Madame Hydrangea was a witch?"

Jack clenched his fists. "Not a witch. I don't believe in them."

"And that's how you feel about psychics? You lump us all together as crackpots and crazies?" She sighed.

"I don't think you're crazy, Kate." Jack reached across the table for Kate's hand and rubbed the inside of her palm softly. "In fact, I think you're pretty wonderful."

Kate inhaled a deep breath, but she didn't pull her hand away. "Even though I'm prying into your life, forcing you to reveal your deepest, darkest secrets?"

"Even then." Jack twisted uncomfortably in his seat. If there weren't other patrons on the patio, he would have come around the table, taken Kate into his arms, coaxed her back into the hotel, into his bed, to do more than kiss. In fact, he'd been trying to find a way to make that happen since their trip to Sydney. But serial killers, murders, and mediums kept getting in the way. His feelings for Kate were growing bigger every day, as was his need for her.

Kate gazed into his eyes with a pensive look on her fabulous face. He was sure she could read him, but he had no clue what she was thinking. Was she as turned on as he was by this foreplay? What was going on in that complicated mind of hers?

"Did your mother ever remarry?" she asked softly.

"No. My dad was her one true love, and she'll follow him to the grave, alone. I don't believe in that kind of commitment. It's not real. Love is an illusion. All you get is hurt when you fall in love."

"Jack," Kate admonished, dropping his hand, breaking the mood. "That's a terrible way to live your life."

"It's gotten me this far."

****

Katherine stared out at the ocean, her pulse still racing from the touch of Jack's fingers. He was at war with himself. He scoffed at love but he made no secret that he desired her and wanted her in his bed. She wasn't misreading the signals. And she was more than ready for him. She recalled what Juliette had told them.

Your love is very strong and so will your passion be, when you finally come together.

What she was starting to feel for the man across the table from her was a combination of things. Lust, certainly, but even more, the stirrings of love, or what she thought was love. But Beauregard Lee Jackson Hale was as stubborn as a mule. Still, she loved the big ox. There it was. Her feelings for him had grown that big and important, and they weren't going away. She'd dreamed about him—them—every night, how they'd be together, in bed and out. Yet she was everything he didn't want. He wasn't looking to fall in love. And despite what he had told Psychic Juliette, he wasn't looking for marriage. He was definitely not looking for her.

Katherine had insisted on separate rooms at the bed-and-breakfast, for propriety's sake. Now she was beginning to regret that decision. Sharing a room would have forced them together, presented another opportunity to get closer. That was what she really wanted.

After lunch, Jack inquired about the reverend at the front desk.

"Most likely he's at home, since it's a weekend," said an attractive young woman behind the desk— Chastity, according to her nametag. "But you can usually find him at the church in the center of town. You really should go hear him preach. It's very moving. He's so spiritual, so pure. It's a truly cleansing experience. He touches your soul, that man. His words will wipe all your sins away."

"Sounds like someone's been drinking the Kool-Aid," Jack whispered to Kate. "I think we should meet the man at his home, in case things get heated. The reverend probably won't be forthcoming at his church."

"How long have you known the reverend?" Jack asked Chastity.

She got a dreamy, glazed look in her eyes as she sighed and smiled. "Oh, I've only just moved here a few months ago, but he made me feel very welcome. He takes a personal interest in every member of his flock, makes us all feel special, and takes the time to make us feel at home and loved."

Jack rolled his eyes. "I'll just bet he does. Hey, can you give us directions to his house? Have you ever been there?"

The clerk blushed. "Everyone knows where the reverend lives. Here's a map. Let me show you." Chastity took a map from behind the desk and explained the route to Jack.

"Well, *Chastity*, you've been very helpful. Thank you." Katherine and Jack got into his car and followed Chastity's directions to the reverend's house. Estate was a better description of the place. It looked like a French chateau. It was set back quite a distance from the road, and beyond the house they could see, smell, and even hear the ocean.

"Wow," Jack said. "Look at this place."

They drove by a stucco sign imprinted with the words *Âmes Sur la Mer*.

"Souls by the sea," Katherine translated.

"The pretentious joker even named his estate. It puts your mansion to shame."

Katherine laughed. "I don't live in a mansion."

"Yeah, you do. Compared to where I was brought up. My whole house could have fit into your kitchen."

"I'm sure it was lovely."

"It's all my dad could afford on his salary. He was proud of it. Now I get to see how the other half lives. The psychic business must be booming, or maybe the reverend has some very grateful followers."

Jack steered the car up to the circular driveway that crossed the well-manicured lawn at the front of the house, where he parked under a canopy of oaks and Spanish moss.

"No valet?" Jack teased.

"Well, the reverend wasn't expecting us," Kate reasoned.

The two stepped out of the car and walked to the front door. Jack rang the bell, and his attention was drawn to the high-tech security cameras. Katherine smoothed her skirt.

Suddenly, the door opened and a tall, imposing man Katherine assumed was the Reverend Carter Coulter appeared. His cape, with the wingspan of a vulture or a vampire, cast a giant shadow across the front porch. An evil aura emanated from the reverend.

Katherine was blown back by the reverend's powerful presence, and Jack caught her to keep her from falling.

He's reading me without my permission. How rude. There's something unholy about this reverend.

"May I help you?" the reverend asked. His eyes widened when he saw Katherine.

Jack tensed. "Are you Reverend Carter Coulter?"

"Yes," the reverend answered curtly.

"We would like to discuss something of a personal nature with you, Reverend Coulter," Jack said. "May we come in?"

The reverend turned his evil countenance on Jack. "How did you find this place?"

"We got directions from a woman at our bed-and-breakfast. One of your flock. Her name was Chastity."

"Ah, Chastity," sighed the reverend, his thin mouth twisting up at the corners.

"Well, I don't do psychic readings without an appointment. You'll find what you're looking for at our Welcome Center."

"That's not why we're here," said Katherine. "We want to talk with you about an adoption you were involved in thirty years ago, in Atlanta."

The color drained from the reverend's already pale face.

"I don't know what you're talking about." His eyes bored into Katherine's and shot out a blast of power that knocked her back again.

She recoiled, then regained her composure and stood firm. "You signed papers and signed a baby over to my father, Judge Tyler Crystal. My parents passed away earlier this week."

"I'm sorry to hear that." The pronouncement was delivered in a monotone that suggested he was most definitely not sorry. And he didn't seem surprised.

"I have the paper right here." Katherine held out the document to the reverend, who glanced at it and frowned.

"Well, you might as well come in," said the reverend, ushering them inside. "Let me get a closer look at that piece of paper."

Katherine sensed he wanted to get a closer look at her. The man was old enough to be her father. His unwavering stare made her uncomfortable.

Jack and Katherine followed the reverend into his cavernous den.

While she felt the reverend's eyes assessing her, she noticed Jack looking around with cop's eyes, probably analyzing possible escape routes in case they were cornered. She saw his right hand rest on his weapon, a motion that did not escape the reverend's notice.

"Are you licensed to carry that firearm?" the reverend asked.

"I am," Jack replied, not giving away the fact that he was a cop—an off-duty cop, but a cop.

The reverend steepled his hands, then flexed them, releasing a hot stream of negative energy.

"Have a seat," he said, directing his guests to a sleek leather couch in front of the fireplace.

Genuine Italian leather, Katherine discovered when she sat down. Soft and expensive. She doubted it got very cold in Florida, but maybe the reverend needed a fire to warm his cold-blooded heart. His aura was suffocating. It blanketed the room like a malevolent fog. She wrestled to maintain her internal balance.

Kate scanned the room. Her expert eye lingered on several masterpieces hanging on the muted walls. She had studied these paintings in art school and learned more about them in her job as an art dealer at the gallery. Some of these painting were of questionable provenance. But there was no doubt they were all originals, all of museum quality. One, in particular, had gone missing from a small European museum three years ago. And coincidentally it—or a damned good copy of it—had ended up in this very house.

The reverend fixed his soulless black eyes on

Katherine's. "Are you an art aficionado?"

"Kate majored in art history," Jack explained. "I don't know a Rembrandt from a Renoir, but Kate used to sell paintings for a living."

"I'm very proud of my collection," said the reverend, gazing at Katherine. "It took me years to accumulate it. What do you think of the Monet?"

"It's fabulous," Katherine admitted, now openly staring at the painting in admiration. "I've never seen anything like it. How did you come by it?"

"At auction," the reverend said.

"And the Chagall?"

"It found its way into my house through a French art dealer. I love the French. They so easily part with their treasures."

Katherine pursed her lips. She'd never seen anything like it in any museum. She wanted a closer look.

"You like Chagall?"

"I love the way he explores fantasy and mysticism in his paintings," Katherine said. Her parents owned an original Chagall, a wedding scene, which held the place of pride in the Crystals' living room.

"As do I. We have that in common, among other things."

"Reverend Coulter," Katherine began, trying to direct the reverend's attention back to the pertinent matter, placing the document in his hands. "About this document."

The reverend appeared to study it.

"I don't recall ever having seen this."

"But isn't this your name on this piece of paper?"

"It appears so. Perhaps I did help one of the

wayward girls who wandered into Casa Spirito, found herself in trouble, and didn't know where else to turn. We're a very forgiving community. But that was a long time ago."

"Has that happened often?" Jack persisted.

"I don't recall."

"Reverend Coulter," Katherine pleaded. "This isn't a trial. I'm just trying to get at the truth. This child, this girl who was put up for adoption, she was born on my birthday. The papers were found in my father's safe, and your signature is on them. My father is no longer here, and so I'm asking you again, what do you know about this document?"

"And I'm telling you, Miss Crystal, that I don't know a thing about any adoption. I suggest you go back to your mansion and get on with your life."

Kate stared at Jack.

"How do you know she lives in a mansion?" Jack asked pointedly.

The reverend cleared his throat. "It's just a figure of speech."

"I think you know more than you're telling us," Jack accused.

"Are you calling me a liar?" The reverend's aura was agitated, and he looked about ready to boil over.

"Are you?" Jack's eyebrows narrowed.

"I think the two of you had better leave. Get off my property, or I'll call the sheriff. We don't like strangers in our town." The reverend stepped to one of his end tables and pulled a gun out of the drawer.

"I believe you are trespassing," he said. "I would hate to have anything happen to such a nice young couple, but if you don't walk out of here now, you'll

157

leave me no choice."

Jack's senses went on alert. "Come on, Kate, let's go. The reverend is obviously hiding something, and we're going to find out what it is. Maybe we should drop in at his church, start asking questions."

"If you go sticking your nose in church business, you'll regret it," the reverend warned ominously.

"Is that a threat?" Jack posed.

"No, that's a promise. You know your way out."

Jack placed his hand on Kate's shoulder and started to lead her out.

She refused to budge and confronted the reverend.

"I need that document back."

"I'm afraid that won't be possible."

"Jack, do something," Kate urged, turning to Jack.

"That's the lady's property," Jack said. "You need to return it."

"Not the way I see it. She handed it to me. You're in my house, and now it belongs to me."

"Kate, we need to leave. It's obvious this man is not going to cooperate. We'll get the document another way."

"But Jack!"

"Don't argue with me, Kate," Jack said in a no-nonsense voice that defied disagreement. He led Kate toward the door, opened it, and guided her out ahead of him. The lock clicked behind them.

"Jack, why didn't you stop him?"

"Six reasons: Smith & Wesson .357 Magnum revolver."

"But you have a gun, too."

"I didn't want to start a fire fight. There are other ways of dealing with people like the reverend."

"Do you have a plan?"

"I always have a plan."

Jack peered through the window in time to see Reverend Coulter slide back the Chagall and place Katherine's document in his safe.

"What did you see?" Katherine asked.

"Where he hid your document. In his safe, behind the Chagall you were drooling over."

"I wasn't drooling."

"Salivating. Lusting after."

"That painting is priceless. It's one of a kind. And it's a beautiful wedding scene."

"Hmm."

"What does that mean?"

"It means we need to get out of his line of sight and wait until he leaves his house."

"How do you know he's going to leave the house?"

"He's afraid. That piece of paper has him spooked, and my bet is he's going to meet with someone, someone who can give us answers. He obviously didn't want us to make the connection between him and that piece of paper. He was wondering if he had covered all his bases."

Kate and Jack got into the car, eased down the driveway, parked behind the cover of a tree, and waited.

Chapter Fifteen

Casa Spirito, Florida

Reverend Carter Coulter reluctantly set the newspapers down on his kitchen table. He couldn't read enough about "Crystal Ball Kate." It was easy to do. Her picture was plastered all over the tabloids and she was the hot topic on the Internet and all the TV talk shows. She had grown into a beautiful, quite remarkable girl. She was the picture of her mother—her *real* mother. And if she had half her mother's spiritual talent...

He was going to have to pay the tempting Juliette another visit. It had been a long time, and he was hungry for another taste of her. Not that he couldn't have his pick of willing young sensitives. They came to town, *his* town, in droves, looking for guidance, and he was all too eager to offer it. His wife was conveniently out of town for the week, and whenever she was gone, his juices started flowing again.

But as for the Crystals, in whose care he had entrusted his daughter, they had reneged on their contract. And they had paid for their indiscretion.

Reverend Coulter strode onto his backyard deck and surveyed his property. He owned the whole damn town and he commanded respect and generated fear. The story of the founding of Casa Spirito was legendary. And he was instrumental in perpetuating that legend. As head of the Board of Trustees for the Casa Spirito Spiritualist Society, he was a tough governor of the unincorporated community of spiritually-minded people. He owned all the land and buildings in the town, including the Casa Spirito Hotel, the Coulter Memorial Temple, the Healing Center, Bookstore, and Welcome Center, and he retained the huge fees and profits generated by the Society because of its federal tax-exempt status.

Anything that got done in this town had to go through him. Anything he wanted was his for the taking. All those innocent runaways, lost and searching, who came to his town were greeted by him with open arms, welcomed into his flock, woven into his web of influence, and eventually, and without much coaxing, wooed into his bed.

Just like Juliette, or whatever her real name had been before she came to Casa Spirito. He had sensed immediately that she was a strong psychic and spiritual healer, and he had taken the beautiful but naïve girl of seventeen under his expansive wing. Back then she had considered him charming. After all these years, apparently the charm had worn off.

He was married, with a family, when he'd first laid eyes on Juliette, but he knew he had to have her. The pull was magnetic. She was reluctant at first, but he had taken his time with her. He recognized her talent right away, and he convinced her they were kindred spirits, destined to be united, or some such nonsense about soul mates.

She was riveted when he'd spun the tale that his spiritual guide had led him to his destiny in Casa

161

Spirito. And that she was *his* destiny, a destiny that could not be denied.

She was his Juliette. He was her Romeo, stuck in a loveless marriage. Star-crossed lovers. She had no money, no family to speak of. No doubt she was running from something or someone. He didn't probe or ask questions. Frankly, he wasn't interested in her past, just her future and what she could do, for him and to him. He'd generously set her up rent-free in an attractive house and shop on the town's main street, a house with several spacious bedrooms on the second story—their love nest. And she had been eternally grateful. His investment had paid off. Psychic Juliette's was one of the most popular and profitable establishments in town. And he got a healthy cut of her profits.

Their first coupling had been mind-blowing. So much so that he had forgotten to use protection. He craved her body and he had to have her again and again. He had never had another woman like Juliette before or since. Her innocence had excited him, and under his tutelage she had blossomed as a medium and as a lover. They had been happy until the day she had come to him and told him about the baby.

He still remembered that day. How could a seer of such talent be so irresponsible? Could she not have foreseen what was about to happen? How could she have allowed it? Her carelessness was inexcusable.

Amid a stream of tears and protests that she refused to give up her child, he fabricated a story that his spirit guide had warned him during a séance that danger would be the child's destiny if they kept her. In the end, he convinced Juliette to give the baby up for adoption.

He secretly arranged for the child to be sold to an Atlanta couple, Katherine's adoptive parents, who couldn't have a child of their own. The price was a hefty sum and a promise of silence. The father had been an attorney and, later, a respected federal judge. The judge's career had been monitored closely over the years.

He had exacted the same promise of silence from Katherine's real mother, because if it were discovered that he was nothing but a lecherous trance medium who had gotten an underage girl pregnant, his reputation would be ruined and the flow of money would abruptly stop. He had become too accustomed to luxury and high living to be run out of town penniless or worse.

If his congregants discovered that their leader, who claimed to adhere to the life-guiding Principles of Spiritualism, which preach eternal life and cleanliness of the soul, had, over the years, seduced and indoctrinated many of the young girls who wandered into the community, he would be ruined. And he would not allow that to happen.

He recalled watching Juliette nurse the baby for the very last time, the tiny hand clutching at her mother's breast while she sucked furiously, before he snatched the newborn from Juliette's nipple and tore her out of her mother's arms.

"Mustn't get too attached to Mommy," he'd crooned, wiping his finger across Juliette's milky breast and sucking the sticky substance off his finger as he cuddled the child. "Save some for Daddy." It still made him hot every time he thought of it. It was at that moment he'd conceived his noble vision of propagating his own stable of psychics in his image.

Juliette never discovered what had happened to her baby, but he knew she continued to long for the girl. The only reason she stayed in Casa Spirito was in hopes he would eventually reveal the location of her baby. He'd teased her with hints of the whereabouts of the child, taunted her with scraps of meaningless information, strung her along magnificently over the years. Was she in San Francisco? Or Chicago? Or was she in New York?

He had warned Tyler Crystal repeatedly to keep the girl's identity hidden from the world or he'd disclose to the authorities how the judge had bought his own child. And what did the man do? He'd allowed her to get tangled up in a high-profile news story, the crash of the Rivers jet, and then the case of the Sydney Strangler. Things had gone along so smoothly for so many years, and now Ty Crystal and his wife had allowed their daughter's identity to be revealed.

If Juliette saw the papers, she'd know. Anyone in Casa Spirito with two eyes and half a brain, seeing the girl's photo, would know who her real mother was, and then Juliette would put the pieces together and start snooping around. He'd had no choice but to tie up loose ends.

Now that he'd gotten a closer look at his daughter and was certain she was truly as talented as her mother, as the newspapers indicated, maybe there was a way he could use her. Reunite her with her "true" family, the family she'd never known. He could easily manipulate her. After all, she was just a woman, and women were naturally drawn to him.

Reverend Coulter went back into the kitchen and crumpled the newspaper pages in his fist. He was still exhausted just thinking about the long drive to Georgia and back.

It was a dirty business, but it was taken care of. There was no trace of his presence anywhere near the Crystals' lake house. No airplane ticket, no hotel stay, no use of credit cards to give him away.

He walked into the library, poured himself a brandy, and replayed the events of the past weeks in his head. Endless hours in the car, tracking down the judge's property. Not difficult with that tacky sign *Crystal Lake House* leading him right to their door. Then there was the matter of tampering with the brakes. Trailing the car around hairpin curves until he witnessed the judge's car careening off a mountain road. The screams amid the burning debris—the judge and his wife had both survived the crash, barely, until the police arrived, led there by an anonymous 9-1-1 tip from a good Samaritan. Never let it be said he wasn't a concerned citizen. He watched the couple being pulled out of the wreckage with the Jaws of Life.

His earlier warning to the judge must not have gotten through. He'd made a phone call, disguising his voice, "Crystal is fragile and easily broken." Still, Crystal Ball Kate remained in Australia and in the headlines.

They'd had an agreement, and the Crystals had broken their end of the bargain. It was as simple as that. The reverend didn't believe in second chances.

The brandy burned, sliding down his throat, settling his nerves. He reached for the bottle to pour another glass. Hands still shaking, he downed a third, until he regained control.

All he needed was a little sleep and he'd be in

tiptop shape. The adoption episode was put to bed forever. His reputation and his considerable fortune remained intact.

Contemplating how he had gotten rid of the Crystals was making him hot. Too much adrenalin in his system to sleep now. Power always made him run hot. Maybe there was time to stop by Juliette's and tempt her with his sudden vision that their daughter would soon be coming for a visit. Or maybe a short rendezvous with one of the younger devotees who was always willing and craving his attention. Or maybe both.

Chapter Sixteen

Jack and Katherine watched the sleek black Bentley careen out of the driveway and onto the road. The handcrafted motor car was driven by none other than the reverend. Jack waited a minute and followed.

"What if he sees us?" Katherine asked.

"He won't. I'm a professional, and he's not expecting us to follow him. We had a standoff and he thinks he's won. So let's see where the not-so-good reverend goes."

Within minutes, the reverend pulled up to a storefront occupied by one Psychic Juliette.

"That's the woman we met with," Katherine said. "She's involved somehow, and we need to find out why."

"Drop me off around the corner. Then take the car back to the hotel. I'm going to see what I can find out," Jack ordered.

"I'm coming with you."

"It's too dangerous. This guy is packing, and I don't think he's afraid to use his firepower."

"This is about me, and I'm going to be there when it happens." Katherine stood firm.

Jack shrugged. He parked the car on the next block, and he and Katherine walked back to Psychic Juliette's place. When they arrived, they heard raised voices in the anteroom behind the blue curtain where Juliette had conducted their session earlier that morning. The reverend and the psychic were having an argument. Jack raised a finger to his lips and with his other hand ushered Kate along. They tiptoed farther into the shop and listened.

"It's her, isn't it?" Juliette's voice. "It's my daughter."

"What are you talking about?"

"That beautiful girl. She came to my shop. After all these years. I knew her. I felt it. Anyone can see she's mine. Katherine Crystal is my daughter."

"You're hallucinating, Juliette, and if they come snooping around here again, I want you to send them away."

"I won't. I've stayed here thirty years waiting—waiting for some word, waiting for you to tell me what you did with her. Now she's come back to me. Of course I'm not going to turn her away."

Katherine's hand flew to her throat and she shifted away, but Jack held her close, wrapping his arms tightly around her so she couldn't move. She was shaking and crying silently, and he tapped her lips softly and shook his head. Don't talk, he was saying.

Don't talk? That woman just said that Katherine Crystal was her daughter, which meant that her beautiful mother was not really her mother. That she, Katherine, was not really who she thought she was. Then who was she?

Reverend Carter Coulter had grabbed Juliette and was shaking her.

"You will do exactly as I say, or I will make sure you never see the girl again."

"But she's your daughter too. Don't you even want

168

to know her?"

Kate shuddered. This man, this evil man was her father? Impossible. But documents don't lie.

Jack held her tighter.

"We agreed thirty years ago that it was best for the girl if she didn't remain here with us. Remember, I told you I had a vision that great harm would come to her if she stayed here. We gave her up for her own safety and well-being."

"That was when I believed in you, when I was in love with you. Now that I know your true nature, I know you never loved her. And you never loved me. You never had a vision. You sold our child for money. How much did Katherine's father give you? When you ripped her from my arms, you ripped out my heart and killed any feelings I had for you."

"If you think I'm so evil, then why did you stay with me all these years? Why did you warm my bed?"

"You used me, you seduced me. I was barely a woman. You made me love you and then you stole my child. And being here, near you, was the only way I knew to get her back. You told me, you swore that you loved me, but you've stayed married to someone else. You promised you'd tell me, one day, what happened to my daughter. And I was foolish enough to believe you."

"I did love you."

"And what about all the other unfortunate young girls, those innocents who have wandered into Casa Spirito? Yes, I know about all the other women you seduced, Carter. And you fed them the same lies. Did you love them, too?"

"I don't know what you're talking about, Juliette."

"Look up and down the street. All these women,

Marilyn Baron

drawn here by your evil spell, forced to stay because you pay their way, set them up in business, seduce them and sell their children."

Kate struggled to get free. Jack held on tighter and refused to release her. He clamped his hand over her mouth.

"You can't prove a thing."

"All the while you grow richer and more powerful. You hide your wealth from the community. You need to be exposed."

"Bitch!"

Reverend Coulter spat out the word as the sound and sting of his slap against Juliette's tender flesh reverberated around the shop.

Katherine recoiled at Juliette's outcry, but Jack never loosened his grip on her body.

"I thought you had learned your lesson. You can't survive without me. I am the leader of this church and this community—and your master."

Juliette planted her feet firmly on the carpet, her bleeding lip protruding.

"You're just jealous," Reverend Coulter said, stroking Juliette's face. "You're jealous because you've seen your daughter, and you know what I see in her. I see you, the you who used to attract me, the you who has become a tired, sad, bitter old woman. And if you don't keep quiet, I will have to handle Katherine. She's really very bewitching, don't you agree? She is a major talent. I've been following her progress in the newspapers all these years. She has our blood and she has surpassed us. Outshone us. I will keep her here, with me, tutoring her, until I find a proper use for her powers. Imagine what I could do with her knowledge of

170

the future. I could rule the world."

"I won't let you. I'll tell your wife. I'll go to the council. And to the police."

"And you think they'll believe you? If you expose me, I will take it out on our daughter. I know you don't want that."

Katherine saw Juliette sag against the back of the loveseat.

"Perhaps once more, for old time's sake?" The reverend moved toward Juliette. His hand fondled her breast. She bit him and he pulled back.

"You'll pay for that, you little hellcat. You're nothing but a used-up whore, and I will have you brought up in front of the council for punishment."

The reverend bared his teeth and turned to exit. Juliette began to whimper.

"Jack," Kate whispered. "You have to do something."

Jack rubbed her back.

"Now is not the time. We're going to have to gather some more evidence."

The reverend turned back toward Juliette. "You've been warned. If you think I'm making empty threats, then you don't know me at all. Katherine's parents proved an impediment, an impediment that had to be removed."

"What did you do to them?" Juliette demanded.

"They had a little accident. And the same will happen to you, if you're not obedient. A shame, about the judge. Now that money source has dried up. I'll be back to check on you after you've come to your senses and stopped your sniveling. You've put me in a mood, Juliette. I think I'll pop in on Psychic Serena. She's so young and naïve, with such a beautiful body. A body made for loving. Reminds me a lot of you when you first came to town."

"Jack, did you hear what he said?" Kate whispered harshly. "He killed my parents."

"It sounds that way."

"I want to go to Juliette."

"We don't want to give our hand away, and she is in danger if we go near her. While the reverend is otherwise occupied with Psychic Serena, I think we'll make a stop at the good reverend's house, snoop around and see what we can find."

Kate hated to hear Juliette's tears. Her birth mother's tears. But Jack made a lot of sense.

When they got out into the sunlight, Kate threw up all over the sidewalk. She saw the reverend's dark car parked outside Psychic Serena's shop. The Closed sign was hanging at an angle in the window. That poor young woman might be a fortune reader, but she was out of luck.

"Come on, let's get out of here," Jack said, a disgusted look on his face.

"Jack, I can't believe this. That woman, Juliette, is my real mother and that evil man is my father? All those years, and I never suspected anything."

"You're nothing like him, Kate. We're going to get him for fraud, for murder, for bribing a federal judge, for whatever other charges we can make stick. That sick bastard's been hiding out here in this quiet little community, building his evil empire, hiding behind his religion, while all the time he was seducing young women and selling their children. And I could kill him for what he said about you. That he was going to—"

Jack couldn't say the words. His breathing was ragged, his face red. "His own daughter."

Kate placed her arm on his shoulder. "Thank you."

"For what?"

"For stopping me. I was going to attack him. I would have confronted him, and you could have gotten hurt."

"Or you. I couldn't take that chance with your safety."

"But he has to pay for what he's done."

"He will. I promise you, he will."

Chapter Seventeen

While the randy reverend, Katherine's real father, was otherwise occupied in some horizontal hocus pocus with Psychic Serena, Jack and Kate retraced their steps and raced back in Jack's car to the reverend's house. When they arrived, Jack veered the car off the driveway and wound around to the back of the property.

"I'm still having trouble wrapping my head around everything that's happened," Katherine said.

Jack grabbed her hand and they walked toward the back door together. "I know, it's unbelievable."

He strode toward the back of the house, with Katherine close on his heels. Spying a barn across a long stretch of lawn, they checked inside the outbuilding to make sure no one was lurking there. They only found several thoroughbred horses in their stalls.

"Oh, these horses are beautiful," Katherine sighed, stroking the mane of a handsome black stallion.

"No time for petting. We need to get moving." Jack pulled her away. When they got to the back door of the house, he glanced up at the alarm system.

"The reverend made a serious mistake. He must either have been in a hurry or preoccupied, because he forgot to arm his security system. The red light isn't blinking, and that will make it easier to find our way in."

"Don't you mean break in?" Kate corrected.

"You say potato, I say potato."

"Let's call the whole thing off," she quipped, managing a half smile.

"No way. We're going in." In one movement, Jack dropped Katherine's hand, took out his gun, smashed the glass, and picked the lock.

"Is that legal?"

"Details," Jack said, and warned her to be careful of the glass as he shut the door behind them.

They walked in through a mudroom and a set of French doors, which led into a spacious kitchen. "Okay, let's head for the den. We need to get into the reverend's safe."

"Breaking and entering *and* robbery." Katherine shook her head.

"Add it to the list," Jack said dismissively as he moved into the den.

"How are we going to open this safe?" Katherine wondered.

"I don't suppose you can conjure up the combination?"

"That's ridiculous."

"First, I'm going to remove this priceless painting you're so hung up on. Maybe we'll take it with us. You deserve it."

"Jack! That's a felony. Anyway, I'm pretty sure it was already stolen."

"Add stolen art to my tab," he said. "Although I'm pretty sure you can't steal stolen art."

Jack was busy removing the painting. He started to toss it onto the couch.

"Jack, be careful! That painting is priceless."

Katherine studied it. She couldn't believe the treasure she was looking at and how much this masterpiece could command at auction.

"Now I remember where I saw this," Katherine recalled. "A thief broke into the Chagall museum in Nice, France, a few years ago and just walked out with this painting. It was never recovered."

"Well, then we're taking it as evidence," Jack stated.

"Give it to me." Katherine lifted the painting from Jack's hands and gingerly placed it on the couch.

"Okay, now we shoot off the lock."

"Will it work?" Kate looked at the safe.

"We'll find out, won't we? Cover your ears. We're so isolated out here, no one will hear the shot except the horses. Hope it doesn't spook them." He aimed his pistol and shot off the lock. The sound reverberated around the room.

What they found inside the safe shocked them both.

"We hit the mother lode." Jack pulled out a velvet pouch full of loose diamonds, some estate-type jewelry, and Kate's birth certificate, along with several other contracts and documents, enough cash to finance a minor war, and several passports, all with different names and countries, all with the reverend's picture.

Jack spread the loot out on the coffee table. "The reverend sure didn't take a vow of poverty. Wonder where he got all this cash?"

"What are we going to do with all this stuff?" Katherine asked.

"Take it back to Atlanta, as evidence in the case I'm going to build against the rotten reverend."

"But this is Florida. Atlanta doesn't have jurisdiction over this case."

"What about selling children across state lines?"

Katherine frowned.

"Go see if you can find some pillowcases we can stash all this loot in."

Katherine set out to explore the rest of the house.

"And don't dawdle or gawk over the paintings. We need to get out of here before the reverend returns. He's dangerous, Kate."

Katherine held up her hand in assent as she walked down a long hallway in search of some bags or pillowcases. Distracted as she came across painting after painting, signed print after signed print—in the hallway, in the bedrooms—she marveled at what she saw. The art in this home could fill a small museum, and she had the feeling that's where most of these paintings had come from. There were several Monets, a Matisse, a Cezanne, even a Fragonard—the Holy Grail. The reverend seemed to favor French artists. Could they be copies? Very fine forgeries, if they were. Katherine looked at the signatures and touched the frames. No, these were originals. She was definitely in the presence of genius, paintings she had only studied in books, seen in museums, or dreamed of owning.

Speaking of dreams, she was here on a mission, in search of a pillowcase. Katherine walked into what was likely Reverend Coulter's bedroom at the back of the house. A spacious master room, overlooking the ocean, with museum-quality decorative arts—an antique French writing desk worthy of Napoleon, French Aubusson rugs, the best satin sheets money could buy. Was this where she got her love of fine things? Her love of art? Only her real father didn't just appreciate art. He stole it and hoarded it so no one else on earth could bask in its beauty.

She put all thoughts of Reverend Coulter as her father out of her mind. Pillowcases, that was what she was after. She threw back the comforter and removed all the pillowcases from the bed. They would fill them with all of the reverend's possessions. How could he even sleep at night?

Katherine scooped the pillowcases up in her arms and ran down the hall.

"Jack, you won't believe what I—"

She stopped short and stared at Jack, whose hands were bound in his own cuffs, sporting a nasty gash on the side of his head. He was face-to-face with Reverend Coulter, who had Jack's own gun trained on his heart.

"Jack, no!" she cried, dropping the pillowcases and running to him. "Did he hurt you? Are you okay?"

Jack nodded and squeezed his eyes with the motion of his head. Katherine reached behind Jack and closed her hand around one of his.

The reverend kept his eyes and gun on Jack, but spoke evenly.

"Katherine, so nice of you to join us. I've waited a long time to get to know you. Our meeting was inevitable. I've watched you, studied you as you grew up. Hungry for any sign of you in the newspapers, as any proud parent would be."

Katherine cringed. Jack squeezed her hand.

"The beautiful young debutante Katherine Crystal is formally introduced to Atlanta society at the Cotillion Ball, dressed in her creamy white designer gown and dripping in her mother's fancy diamonds. Katherine

Crystal graduates from the Pratt Institute. Oh, yes, I was there. Katherine Crystal joins the Freyer Gallery in Midtown. It's all there in the scrapbook your friend Jack discovered as I walked in and surprised him. I call it the Katherine Chronicles," said the reverend proudly.

Katherine looked down at an open scrapbook with pictures of her with her parents on vacation—skiing, at the beach, on safari, with friends, intimate photos with Justin Bamberger. She released Jack's hand and leafed through the scrapbook—pictures of her from grade school to college, news clippings after Ocean Rivers' death, stories about capturing the Sydney Strangler.

"You were always the goal, Katherine, the prize," acknowledged the reverend, smiling. "I knew the minute I held you in my arms that you would grow up to be special. How could you not? The union of a talented trance medium and a strong psychic and spiritualist. I have had many offspring, with many women, but you, Katherine, are the realization of all my hopes and dreams. The first moment you realized your pent-up talent, when you predicted the death of little Ocean Rivers—that's when I began to consummate the plan. You and I together—think of what we could accomplish, Katherine. You are just beginning to come into your true powers, and I will be your spiritual guide, help you realize your potential. With your psychic ability and my...talent, there are no limits. My lifeblood flows through your veins."

The reverend's beady eyes sparkled. "Come, closer child. Come over where I can gaze upon you at long last in the flesh. Come, don't be afraid. Come to your father."

Katherine choked. But when the reverend waved

the gun at Jack, she complied.

"I've never gazed on such beauty. Ah, your mother, now, she was a beauty, but you far surpass her. I understand you've already met your mother."

"She is not my mother and you are not my father," Katherine said, her jaw set stubbornly.

"Of course you will need time to digest and accept reality," said the reverend. "But we'll have plenty of time together for you and me to become intimately acquainted, to get to know each other in every sense."

The reverend's words were creepy, his tone not the way a father spoke to a daughter.

"You must know that the girls and women who came before, they mean nothing to me. They were just a sideshow. But you are the main attraction. You are my creation, you are above the rest. I have power, Katherine, and untold wealth, as you can see. I can give you everything. You're going to love it here at *Âmes Sur la Mer*. We'll keep you tucked away here at the estate for a while until you get used to our arrangement, and then, if you're good, you can venture out into the community. I have horses. Can you ride, Katherine?"

Katherine didn't answer.

"Of course you can ride. There's a picture of you riding, right here in the scrapbook." He flipped the book's pages to the one he was referencing.

"I've collected all of your favorite artists, all of your favorite things. I did it all for you. We're just about to start our journey together. I can't wait. My beautiful Katherine. Created in my image. My darling daughter. Ours will be a perfect union. Think of the children that will spring from our loins. They'll be magnificent."

Reverend Coulter reached out his hand and touched Katherine's face, slowly toyed with a lock of her dark curls and let his hand slide farther to skim across her breast.

"I could never—I would never—" Katherine shuddered, shrinking away from the monster before her.

"Oh, you will, and you will love it. Trance sex is delightful. No inhibitions. Once I put you under, you will stop struggling, and I will take you to levels you've never dreamed of."

Jack started to lunge forward.

Katherine dropped back to stand next to Jack in a show of unity, taking one of Jack's hands in hers once again. Jack squeezed her hand, almost cutting off the circulation as his muscles strained against his restraints.

"Uh, uh, uh," the reverend cautioned, waving the gun at Jack's heart. "I'm in control here. Jack has been a very naughty boy, and he will have to be taught a lesson. But I'll deal with him later."

"Like you dealt with my parents?" Katherine accused.

"Where did you get that notion, child?"

"We were there, when you went to visit Psychic Juliette. We heard everything, just not the details about how you murdered them."

"Oh, I suppose it can't hurt to reveal my triumph," said the reverend. "I'm actually pretty proud of my handiwork. I simply tampered with the judge's brakes and, unfortunately for them, the car careened off a mountain road and exploded. The fireworks were magnificent," recalled the reverend, as if he were remembering a pleasant Fourth of July night on the National Mall.

"You bastard," Katherine whispered.

"Now, now, it had to be done. Don't you see? To fulfill our destiny."

"You'll never get away with it," Jack said, struggling to maintain his temper.

"Oh, but you see, I already *have* gotten away with it. You have no proof of anything. It was a nasty accident. But the judge had suddenly developed a conscience. He was going to turn me in, turn himself in, admit to everything. I couldn't let that happen."

The reverend rested his free hand on his chin and tapped his mouth, deep in thought. "Jack is an obstacle I hadn't counted on. But, no matter. I will think of a way to dispose of him, too. I was going to come to Atlanta to get you, but you came to me. Come, child, I'm anxious to get started. We have a lot of catching up to do."

Katherine folded her arms and stood her ground. "I'm not going anywhere with you."

"Don't be difficult. You're trying my patience. But if that's the way you want to play this game..." The Reverend pulled out a hunting knife and held it up to Jack's neck, pricking it and drawing blood.

"Jack!" Katherine screamed and faced the reverend. "Leave him alone. I'll do whatever you want. Just leave him alone."

"Oh, so that's the way it is. Two lovebirds. Maybe I should let you watch while I gut him like the pig that he is."

Katherine moved forward and reached for the knife.

The reverend grazed her arm, and she pulled it back, wincing.

"Don't drip on the Aubusson," the reverend said, grabbing Katherine's flowing hair and pulling it tightly into a knot around his hand until she cried out in pain. With his other hand, he loosened the grip on his gun and picked up a coil of rope resting on the coffee table next to a pile of cash. He released his grip on Katherine's hair and tossed her the rope.

"Now tie him up in that chair, at the waist and feet, and do it quickly. I'm losing my patience. I'd just as soon put a bullet in his brain."

"Do it, Kate," Jack said. "Just do what he says." Katherine hesitated.

"We can make this easy or we can make it hard." The reverend smiled at his off-color joke. "Personally, I love a good struggle. You know what daddies do to naughty little girls. I hadn't wanted to use the strap, but..." His eyes twinkled at the prospect.

Katherine's hands trembled as she started to tie Jack to the chair.

"Make it tight," the reverend ordered. "Cut off the circulation, that's it. I'm going to check your handiwork."

Katherine placed a kiss on the top of Jack's head after she'd tightened the knot. "I'm sorry I got you into this mess. I love you, Jack."

Jack looked up into Katherine's eyes, trying to remain confident when she could see how agitated he was.

"Come along to the bedroom, sweetheart," cooed the reverend. "It'll go much easier on you and your boyfriend if you cooperate."

Kate's eyes pleaded with Jack.

"Kate, it's okay. I'll be okay. Just do as he says."

"But, Jack..."

"I'm the man with the plan, remember?" Jack grimaced as he tried to smile. He was tied up tight, knocked almost unconscious with the butt of a gun, blood was trickling out of his neck, and he was talking about a plan?

****

Jack forced himself to remember his training. Studies he'd read of officers killed in the line of duty showed they were too nice, they waited too long to put a person in a control hold or contain the situation. The man who had killed his father had equated hesitation with weakness and it had gotten his father killed. Jack was not going to make the same mistake.

"Don't hurt her, Coulter," Jack barked. "I'll kill you if you do."

"You're in no position to threaten me." The reverend smiled. "Keep making a fuss and I'll make you watch."

"I'm a police officer," Jack said.

"You don't think I know that? I'm going to take my time with her, and I would advise you to use your last moments on earth to ask for forgiveness for your sins."

"You said if I cooperate, it would go easier on Jack," Kate protested.

"I lied," said the reverend, pulling her down the long hall into the bedroom, farther away from Jack.

The man was demented, and unfortunately Kate was going to pay the price. This might be the last time he saw her alive.

"Kate," Jack called out mournfully. "Kate, I love you."

****

He loved her. How bittersweet to finally hear the words pour out of his mouth when they had no future together. Bile rose up and threatened to spill over. This couldn't be happening to her. The reverend was a monster. He was going to rape his own daughter. Who knew how many other times he had done this to how many other innocent women in addition to her birth mother.

If she had one regret besides losing Jack, it was not getting to know Juliette. Now that she'd met the reverend and knew what kind of man he was, she realized Juliette was no match for him. He wouldn't hesitate to kill her, too, to keep her quiet.

She could scream out, but the house was so far from the road and any other house that no one would hear her but Jack, and she couldn't make him sit there helpless and listen to her screams.

She would find a way to outwit the reverend. She looked around for something to use to defend herself. If she were as talented as he claimed, surely she could use some of her powers to get herself and Jack out of this mess. But what were those powers? Should she try to read the future? What good would that do? Should she attempt to distract him? What was about to happen to her was a fate worse than death. A fate she didn't know if she could endure.

The reverend tossed her onto the bed. She massaged her head where he had practically pulled her hair from its roots.

"Now, take off your clothes slowly and let me see you, all of you. See how sensitive you truly are."

"I won't," Katherine said stubbornly, scooting

away from him on the bed.

The reverend rolled his eyes. "You dare disobey me?"

The man was seriously deluded.

He inched closer to Katherine and lifted her blouse. She winced and covered herself with her hands. He ripped off her blouse with a slice of the knife.

He began to breathe hard as he stared at her.

"You're a vision," said the reverend. "Just like Juliette. I loved your mother, you know. And she loved me, until I took you away from her. She never forgave me. But things will be different between you and me. Now stay still."

Katherine felt a sting in her arm, and her legs went rubbery.

"What did you do?" she implored.

"I've given you something to take away your inhibitions. Things will go much easier for you now."

Katherine's muscles felt loose, and a feeling of lightness invaded her senses.

In her haze she saw the reverend's body come down to cover hers.

She tried to move, but she was trapped and immobilized by the drug he'd administered.

The last thought she had was of Jack before the vision appeared before her.

A dark, avenging angel swooped down, aiming the business end of a gun at the reverend's back. A shot exploded, and then another. How many cartridges did her weapon hold? The angel was using the reverend for target practice. A red stain bloomed on the reverend's shirt, and then the world went dark.

Chapter Eighteen

When Katherine came to, Jack was standing over her.

"Is this a dream?" Katherine wondered.

"No, I'm here, and so is your mother—I mean, Juliette," said Jack.

"I don't understand." Katherine looked over Jack's shoulder and saw the psychic, Juliette.

Reaching for Katherine's hand, Jack filled in the blanks. "Juliette was right behind us. She suspected something, so she followed him in her car after he left Psychic Serena's. She has a key to the reverend's home, so when she let herself in I told her not to waste time untying me but to get to you."

Jack brought Katherine's hand to his mouth and kissed her palm. "Thank God she did. She untied me and unlocked my cuffs, but when I confirmed what was about to happen, she picked up the reverend's gun. She knew he kept a gun hidden in his drawer. I wanted to use my fists on him," Jack continued, his jaw clenched. "I wanted to strangle that bastard for what he did—and what he was about to do—to you. God help me, I wanted to kill him, send him straight to hell where he belongs. I was going to do it, too, when Juliette stopped me."

"I told Jack this was my fight, my daughter," Juliette explained.

"So I followed Juliette into the bedroom and walked in on his last, gasping breaths," Jack said. "I wanted to put another bullet into that slimy bastard. Instead, Juliette and I together watched the life seep out of him. And did nothing to save him."

Katherine flinched. "What will happen to Juliette?"

"Nothing, if I have anything to do with it," said Jack. "She killed the reverend in self-defense, trying to protect you. She saved our lives. I've already called the local police and an ambulance. I'm going to fill them in on what happened and make sure everyone in town knows they were worshipping a false god. We have all the proof we need about your adoption, the bribes, the other girls he trapped in his web of lies, how he stole from the church, the missing masterpieces. It's all documented in very detailed records he kept in the safe. He was fixated on you, Kate, and if Juliette hadn't shown up when she did, I don't even want to think what would have happened."

Katherine looked up into her birth mother's eyes— her eyes, in her birth mother's face, so like her face— and smiled.

"Did he hurt you, child? Are you really okay?" Juliette asked, smoothing her hand over Katherine's head.

"I am now, thanks to you," Katherine said. "How did you know we were in danger?"

Juliette smiled. "That's a funny question to ask a psychic. Call it intuition, but I felt the vibrations of his evil energy. He told me what he did to your parents. I believed he had the capacity to hurt you, and I couldn't let that happen."

"You were my avenging angel."

"I don't know about an angel, but I *was* seeking vengeance. Carter was an evil man. He lured me and many other women who stumbled on Casa Spirito into his dangerous web of evil with his trances and his sweet talk and his threats. He had to be stopped. The women of Casa Spirito will sleep easier tonight."

"He said he loved you," Katherine revealed.

Juliette sighed. "There was a time when I believed that, and maybe in his twisted way he thought he did. I was certainly in love with him. But Carter Coulter was only ever in love with himself."

Katherine sat up against the headboard. "You have a beautiful home and shop. But when he treated you so badly, why didn't you leave the reverend? Leave this place? Why did you stay in this town all these years?"

Juliette twisted her hands together in her lap. "It's complicated. This place is my home, for one thing," Juliette explained. "And this house, well I own the house now, but The Casa Spirito Church retains ownership of the land. And the church was owned and controlled solely by Carter. If I left, I'd lose everything I've built." Juliette got a faraway look in her eyes. "Where I came from, who I was before—I had nothing to go back to."

Katherine placed a comforting hand on Juliette's. She was sure there was a story there when Juliette was ready to discuss it.

"But the main reason I stayed was because I hoped one day I'd find you. Carter said he knew where you were. He said he would tell me. That's how he held me here. Then when I saw what he was doing with the other women, I couldn't abandon them. For a long time after you were born, he was content with just me. He didn't bother anyone else. It was just recently he started up again with his dangerous seductions. That's when I knew I could never be with him in that way again. I threatened to go to his wife and to the Council and expose him, but he said I would never see you again, never know what had happened to you. I took care of the other women, comforted them when he took their children away from them, like you were taken from me."

"So there are other children, like me, out there?"

"I'm afraid so," Juliette said. "I'm going to work with the police, the FBI, to track them down."

"What if they'd rather not know? I know this will hurt you, but I would have preferred to be kept in the dark. I was happy."

Juliette sighed and nodded. "I understand."

Sirens screeched, and Katherine could see flashing blue lights out of the front bedroom window.

Jack cradled a shaking Katherine in his arms. "Let's go get you checked out, and I'll take care of some of these cuts, and then we'll go down to the police station and to the Council and make our statements. The FBI team is on its way to Florida to sort out all the 'adoptions.' The reverend kept very thorough records. Juliette is right. We will find those children and return them to their real mothers."

"What a mess," Katherine said. "What about the adoptive parents who love those children? How are they going to give up their babies?"

"They'll work it out," Jack assured her.

"I won't stop until everything is put right," Juliette agreed. "I should have gone to the authorities sooner. Maybe I could have prevented this, done something—"

Jack interrupted her. "Juliette, you would have risked your life if you did. Carter Coulter was a tyrant, an adulterer, and a murderer. He had too much to lose to let you expose him. No one would have believed you."

"And Jack, all those children, they could be related to me," Katherine said, anguish in her eyes.

Jack nodded. "It looks that way, honey."

Juliette heaved a sigh and turned to Katherine. "There were so many times when I wanted to kill him, but I was afraid if I did I'd lose all chance of finding you, forever. I'm so sorry. I never stopped loving you. From the moment Carter ripped you from my arms, I've wanted to find you. And now, by a miracle, I have. Can you ever forgive me?"

Katherine put her hand on Juliette's arm. "You saved my life. You have nothing to be forgiven for."

"I murdered a man," said Juliette calmly. "I have to suffer the consequences."

Alarmed, Katherine looked up at Jack. "Please talk some sense into her." She turned to Juliette. "You are not a murderer. You are not going to jail."

"How can you be so sure?" Juliette asked. "Carter Coulter was very powerful in this town. They might not be so forgiving."

Jack took Juliette's hand. "When they hear the full story, see the safe with his papers and all his ill-gotten gains, this will be a scandal, no doubt, but the blame lies solely with the reverend, and nobody else."

Chapter Nineteen

Jack and Katherine sat side by side on Psychic Juliette's loveseat.

"Jack, Katherine, would you like some herbal tea?"

"I could use something stronger," Jack said, laughing.

"That can be arranged," Juliette said, reaching into her kitchen cabinet and pulling out a bottle of Jack.

"Your namesake," Juliette joked.

"Tea will be fine for me," said Katherine. "I need something to calm my nerves. Just promise me you won't read the leaves. I think I've had enough adventure for one day."

Juliette smiled, poured a cup of tea for Katherine, and filled a shot glass and handed it to Jack.

"Katherine, thanks for agreeing to see me. I was so sorry to hear about your parents and horrified to know that Carter was responsible. What a grievous loss."

Katherine sipped her tea and paused. "I don't think I'll ever get over it."

Jack was silent.

Juliette settled sympathetic eyes on Jack. "Jack, it's been a while since your father died."

Jack swallowed the glassful of liquor. "I was ten when it happened."

Juliette folded her hands in her lap. "I feel his presence around you."

"No offense, ma'am, but I don't exactly believe in this stuff."

"That's understandable. Not many do. There are a lot of imposters who give our profession a bad name. But there is an aura hovering around you. It's always been there. It was glowing strongly at Carter's house when I first arrived and saw you tied up. A protective spirit? Call it what you will. Your father was watching over you."

At a loss for words, Jack rubbed his chin, still not quite used to not having the beard he'd worn when Katherine first met him.

"He's waiting for your mother. Oh, it's not her time yet, but he will wait forever. Theirs was a deep love."

"I never had much use for love," Jack admitted, shaking his head.

Katherine looked at Jack. His last words to her as Reverend Coulter dragged her off to the bedroom were, "I love you, Kate." Spoken in the heat of the moment. He obviously regretted those words. Maybe he didn't even remember shouting them.

"Oh, I think you do know love, Jack," whispered Juliette. "Love for your mother, love for someone else in this room. It's so strong, the energy crackles. The spark is electrifying."

Jack looked at Kate.

Juliette fixed her violet eyes—Kate's eyes—on Jack. "Do you deny it?"

"I can't," he admitted.

Juliette smoothed her flowing black skirt. "When I did the reading for the two of you, I meant every word. You are destined for each other."

193

Jack cleared his throat, looked away from Katherine, then started to rise. "Well, Juliette, we'd better get going. I've got to get back to my job. It was a pleasure to meet you. And thank you again for all you did for Kate and me."

Juliette got up from her seat and shook Jack's outstretched hand. "I look forward to seeing you again, soon."

Jack doubted seriously his path and Juliette's were going to cross again. Why would she say a thing like that? Oh, right, she was a psychic. Jack smothered a smile.

Katherine got out of her seat, hesitated and placed her hand firmly on Jack's arm.

"I'm going to stay for a while. I have nothing to go home to. My parents are gone. I don't have a job. I'm not ready to rattle around in my house alone. You need to get back to work, but there are a lot of things Juliette can teach me. A lot of things I want to learn. I might want to become a member, attend some development classes, become an official student of Mediumship, at least find out more information. And Juliette and I have a lot of catching up to do."

Katherine didn't have to be a psychic to read the disappointment on Jack's face.

"Maybe I'll see you around, Kate," he said, pulling his hand out of Katherine's grasp, inclining his head politely toward Juliette and walking out of the shop.

Suddenly, he stopped and turned. "Oh, Juliette, I almost forgot. I have something for you. He handed Juliette the scrapbook he'd found in the Reverend's safe.

"What is this?"

"Reverend Coulter collected pictures of Kate throughout her life. It's all there. He recorded every important date. There are pictures and newspaper clippings back to when she was just a baby. There's even a lock of her hair."

Juliette's eyes lit up, and she flashed Jack the biggest smile. Her gratitude was evident in the tears that spilled down her cheeks. She clasped the scrapbook to her chest with a high-pitched keening sound. "Thank you, Jack."

"I got the book out of evidence down at the police station. They've already dusted it for prints. They don't need it anymore, and I thought you deserved to have it."

Then he turned away and walked out the door.

Katherine's hand flew to her heart.

"Your Jack is uncomfortable with emotions," Juliette said, turning back to Kate and sniffling. "I missed so many years with you. Thank you for giving us another chance."

Katherine reached for Juliette's hand. "I'm here now. And you're wrong. He's not *my* Jack. I thought he would stay, but I guess I was wrong."

Juliette shot Katherine a skeptical look. "I know what I see. Well, let's talk about something else. What are your plans?"

"I plan to spend as much time as possible with you. I want to learn more about reading tarot cards. I want you to teach me everything you know."

Juliette clutched Katherine's hand as she hugged the scrapbook to her breast. "I'll look forward to that."

Katherine desperately needed someone to talk to about her life, her future path. And she felt close enough to Juliette to confide in her.

"I've been having these overwhelming visions my whole life," Katherine began. "Sometimes they come crashing into my consciousness at all hours of the day and night. I can't always make sense of them."

"I can help you with that," offered Juliette. "It's just a matter of focus and control."

"Sometimes I feel like I want to break something, that if I don't, my head will explode. When my mother was alive, she used to call these episodes headaches. My premonitions, my visions, they were a bad thing, not to be discussed. She would give me aspirin and send me to bed to block out the pain."

"The secret is to control it, don't let it control you." Juliette gave Katherine a knowing look. "I find that sex helps."

"Sex?"

"Yes, it's a powerful blocker, and a hell of a lot more fun than aspirin."

Katherine laughed. This was not a conversation she thought she'd be having with her birth mother so soon in their fragile relationship.

"Is this your version of the birds-and-bees talk?" Katherine asked, and then the words tumbled out. "I haven't had anyone to discuss my feelings with, until you. I would very much like to explore my—my sensitive side. I want to contact my parents. Is that even possible?"

"Anything's possible, child. But are you sure you're ready for that?" Juliette led Katherine back to the couch. "Come, let's sit awhile. I'd love you to show me through the scrapbook of your life."

Katherine sat side by side on the couch with her birth mother as Juliette opened the book to a page where Katherine stood in front of The Crystal Palace.

"My, this is some house," Juliette said, her eyes widening.

"Yes. Atlanta's been my home for so many years. Our house is too big for one person. There's plenty of room. How would you feel about coming to stay with me for a while so we can get to know each other better?"

Juliette burst into another episode of tears. "Katherine, I would love that. Thank you."

Katherine looked into her birth mother's eyes. "If you can read the future, I'd like to ask you a question about Jack."

"Have you and your young man not declared your love for each other?" Juliette asked.

Katherine hesitated. "I told him I loved him. And he told me, when he thought he was about to die, but..."

"Yet you just dismissed him like he meant nothing to you."

Katherine's voice rose. "And he walked out like I didn't matter to him at all."

"You don't have to be a psychic to see that boy is head over heels in love with you. He's just hurting. There is a piece of him that's broken. He hasn't accepted the importance of love in his life. I'm not saying anything your mother wouldn't say if she were here. But if you truly love him, Katherine, go after him, and do it now, before it's too late."

Juliette was right. Who cared if Jack didn't realize it yet? In her heart she knew without a doubt how she felt about him. The pang she'd felt when she watched him walk away only convinced her how much she'd miss him. She could read the minds and predict the future of others, but she hadn't known her own mind, until now.

Katherine ran out of her mother's home. "I'll be back," she promised, calling over her shoulder.

"Jack, wait," Katherine shouted as she watched the giant, her giant, amble down the street. She closed the distance between them.

Jack turned. "Did you forget something?"

"Yes, we both did."

They met in the middle of the sidewalk. Katherine reached up and caressed Jack's face. "I forgot to tell you how much I love you, and that I'll miss you if you go, and how much I want you to stay."

Jack's face registered the gamut of emotions. "Kate, I don't know what to say."

"Just say you love me."

"But..."

"I know you're scared. You thought I'd walk away, that love would walk away again, so you're walking away first. You can count on our love, Jack."

"Kate, when you told me to go, I thought you wanted me out of your life." Jack's face was a mask of pain, his voice faltered.

"You forget. I am a psychic. And I predict we're going to have a wonderful life together. And you heard what my mother, what Juliette, said—we're soul mates."

****

Jack grabbed Kate and crushed her to him, devouring her lips. This was no place for seduction but he wanted to take her now, right here in the middle of town, where everyone could see. But he exercised some patience before rushing her back to the bed-and-breakfast. He was eager to get started on their life together, on the picture Kate painted in his mind.

When they were finally alone in his room, Jack felt a little like he was in a fairy tale. Kate was Beauty and he was the Beast. He was an ungainly giant, too rough for her. His crass was not nearly good enough for her class. But, somehow, they had made it to this place. Somehow, miraculously, she loved him. And, although he'd never said those words to any other woman, never thought he ever would, had never really said it yet to Kate, except under duress, he loved her back with all his heart.

In their haste to be closer, clothes were flung across the room. But when they were completely undressed, Kate looked down at him, her eyes wide and her mouth open.

"H-how exactly is this going to work?" Katherine stuttered, biting her bottom lip. "I mean you're so…and I'm so…"

"Here," Jack suggested, breaking out into a big grin. "Touch it. It's not so bad. It won't bite, but I might."

Katherine laughed nervously.

Jack brought her hand down to feel him, to a place that was swollen to twice its normal size.

"Oh, my god," Katherine exclaimed when she felt Jack and connected to the throbbing, pulsing sensation under her fingers. Justin Bamberger, though tall, had been slim and tidy, whereas Jack was, well, manly and messy, and all thoughts of her schoolgirl fumbling with Justin Bamberger flew out of her mind forever.

Jack kissed her softly and whispered against her ear. "Is it true what they say about sensitives?"

"I don't know. What do they say?"

"That they're, um, more sensitive. For example, if I were to touch you here?" His finger toyed with her nipple and he moistened it with his mouth. "Or over there?" His finger moved to her other nipple and his mouth followed. "Or down there? His finger rubbed and moistened her center and then his mouth—

Kate gasped.

"Why don't we try a little experiment?" Jack suggested. "I think, in the end, you'll find that there's no problem we can't overcome and that we fit together well."

Jack placed the heel of his hand over Katherine's heart and felt it quicken. She looked nervous, but she also looked distracted, and he wanted her undivided attention.

"Jack, I'm beginning to see things, to feel things. I can't focus."

"You're on information overload, you're overstimulated," Jack whispered.

"I can't help what my mind sees, or the signals I'm picking up."

"Block it out. Get rid of all that outside stimuli. Let me stimulate you." He put both hands on either side of her head and forced her to face him. "See only me."

Katherine moaned.

"That's my Kate. That's my love."

"You love me?" she whispered, looking up at him.

"How can you doubt that?"

Jack was prepared for a struggle, but the funny thing was, Kate wasn't putting up much of a fight, not if those sighs and moans coming out of her mouth were any indication.

After they made love—stormy, magnificent, mind-bending love—they lay in bed facing each other, wrapped in each other's arms.

Katherine turned her face up to Jack's, her eyes searching, hopeful. "What happens now—I mean to us?"

"I'm going to stay with you as long as you need me to," Jack assured. "And Kate, I think it's about time you met my mother."

Kate looked warily into Jack's eyes. "What if she doesn't like me?"

"I predict she's going to love you," Jack said, smiling and toying with the ringlets on Kate's head.

"You predict?" Katherine asked.

"You're not the only one with powers in this room. I have abilities you never even dreamed of," Jack crowed.

"Oh, I've dreamed of them," Katherine said, rubbing Jack's naked shoulder. "Why don't you show me just what I've been missing?"

Chapter Twenty

Atlanta, Georgia

"Beauregard, is it really you?"

"Yes, it is, Mama. It surely is."

"Come over here and give your Mama a proper hug."

Mrs. Hale lowered the heat on the stove and ran up to Jack, who scooped her up in his arms, like she was as light as a young girl. Which she probably was. Mary Ellen Hale looked like a munchkin compared to her strapping son. How someone as big as Jack could come from such a tiny woman was beyond belief. Kate wondered if Jack's father had been big, too, like his son.

"It smells like a diner in here, Mama. What are you cooking?"

"I've been in the kitchen all day, making your favorites," said Mrs. Hale. "Fried chicken, black-eyed peas and bacon, and for dessert, I'm even frying blueberry pies."

"The kitchen's a mess."

"It's a good thing you weren't here three hours ago. There was flour everywhere." Then she noticed Katherine.

"And who do we have here?" Mrs. Hale asked, looking at Katherine, who had virtually disappeared behind Jack's bulk.

"This is my girl, Mama. This is Kate."

Mrs. Hale embraced Katherine. "Any friend of Beauregard is a friend of mine. Where have you been hiding this girl, Beauregard?"

"I haven't been hiding her. We've been out of town, in Florida."

"Well, I don't know what to think."

"You'd better watch out, Mama. This girl can read minds."

Mrs. Hale faced Katherine. "What am I thinking right now?" she challenged.

Jack answered for her. "She's thinking you'd better hurry down to the nearest bridal shop and get a mother-of-the-groom dress."

"Oh, my gracious. Beauregard, do you mean it? You've finally found the one? And you weren't even looking. That's usually the way it happens with true love. That's the way it happened with your father and me." To Katherine she said, as though in confidence, "I always told my son. I said, 'Beauregard, when you finally fall in love, you're going to fall hard.' Isn't that what I always said, son?"

"Mama, you're babbling."

"A mother has a right to babble when her son brings home the girl of his dreams. Isn't it kind of sudden, though?"

"Maybe, but she just bowled me over. I knew it from the moment I saw her. There was something unusual about her."

"He thought I was a quack," Katherine corrected.

Jack laughed.

"Well, the Hales are all a bit crazy," Jack's mother

said, "so you'll fit right in."

"And the more I was around her, the more I knew how special she was and that I wanted to spend the rest of my life with her."

"Don't lie to your mother, *Beauregard*," Kate explained. "It didn't exactly happen that way." Since the Hales were speaking around her, she made an end run toward Jack. "Jack, is that a proposal?"

"Yes, Kate. It is. It surely is."

Kate flew into his arms, and he scooped her up and gave her a big kiss. "Is that a yes?" Jack asked.

"It surely is, Beauregard, it surely is."

Mrs. Hale hugged her. "Welcome to the family, Katherine."

"Thank you, Mrs. Hale," Katherine said shyly.

"Please, call me Mary Ellen."

Katherine bit her bottom lip. "Mary Ellen."

"This calls for a celebration," Mrs. Hale said. "Here, Kate, try one of my fried blueberry pies." She handed Kate a miniature pie on a napkin. Kate took a bite.

"Ummm. This is delicious."

"They're fantastic," Jack agreed, wiping a powdered sugar mustache off Katherine's upper lip before kissing her.

"Glad you like them," said Mary Ellen. "Katherine, now that you're going to be in the family, I'm going to give you my secret recipe."

Katherine smiled and looked up at Jack. She didn't have to be a mind reader to know what her fiancé was thinking. They'd already found their secret recipe for happiness.

Chapter Twenty-One

Katherine pushed her plate aside and sat with her head in her hands, slumped over the Hales' cloth-covered dining room table.

"What's wrong, Kate?" Jack asked, looking up from his plate with a concerned frown.

Pouting, she stared at his plate. "Is that your second helping of fried chicken?"

Jack grinned. "I'm a big guy, and I have big appetites. And my Mama makes the best fried chicken in the world."

"Don't let The Colonel hear you say that," Katherine said.

"It's one of our family's secret recipes."

"Are all the recipes in your family secret?" Kate asked, lifting her head.

Jack nodded. "Pretty much. Now what's wrong, honey? I just proposed and you're sulking already. Having second thoughts?"

"Of course not," Katherine said, rubbing Jack's arm. "It's just that your mother is so excited about the wedding, she's off calling half the people in Atlanta to tell them the news."

"Anything wrong with that?" he said, with his mouth full.

Katherine chewed on her bottom lip. "I think it's wonderful how your mother is so excited about our plans. But I've just lost my mother. And at a time like this, a girl needs her mother. My first instinct was to pick up my cell phone and call her...but I can't. I guess I'm just feeling sorry for myself."

Jack stopped, cleaned his hands on his napkin, grabbed Katherine's hand, and wiped away her tears with the edge of his wrist. "Kate, how stupid of me. I didn't think."

"This is something I would have wanted to share with her." Kate stifled a sob. She'd been so excited about Jack's proposal, she'd wanted her mother to be the first to know, until she realized this was just the first of a long line of special occasions she wouldn't be experiencing with her mother. She didn't want to spoil Jack's happiness or infect his upbeat mood. But she couldn't pull it off, couldn't mask her sadness.

Jack's face was flush with regret. "I know. But my mother will be there for you. You heard what she said. You're family now."

Katherine shook her head. "It's not the same."

Jack moved his plate aside and lifted Kate onto his lap. "Sorry, baby," he said, engulfing her in his arms.

Katherine hugged him back for dear life and let her tears spill all over his shirt. "I miss her, Jack. I miss them both so much."

Jack squeezed her tightly. "Of course you do. But you have me now."

"And I don't know what I'd do without you," Katherine said, rubbing her face against his cheek. "But you can't fix this."

Jack brightened. "You haven't told Juliette. Why don't we call her together?"

"Jack, Juliette is my birth mother. She can't take

the place of my mother. It doesn't work like that." Juliette was a lovely person, but she hardly knew the woman. She wanted to get to know her, but her emotions about losing her mother were still too raw to let her in completely.

"I know," Jack sympathized, "but she would be happy for us. She would want to be included. It would mean a lot to her."

"Maybe." Katherine sniffled.

"You said you invited her to stay with you at your house, so let's make it official. Let's call her and invite her up to help out with the wedding. It would be a chance for you to get better acquainted. It would be good for both of you."

Katherine hugged Jack. Her Beauregard was full of surprises.

Chapter Twenty-Two

Juliette sat back in a green wingback chair and surveyed the Crystals' living room. She had been in disbelief over the house since her arrival the night before, wandering in and out of each bedroom, oohing and aahing, touching fabric on the beds, the windows, smoothing her hands over the couches and chairs.

"It's a castle," she announced when Katherine finished giving her the grand tour.

"Not a castle," Katherine said. "Although the media call it The Crystal Palace. To me, it's just home."

"Katherine, I don't know what to say. This house—your home—it's everything I could have wanted for you. Knowing you had such a good life, such wonderful parents, makes me happy. If I had kept you, I could never have offered you anything like this. Horrible as your birth father was, he did the right thing by giving you up."

Katherine rounded on Juliette. "How can you say that? He did it for all the wrong reasons. He took a child away from her mother. What kind of person gives up their child?"

Juliette looked like she'd been struck.

"I didn't mean you," Katherine apologized. "I know you didn't want to give me away."

"You were better off here. I see that now. I know I could never take your mother's place, and I wouldn't want to, but I'm here now and I love you, and whatever I can do to help, I'm more than willing."

Katherine knew she'd offended Juliette, even if unintentionally. She'd have to do her best to make it up to her special guest. "I'd like you to be a part of the wedding. I don't know where to begin."

Juliette looked at her with loving eyes. "To tell you the truth, neither do I, but we'll do it together. I'm just getting used to having a daughter. I hope you don't mind if I think of you that way. I've been waiting for you my whole life."

Katherine smiled. "That's a lovely thing to say. I'm glad to have you in my life."

Juliette's expression brightened. "Have you thought about where you might want to have the wedding? Whether it will be a large or small affair?"

"You know, if my parents were here, it would be a big society affair, the wedding of the decade. They would make a big deal, invite all their friends, but a small ceremony sort of appeals to me. And it wouldn't be right to have a big celebration so soon after I've lost them. So—smallish, I think."

"That sounds wonderful. I can handle small."

"Jack's mother has been fabulous. I want you to meet her. I offered to have the wedding here at the house. We have so much room. It would mean a lot to me. We could have the ceremony outdoors in the garden and then come inside for the reception."

Juliette's eyes teared up. "I don't think you could have it in a more meaningful setting. The home where you grew up." She wiped her eyes with the back of her hand. "Of course, we need dresses. I know I don't have anything fancy enough."

"Why don't we run over to a bridal boutique today and try on some wedding dresses and mother-of-the-bride dresses?" Katherine suggested. "I'll call and make us an appointment."

"Mother of the bride?" Tears glistened again in Juliette's eyes and threatened to spill over.

"That's what you are, Juliette."

"Lord, you need an appointment to go shopping? This *is* the big city. I'm sure a store like that would be out of my price range."

"It will be my treat," Katherine announced. "I will take care of everything. You don't need to worry about a thing."

Juliette walked over to a buffet table and picked up a picture.

"Is this your mother, Jessica Crystal?" Juliette asked. "And your dad?"

"Yes."

"She looks like Grace Kelly. She's very beautiful. And he is so handsome. I'll be forever grateful that they took such good care of my baby."

And now it was Katherine's turn to cry. Then she dried her eyes and got up out of the chair. "Okay, enough sadness for one day. We need to get out of this house. Let's go shopping."

****

Juliette and Katherine entered the bridal shop on Peachtree Street.

"Is everything in Atlanta on Peachtree Street?" Juliette wondered.

"Most everything."

"May I help you?" A stern-looking woman in a tailored dress approached them. She didn't look like she belonged in a bridal shop. Her entire demeanor was off-putting.

"We had an appointment," Katherine said. "Crystal?"

"Yes, Miss Crystal. We spoke on the phone. I'm Ingrid Frost. I was so sorry to hear about your mother. She was one of our best customers. It would be a privilege to help you find a wedding dress."

"And this is Juliette." Katherine hesitated, adding, "A close family friend."

"I see. Now, you told me your size, and I know your mother's taste, so I've started a fitting room for you. There's one in particular—a satin gown with tulle cap sleeves and a glamorous tulle back train—that your mother would have loved. It's dramatic and elegant, like Jessica."

"Well, Miss…Frost, is it? My mother isn't the one getting married. I am. I have completely different taste than my mother had. Not to mention that my mother was a size two and I'm a size eight. May I look through the shop and pick out some dresses?"

"Of course," said Miss Frost, properly rebuked.

The wedding consultant stared at Katherine's naked ring finger and look at her inquisitively.

Katherine followed the stare and stammered, "I, um, my fiancé, that is, we haven't picked out the ring yet."

"Does the girl need a ring on her finger in order to shop at your establishment?" Juliette asked, barely disguising her irritation.

"No," Miss Frost stated flatly. "It's just that girls are always eager to show off the size of their engagement rings. It's a status symbol, a symbol of their husband's success."

Juliette's brows narrowed, and she looked like turning Miss Frost into a toad would have been a pleasure, if only she were capable.

"The young lady's status is that she and her fiancé are deeply in love and they don't need a ring to prove their commitment to uptight shopkeepers such as yourself. So if we don't meet your manufactured qualifications, we can take our business elsewhere, can we not, Katherine?"

Katherine smothered a smile. This outing was proving more fun than she'd expected.

Miss Frost choked and ignored the remark. "Let me show you our selection." She led the way farther into the store, where she showed Katherine and Juliette dozens of dresses, each of which they summarily rejected. Miss Frost was growing more and more impatient.

"These are very luxurious," Katherine began, "wonderfully designed. But I had something else in mind."

Juliette located a diaphanous pink gown on the rack and exclaimed, "Oh, my. What about this one?"

Miss Frost shuddered. "Oh, no. That won't do at all. That would make you look like Tinkerbelle or Glinda, the Good Witch of the East."

"I love Glinda," Katherine said.

Katherine took another dress off the rack and held it up against her body. She twirled over to the mirror. "What about this one?"

"The strapless Vera Wang taffeta gown with asymmetrically draped bodice, a scoop neckline, and a full ball-gown tulle skirt." Miss Frost recited the description in a monotone as if she were reading it from an advertisement.

"I love it," Katherine stated. "What colors does this come in?"

"Champagne/ivory and blush/ivory," Miss Frost said.

"I like the blush bodice with the ivory skirt, the one I'm holding. And I love this floral sash and the cathedral-length train."

"The floral sash is removable," Miss Frost pointed out.

"No, we'll keep it. It's exactly what I'm looking for. Juliette, what do you think?" Katherine twirled around one more time with the gown pressed against her body and turned to Juliette.

"I think it's magnificent. It looks like spun sugar. You'll look like a princess in it, like you're floating on a cloud."

"Jack will love this. He always says I remind him of a fairy. Juliette, I think we have the same taste."

"Isn't it a little...flamboyant?" Miss Frost remarked coldly.

"No, I think it's just right. My mother would have hated it," Katherine smothered a laugh and looked up. "Sorry, Mother." To Miss Frost she said, "I'll take this one into the dressing room and try it on. It's my size, and I'm betting it will be a perfect fit. It was meant to be."

"Let me have my seamstress come into the fitting room. I think it's a little tight in the—"

"It's all that fried chicken I've been eating lately," Katherine explained.

"I was referring to your, I mean, are you sure you

want to wear strapless?"

"Why not?"

Miss Frost's eyes focused on Katherine's breasts like a laser. "Perhaps it would make you appear a bit... top heavy—"

"Are you saying my boobs are too big? Well, I always thought so, too, but my fiancé really likes them the way they are, and he would want me to celebrate them." Katherine snuck a private look at Juliette.

Miss Frost turned pale and looked like she'd swallowed an egg.

"Big breasts run in the family," said Juliette, whose breasts were fairly obvious in her tight bargain-basement T-shirt.

"Very well, then. Let's see what you look like in it. If it suits you, I will have the gown cleaned and pressed and delivered to your house."

"Wonderful. Now my— Juliette needs a gown, as well. Something on the order of a mother-of-the-bride dress."

"Do you have anything in purple?" Juliette asked. "Purple is my color."

Miss Frost shuddered. "Purple is yesterday's color," she said. "We don't have much call for it. Perhaps we may have one or two on the *sale* rack." Miss Frost frowned on the last words.

"I never buy anything *unless* it's on sale," said Juliette. "Lead the way."

Katherine laughed. "My mother never bought anything if it *was* on sale. She went to great lengths to pay full price."

"We have a Calvin Klein pleated taffeta in cerise," offered Miss Frost.

"I knew a psychic once named Madame Cherie," Juliette said.

"Or an Adrianna Papell in deep mulberry," Miss Frost added, her eyes rolling.

"Is that purple?" Juliette asked.

"I think it would be best if I showed you. Smoke might be a nice color on you, or an elegant gray hue for a touch of glamour, or a Nicole Miller metallic, which would look great on a full-figured woman such as yourself."

"I don't know who Nicole Miller is, but I think I've just been insulted." Juliette laughed. "And I've never had such fun in my life."

"If we can't find the perfect dress here, I'm sure Nordstrom's Bridal Shoppe could accommodate us," Katherine said.

Miss Frost stiffened. "Ladies, I think we can work together."

"Wonderful," said Katherine, taking Juliette's hand.

Chapter Twenty-Three

"Jack, this was a great idea you had, this little getaway to North Carolina," Kate said, leaning back on the headrest in Jack's car as she watched the world fly by.

"I know how stressed you've been lately, honey, with your parents' funeral, discovering your birth parents, planning the wedding, and all. I know I haven't been much help. I thought a nice drive to the mountains would lift your spirits."

"And you were right. I feel like I don't have a care in the world. No voices in my head, no premonitions. It's great."

"We're almost there. You're going to love the little place I've booked. We'll be all alone, no Mama, no Juliette. Those two are driving me crazy, and I'm sure they're doing the same to you."

"Well, just a little, but I kind of like it. And the wedding's almost here."

Jack reached over and touched Katherine's face. "I can't wait, which is why I've booked this little romantic getaway, because I can't wait."

Katherine blushed. Since she and Jack had made love in Casa Spirito, she couldn't get enough of him. They couldn't get enough of each other. Each day was a revelation, each night a wonder. She couldn't believe how lucky she was to have Jack in her life.

"I'm so lucky I found you," Jack said, as if reading her thoughts. Strange how they were bonding, connecting, getting closer every minute.

"I love you, Jack," Katherine mused dreamily, eyes half-closed. "Love you, love you, love you. I must have love on the brain. I keep seeing love everywhere."

Katherine squinted up through the moon roof. The tops of the trees flitted by, closer than the blue sky and puffy clouds, and she relaxed, possibly for the first time since Jack had proposed.

Suddenly, the sky darkened and the canopy of trees felt like they were closing in on her. Her thoughts darkened with them.

"Jack, stop the car," Katherine cried out. "Stop the car right now."

"Honey, we're on a small country road in the middle of nowhere. There's nothing out here but woods."

"Stop it. I have to get out." Katherine was becoming more agitated by the second.

"Okay, okay, let me pull over. Are you feeling all right? What's wrong? You look like you've seen a ghost."

Katherine jerked open the car door and stumbled out. Jack followed. She had walked only a few feet when she found herself in a small overgrown family cemetery, just a fenced-in area with some old family plots, not a house or a living creature in sight except for two giant ravens perched on a gravestone.

"I think those are the same birds we saw in Casa Spirito, Kate."

Katherine frowned. "Don't you see? It's a sign. I'm cursed."

217

And what she saw inscribed on the crumbling gravestones shook her to her core.

"What the hell?" Jack stared at a cemetery no one had tended in decades.

"Jack, do you see?" she shrieked. "Do you see this? This is what I was visualizing in my mind. Every stone engraved with the word LOVE. This is the Love family plot. Love, Love, Love. This is what I was thinking in the car. My god, will I ever get away from it? I can't stop the voices. I think I am going insane!"

"Kate, this is freaky," he admitted. "You are one scary woman."

She massaged her forehead. "See what you're going to have to live with? This is what your life is going to be like. You're about to marry a woman with serious issues."

"And I can't wait." Jack enveloped her in his arms. "Whatever you're going through, whatever happens, I am going to be with you, loving you. Celebrating our love."

"You are going to grow tired of me. You're going to regret marrying me. You may not think so now, but give it time. It's just like Justin Bamberger. He—"

"Please don't compare me with that snobby blueblood bastard Justin Bamberger. His loss was my gain. I will never grow tired of you, Katherine Crystal. And I love you just the way you are."

Then he kissed her, right there in the middle of the cemetery.

"I love this woman," Jack shouted. "Anybody listening? I love you, Katherine Crystal."

Katherine returned Jack's kisses and nestled against his warmth.

"Who says this is a bad thing?" Jack asked quietly.

"They, the voices, wanted me to stop. For some reason, they wanted me to stop. What does it mean?"

"Baby, everything doesn't have to *mean* something. You felt a presence, you felt the name Love, and we stopped, and this is what we found. Nothing sinister going on here. Why don't we take it as a good sign? That the world approves of our love."

"Jack, you don't really believe that, do you?"

"I sure as hell do. I believe in us. Now, let's pay our respects to this lovely family, pick some of these lovely wildflowers to put on their graves, and be on our way. I don't think I can wait to be with you one moment longer. And I don't think you want to make love in this graveyard, do you? Although that would make a nice memory."

"Jack, you're crazy."

"Crazy in love with you, Kate. As a matter of fact, I think I'll move up the timetable."

"What do you mean?"

"It was going to be a surprise, but I think the occasion calls for a little change in plans. Never let it be said that Jack Hale cannot be flexible."

Katherine smiled.

He turned to Kate, took her hand and bent down on one knee.

"I never did this properly before. Katherine Crystal, will you do me the honor of being my wife?"

Katherine flushed.

"Yes, oh, yes, Jack."

"Now close your eyes."

Katherine complied.

Jack massaged her ring finger and brought it to his

lips. He kissed her finger and slid a ring on it. Katherine's heart skipped a beat.

"You can open your eyes now."

Katherine's eyes fluttered open, and on her ring finger sat the most beautiful emerald-cut diamond, in an exquisite platinum setting.

"Oh, my, Jack. It's absolutely beautiful! You didn't have to. This must have cost a fortune. I don't want you to spend that kind of money on me."

"Kate, a special woman deserves a special ring. I hoped you'd like it."

"Like it? I love it." The sun broke through the clouds, and when Katherine held up the ring to admire it, it sparkled and flashed in the sunlight. The biggest grin spread across Jack's face, and she jumped into his arms.

Spirits lifted, they walked back to the car, arm in arm, back into the light.

Katherine buckled her seat belt and looked over at Jack. He was understanding now, but how tolerant would he be if he had to face her quirky outbursts on a regular basis and put up with her premonitions day in and day out? Night after night? Would it start to wear thin like it did with Justin? Would he regret his decision to marry her? She wished she could take a quick peek into their future to see if they got their happy ending.

Chapter Twenty-Four

Jack looked over Katherine's shoulder at the proofs of the wedding invitations spread out on the coffee table in Katherine's living room. He had just started a fire to take the chill off the room.

"Are these okay with you?" Katherine held up the proofs so Jack could get a closer look.

He picked up the invitation with its response card and envelope. "Sure. I don't know anything about invitations. If you like them, then they're fine with me."

"You're certainly agreeable."

"I try to be."

Katherine gathered up the proofs and placed them in the envelope from the printer. "Well, while you're in such a generous mood, I'd like to ask you something."

"Ask away," Jack said, ruffling Kate's hair.

"I'd like to ask you about the day your father died."

"I don't talk about that," he stated emphatically, moving away from her chair to stoke the fire in the grate.

Katherine rose from the chair and turned to face Jack. "Not even with me?"

"Not with anyone."

"I'm not just anyone, Jack. We're going to be married."

"It happened a long time ago."

"And it's still affecting you. I think we need to talk

it out. If I'm going to marry you, I want to understand you."

"If?" Jack frowned.

"When," Katherine corrected. "I'm not going to leave you, Jack, like you think your father did."

"What do you want to know?"

"Losing my father suddenly, the way I did, was traumatic, but for a ten-year-old boy, it must have been devastating."

Jack paced to the green leather recliner and sank into it, sulking, like a little boy. She could see what a young, rebellious Beauregard Lee Jackson Hale might have looked like. She waited patiently for him to speak.

"It was getting dark, and Dad wasn't home yet," Jack began, his head pressed against the back of the chair, his eyes lost in the past. "It was my parents' anniversary, so Mom knew he wouldn't miss it for anything in the world. My mom was all dressed up. They were going to go out to their favorite restaurant— a steakhouse—for a special dinner, but he was late and she was worried. She didn't want to upset me, but I could tell she was getting frantic.

"She called the precinct, and they said Dad had left an hour ago. Mom and Dad were, like, connected. She could tell something was wrong. Sort of like you can."

Kate nodded.

"I got on my bike and rode the route he would normally take to get home. I stopped when I saw his police cruiser at a jewelry store. I figured he'd stopped by to pick up an anniversary gift for my mother. We both knew she'd been looking at a necklace there. So I parked my bike in front of the store and waited for him to come out. No one was going in or out of the store, so

I looked through the window. My dad was standing there holding a gun on two men. I guess they were robbing the store. I ran to my dad's car and used his radio to call for backup."

"How did you know what to do?" Katherine interrupted.

"My dad taught me. He taught me a lot about being a cop. He wanted me to grow up to be just like him."

Katherine's heart broke when she looked at Jack and heard his voice crack as he continued the story.

"What happened then?" she prompted.

"I couldn't just leave my dad there. He needed my help, so I walked into the store. Everyone—the customers, the salespeople, the robbers, and my dad—looked up when the bell over the door rang. After that, everything happened so fast. One of the robbers grabbed me and picked up a gun from the floor and held it to my head. He told my dad to drop his gun or he would blow my brains all over the plate glass window. Those were his exact words.

"I looked at my dad. And in that moment I knew what he was going to do. 'Don't do it, Dad. Don't surrender your weapon!' That was one of the first things they teach you in the Academy. Don't give up your gun. But he didn't hear me—or he didn't want to hear me. I saw it in his eyes. I saw him hesitate, and so did the gunman.

"I tried so hard not to cry, I tried to be brave in front of my dad, but I did cry. 'Jack, it's okay,' he said calmly. 'I love you, son. Tell your mother I'm sorry I missed our anniversary.' And then he dropped his gun, and the second robber picked it up and shot him in the head, just like that. I was sure he was going to shoot

223

me, too, but he didn't. I wish he had."

"You don't mean that. What happened next?"

"The police arrived, and they arrested the robbers and took my father away in an ambulance, but I knew he was already dead. I rode in the ambulance with him to the hospital, and then my father's fellow officers drove me home and we told my mother. She was still in her fancy dress, waiting for me and my father.

"A few days later, after the funeral, a package arrived. It was from the jewelry store, a gift from my father with a love note, all wrapped up in white paper and a blue bow. My dad had bought my mother the necklace she wanted. That's why he was in the store when the robbery happened. He died on their anniversary. She hasn't taken it off since."

Katherine perched on the arm of Jack's chair and enfolded him in her arms. "You had to watch your father die," she choked. "I can't imagine how horrible that must have been for you. I don't know what to say. I'm so sorry."

"And it was all my fault," Jack said. "If I hadn't come into the store, my father would still be alive."

Katherine sat on the arm of the chair and massaged Jack's elbow. "Jack, you can't know that. And you called for police backup. If you hadn't been brave enough to walk into that store to help your father, other innocent people in the store might have been harmed."

"Why did he drop his weapon, Kate?"

Katherine didn't hesitate. "To save your life, because he loved you. That's what parents do."

Jack barely managed a bittersweet smile. "They said my dad was a hero, but there's not much comfort in a dead hero."

Katherine blew out a breath and slid down to sit in Jack's lap. "Thank you for telling me, honey. You know, at the reverend's house, you had your gun, and when I came back into the living room, you were tied up. You're twice as big as he was. You could have overpowered him. Obviously, you gave up your weapon for me, Jack, when he threatened to harm me. I know you did, because you loved me. You went against your training and all your instincts, you broke the rules—to keep me alive, even for a moment longer."

"He surprised me," Jack objected.

"Do you deny it?"

He sighed.

"Feel a little better, now?" she said softly.

Jack nodded. "I guess I needed to get that out."

"What about that psychic you told me about, Madame Hydrangea?" Katherine wanted to know. "What ever happened to her?"

"After a couple of years of holding hands around the table, the psycho bitch tried to put the moves on me, a twelve-year-old kid. I had lost my father, and then she made it worse."

Katherine pursed her lips in clear disapproval. "She didn't—"

"No."

"Did you ever tell your mother?"

"No. She believed in Madame Hydrangea. It would have broken her heart."

Katherine hesitated, but had to ask again, "And she never got through even once? She was never able to contact your father on the other side?"

Jack shook his head. "Of course not. I told you before. It was all a con. She was nothing but a scam artist. But my mother believed it. She believes to this day that she can communicate with my father. That love lasts forever, even beyond the grave. I always thought that was bullshit—until I met you. I told Madame Hydrangea if she didn't leave I would tell some of my father's friends on the force what she was doing. She got the message, because she just disappeared, along with most of my father's savings."

"Then what happened?"

"I was a mess. After that night, I was the biggest juvenile delinquent on the block. I caused my mother a lot of grief for a lot of years. Losing my father like that really messed me up. Eventually, I worked it out myself, but what I really needed was professional help. Finally, one of my father's friends set me straight and got me back on the right path. And I decided that when I became a cop I was going to follow the rules to the letter. I was convinced that was the only way to stay safe. But I always associated psychics with my father's death."

Katherine kissed Jack's nose and smiled. "Now I understand why you hate psychics. It makes perfect sense."

"But you're different. You're real." Jack hugged her. "And speaking of psychics, there's something I want to talk to you about."

"What's that?" She snuggled up against him.

"You know, ever since I met you, my luck has changed. We make a pretty good team. Do you want to make this arrangement permanent?"

Katherine tilted her head in confusion. "I thought you already asked me to marry you?"

"I'm talking about a business arrangement, Kate. I

was thinking we could combine our talents and start a psychic detective agency. Hale & Crystal."

"Crystal & Hale," Katherine proposed, her eyes sparkling.

"Crystal & Hale, then," Jack agreed. I've given this a lot of thought, Kate. I'm serious about us forming our own agency. I'm quitting the police force."

Katherine pulled back from Jack's embrace. "Where did this come from? I don't want you to give up something you love, something you worked so hard for. Wouldn't your father have been disappointed?"

"That was my father's dream. I don't want you to go through what my mother went through. Being married to a cop is rough. I don't want you to be a widow like my mother. And I don't want my child to ever have to go through something like I did."

"You're already thinking of children? We haven't even walked down the aisle."

"Hell, yes," Jack answered, his face exploding into a grin. "I can't wait, Kate. I want us to get started on a family right away. As long as we don't name him Beauregard, after me."

Katherine crinkled her nose. "What if Beauregard turns out to be a girl?"

"Hell, we'll have one of each. I'm turning my resignation in right after the wedding. And we're going to build a new business and a new life together."

Katherine twisted a lock of Jack's hair. "But we don't know anything about being in business."

"I'm a hell of a detective, and you're the most talented psychic I know. We'll need an office, though."

Kate pursed her lips in thought. "The Crystal Palace is big enough for us to live in and work there too. We have a huge guest house, with a private entrance, that I could redecorate. It would make a great office space."

"We'll need a receptionist."

"What about Juliette? If you can stand working with two psychics. She can also help us on cases, with her special abilities. She's been working with me to hone my skills. She really is talented."

"Perfect."

"Do you think we'll get enough business?"

"Kate, your phone is still ringing off the hook with people and agencies wanting your services. Business from the APD alone would be enough to keep us going."

"You've really thought this through, haven't you?"

"I have."

Katherine placed her hand on Jack's cheek. "You're still thinking about your father, aren't you?"

"I miss him something fierce," Jack admitted. "It's like a dull ache that never goes away."

Kate took Jack's hand in hers. "You know, Juliette says she really can communicate with the world beyond—the spirit realm."

"You know how crazy that sounds."

"Juliette says she can bring back our loved ones, that they're still around us and are able to communicate with us, that they still care about us. I'm going to get her to try to contact my parents. She can try to reach your father."

"You don't really think that's possible, do you?"

"Yes, I do, Jack. I trust her and I think she can do it. I think we should give it a try. It might give us both some closure."

Chapter Twenty-Five

Jack, Mrs. Hale, Juliette, and Katherine held hands around the dining room table in a darkened room at the Hales' house. Katherine was nervous. She had arranged the séance because she thought she was doing the right thing. But it could easily backfire and send Jack and his mother hurtling back to the worst time in their lives, just when Jack was finally beginning to put the past behind him. If it didn't go according to plan, it might reignite his hatred of psychics, maybe diminish his feelings for her.

Mary Ellen Hale was smiling dreamily as if she knew how the evening would turn out. She would soon be communicating with her beloved dead husband, if only in spirit, and she looked as anxious as a schoolgirl with her first crush.

What was Jack thinking? His big hands were sweaty, but who knew where his head was? Perhaps he was hopeful, perhaps doubtful. But he had agreed to go along with it, for her sake.

Juliette, on the other hand, had already crossed over into the spiritual world. She was making mental preparations to communicate with the dead. Juliette had insisted they conduct the séance in the house of the dearly departed. She said that spirits stuck to their houses, to the people they loved and had been ripped from, in this world. That made sense to Katherine.

Juliette had taught her the basics about how to conduct a séance, and she felt she could do it herself, but this was too important. This was Juliette's show.

The lights were low. Candles were glowing and flickering around the room, throwing shadows across the table. The setting was serene. She was surrounded by love and family, her new family. And she was harboring hope that maybe she would get a visit from her parents.

Mama. She prayed silently. *Mama, if you're here, if you can hear me or see me, give me a sign.* Jack squeezed her hand. Could it be? Could her mother's presence be in the room? Katherine swallowed hot tears.

Juliette said they all had to believe. And Katherine thought they all did. With Juliette's guidance, they had picked an auspicious date. The night before Katherine and Jack's wedding. She was sorely missing her parents, especially her mother. They were to be married on the same date as Jack's parents' anniversary. That way, the date would take on a new, happier significance in their lives. This evening was the day before Jack's father had died, the last day the Hales had all been together as a family.

Katherine heard the steady beat of the clock, tick-tock, tick-tock, as if they were being collectively hypnotized. And Juliette had likened the state of mind in the room to hypnosis. Reality was suspended, belief in a higher being reinforced. They were about to enter a new realm, take a journey to the unknown. Would it work? She desperately wanted it to, for Jack's sake.

Juliette spoke. But, at first, her chanting seemed unintelligible to everyone but Mary Ellen.

"I feel the spirit of Jackson Hale in the room," Juliette continued. "Jackson is trying to tell you something, has been trying to tell you something. He's sending us a message, a message of love and hope and happiness about the upcoming wedding of his son."

"Jackson, is that you? Jackson?" Mrs. Hale was agitated. Katherine saw Jack squeeze his mother's hand when she called out her husband's name.

A hush fell over the room. The temperature dropped precipitously. A benevolent fog seemed to envelop them. Their hands were linked, each participant murmuring a secret prayer.

When Juliette next spoke, she had assumed another presence, a deeper, masculine voice.

"Jackson," Mrs. Hale cried out when she heard his words. "Sweetheart, I love you. If you are hearing this, please, give me a sign."

A picture frame fell over on the bureau in the dining room. The vintage wedding picture of Jackson Hale and his new bride, Mary Ellen.

"He's here," Mrs. Hale cried out in happiness, tears flowing. Katherine could feel Mrs. Hale's emotion, predict that her hand was going to fly to her mouth.

"Don't break hands, don't break the bond," Juliette's spiritual guide channeled.

The chain held.

"What is it, Jackson, my love?" Mary Ellen implored. "What are you trying to tell us?"

"I love my little honey bunch. I've loved you since I stole that first kiss on the Halloween hayride."

Katherine's jaw dropped. If that were true, how could Juliette have known something like that?

Jack squeezed her hand, indicating that it was true.

Mary Ellen's eyes were tearing up again.

"Honey bunch. That's what you used to call me. Your little honey bunch, because I'm so tiny and because you love me a bunch."

Juliette spoke again and again, but it was not Juliette speaking. "I wish I could be there with you at the wedding, on our anniversary. But I'm never far away. I've been with you all these years. I've been right here."

"I felt him. I knew he was near," Mary Ellen sobbed.

"Mama," Jack said. "Don't cry, now."

"I'm so proud of you, Jack, the way you've watched over your mother all these years, the man you've become, the partner you've chosen."

Now it was Jack's turn to be heard. "Daddy, is that really you? Give me some proof. I have to know. Is this for real?" The anguish in Jack's voice was genuine.

The room went silent and then Juliette was back.

"He says the night he died you called for backup using your special code—Jack Sprat."

"No one else knew that code," Jack exclaimed, "no one around this table."

"He says when you were a little boy and you threw a temper tantrum, you always went to your special hiding place, the tree at the old Watson place."

Jack raised his voice. "Why did you give up your weapon, Daddy? Why did you let them shoot you?"

"He says he would do whatever it takes to save you, because he loves you more than life itself," said Juliette, adding, "and he says he would do it again."

Jack was openly weeping. "Daddy, I love you."

Jack's hand was squeezing Katherine's so hard it

hurt. Mary Ellen was sobbing in happiness.

Juliette's voice broke through the stillness. "Did he come? Was he here?"

"You did it, Juliette," Katherine said. Even though she hadn't gotten to reach her parents, she was thrilled for Jack and Mary Ellen. She couldn't have wished for a better outcome. It would make their wedding day so much more meaningful.

After the séance broke up, Jack pulled Kate aside.

"That was him. I know it. It was my father. The words he used... My father said he was proud of the partner I'd chosen. That's you, Kate. Do you think that means he approves of our new business venture, that maybe he's not disappointed in me?"

"It certainly sounds that way. It's not like you're giving up law enforcement. We're going to be helping people. You're going to be doing what you always did, just independently. And you'll have more time to finish law school like you always wanted. I think we're doing exactly the right thing for our future."

"Thank you for suggesting this, Kate. It meant a lot to my mother, and to me."

Chapter Twenty-Six

Something old. Something new. Something borrowed. Something blue. A wedding tradition to be shared with a mother. Katherine stood at the cheval mirror in her parents' bedroom, trying not to cry.

"I'm getting married today, Mom, Dad. I wish you could have met Jack. He's great. I know you would love him as much as I do. I wish—so many things. I wish you could be here. I hope you'd be happy with the wedding we've planned. It won't be the same as you'd do it, Mom. It will be small but intimate, still lovely."

Suddenly, Katherine sagged on the bed, devoid of energy.

"Katherine, dear, don't cry, you'll muss up your makeup," said Juliette, sweeping into the room in her eggplant-hued gown and examining Katherine. "I've been looking all over for you. What's wrong? You're missing your mother, aren't you?"

It was uncanny the way she and Juliette could communicate. They didn't need words. They always knew what the other was thinking, feeling. Not just because they both had the gift, but because they were truly mother and daughter. Katherine was fighting it, felt it was disloyal to her parents, but the bond she shared with Juliette was real and growing stronger every day.

Juliette pulled Katherine up from the bed and

wiped her tearstained face with a tissue she plucked from a box on the nightstand. Katherine had left the room exactly as she'd found it when she got home from Sydney. She couldn't bear to change anything. The judge's robes still hung pressed and encased in plastic in the closet along with her mother's work clothes, gowns, her shoes and purses.

"I know I'm a poor substitute, but here I am," announced Juliette. "So, I know the wedding tradition is something old, something new, something borrowed, something blue. That's why I invited Mary Ellen up here to be a part of this."

Mary Ellen Hale walked into the room in a lovely cream-colored floor-length gown. She smiled at Katherine. "There you are, Kate. Now we can do this right."

Juliette began. "For the something old, I've got this antique diamond bracelet a wealthy client gave me in a trade for my services. I gave her some investment advice and she made a lot of money, so she was grateful. Now it's yours." She put the bracelet on Katherine's wrist.

"Juliette, you don't need to do that. It's beautiful."

"Are you going to take away my happiness? Now hush, and let us finish."

"We'll save the something new for last. Mary Ellen, it's your turn."

"Kate, my new daughter, for something borrowed..." She removed a delicate necklace with a single diamond enhancer from around her neck.

"But that's the necklace Jack's father bought you the night he, the night that he—"

"Go ahead, you can say it. The night he died."

"But Jack said you'd never taken it off."

"I know, but Jackson is always with me, in here," she said, touching her heart. "And he would want you to wear it. So, something borrowed, something meaningful, something tangible to connect our families. Here, let me put it on for you."

Mary Ellen fastened the necklace at Katherine's throat.

"Thank you," Katherine said gratefully. "I love it."

"For the something blue, I have this garter," beamed Juliette proudly, lifting Katherine's dress and sliding it up her leg. "I got it at a fancy lingerie shop and it *wasn't* on sale."

Katherine laughed.

"Now, for the something new." Juliette's eyes teared. "I told myself I wasn't going to cry."

Katherine was puzzled.

Juliette held out a small oblong box, beautifully wrapped, and handed it to Katherine.

"Juliette, you shouldn't have! This is from Tiffany's. That's way too expensive."

"I didn't. Your mother did."

"I don't understand."

"I walked into your room earlier, looking for you, and there, on your bed, was this box with your name on it."

Katherine wanted desperately to believe. She smoothed her hands over the wrapping. Tiffany's was her mother's favorite store. She always bought a piece of jewelry for herself or for Katherine to mark special occasions, often without her father's knowledge.

"There's a note," said Juliette.

Katherine quickly opened a miniature white

envelope that was fastened under the turquoise ribbon and read the inscription.

To My Darling Daughter "KC" on Her Wedding Day.

Love Always, Mother

"But how?" Katherine stammered.

"She must have bought these for just such an occasion," said Juliette.

"I think my mother was beginning to despair that I would ever get married."

It was her mother's handwriting. And "KC" was one of her mother's pet names for her, an abbreviation of Katherine Crystal. No doubt about it. The gift was from her mother and it was meant for her.

"Go on, open it," Juliette urged.

Katherine tore at the paper and opened the blue box, a box her mother had last touched. She removed a blue felt pouch and emptied the contents carefully into her hands.

The delicate Tiffany teardrop diamond earrings sparkled with an almost heavenly light.

"Oh, my," Katherine said. "They're absolutely stunning. This is definitely something my mother would have chosen."

"And they go so well with your dress. Let me help you put them on." Juliette fastened the earrings on Kate's ears.

Katherine choked up when she looked in the mirror.

"No tears, now," Juliette warned. "Your mother is with you after all. She's right here in this room. There's no doubt about it. Don't you feel her love?"

Katherine looked up and nodded. "But tell me, did

you really find these on my bed?"

"Would you believe that your mother came to me in a dream last night—perhaps she was close because of the séance—and her spirit led me right to the place where I found the wrapped present. That gift was meant to be found. It was meant for you, meant to be positioned where you would find it at just the right moment."

"Did she say anything else?"

"Something about 'much better than Justice or Justine.' I didn't understand it."

Kate laughed. "Justin Bamberger. The son of one of my parent's closest friends. She was always trying to push us together, and we were engaged for about a minute, but he didn't love me for who I was. My psychic episodes totally freaked him out. So I broke it off. I think he was relieved. My mother must have ordered these in anticipation that we'd get back together."

"Justin Bamberger?" Mary Ellen repeated.

"Yes. He was perfect on paper, just not in person."

"No one could be better than my Beauregard," Mary Ellen said.

"I agree," said Katherine, smiling. She turned to Juliette. "Was she—is she still—her face—how did she look?"

"As beautiful as a princess. Her spirit shone through. She was magnificent, and so happy you'd finally found your soul mate."

"That's you, talking about soul mates."

Juliette denied it.

"Was she alone?"

"The judge, your father, was looking over her

shoulder, proud as a peacock. They were together, he had his hand on her shoulder. Acted like a couple of newlyweds. They were much younger than they were in the photo downstairs."

"How could that be?"

"Oh, that's very common when we see spirits that have passed over. We almost always see them at their adult youngest and healthiest and happiest, because that's the way they are in heaven."

"You really believe that?"

"Most definitely. Now, let's get out of here, child. We have a wedding to go to. We don't want to keep your groom waiting."

Mary Ellen and Juliette each folded a hand through Katherine's elbow and together escorted her to the head of the stairs to the strains of the wedding march. The two women would be giving her away.

Katherine started down the spiral staircase, enfolded in love in this realm and from the realm above. She could feel it. She could feel her parents' love and encouragement.

But when she got to the landing, she was focused on Jack. He looked so handsome in his tuxedo. She could see him, but he couldn't see her—yet. Would he like the dress? Was it too much? Should she have gone with something simpler or more elegant, something more to her mother's taste?

All doubts were banished when Jack looked up and saw her. His jaw actually dropped. His expression was one of sincere appreciation, and of love.

As the women handed her off to her husband-to-be, he whispered, "My god. Katherine Crystal, you look like a fairy princess. I can't believe how lucky I am."

That was the effect she was looking for. She took Jack's hand and everyone else vanished—the large contingent of Hales that had come in from all around the South, her parents' friends, her friends from the gallery, even some of Juliette's friends from Casa Spirito, and the judge who was going to marry them. Justice Harvey Bamberger. Probably Justin was here, too, but she didn't care. All she cared about was Jack.

The voices in her head were stilled. But she hardly heard the vows. She only hoped she said the right things at the right time. All she could see was Jack in front of her. She was remembering the words he spoke when they made love for the first time: "See only me."

Jack's eyes were shining with love. He was reciting his vows, putting the ring on her finger, and then he had her in his arms and was kissing the breath out of her. Everyone was laughing. She was married, then. She hung on to him for dear life as she walked back up the aisle with her groom, yes, her soul mate, and into their future together.

The reality was better than any vision she could have had of her wedding and her future life. It was glorious, unexpected and totally unpredictable.

Chapter Twenty-Seven

"You're back from your honeymoon!" Juliette exclaimed, sweeping Katherine up in her arms, then hugging Jack, as the newlyweds walked into the new offices of Crystal & Hale. "You look tan and rested. Did you two have fun in Bermuda?"

"It was wonderful," Katherine sighed.

"Way too short," Jack complained. "But the honeymoon is not over." He grabbed Kate and bent her backwards in an exaggerated kiss.

"Jack, not here. Juliette is watching."

"I don't care if she is. I am going to kiss my wife wherever and whenever I like, and as long as I like."

Katherine rolled her eyes.

"What did you see there?" Juliette asked. "Tell me all about it."

"We saw a lot of Bermuda...from our hotel room," Jack said.

"Jack, stop," Katherine admonished.

"That's not what you said on our honeymoon. In fact, I wouldn't be surprised if we haven't already conceived a little Jack, Jr., or a little Kate. Those Hale swimmers are really hearty."

"Jack Hale, you're embarrassing me in front of Juliette."

Jack threw his hands up. "Okay, I can see that you two women are going to work me to death, and you know what they say—all work and no play makes Jack a dull boy."

"Jack, stop being silly."

Katherine looked around the room. "Juliette, you've done wonders with this place in just two weeks. And I love the sign out front. It's so official—Crystal & Hale—Psychic Detective Agency."

"Well, all the interior decorating is not complete, but I think you're going to like your individual offices. And we've already gotten some messages, including a dozen media calls, all wanting to know what Crystal Ball Kate is going to do next."

"How does anyone even know we're in business?" Katherine wondered.

"Word travels fast. Talk of your honeymoon and the new agency is trending on Twitter. In fact, we already have a new client, in a manner of speaking."

"Tell us, who called?" Katherine asked.

"Well, it was a Mrs. Yardley. She wanted to hire you to find Bo."

"Is Bo her son?"

"No. Bo is her pet boa constrictor who got loose from his cage."

"Who would name their boa constrictor Bo?" Jack asked.

"Your mother named you Beau," Katherine pointed out.

"We don't look for lost pets," Jack said. "This is a respectable detective agency. Lost pets don't constitute a crisis."

"To Mrs. Yardley, losing Bo was a crisis," Juliette explained.

"What did you tell her?" Katherine asked.

"I called animal control, and they found Bo up in a magnolia tree in the neighborhood and brought him back to Mrs. Yardley."

"That was nice of you," Jack conceded. "But you shouldn't be spending time tracking down missing pets. We have an office to run. And cases to solve."

"Actually Mrs. Yardley is officially a client. She was so grateful she had her driver bring down a check for a hundred dollars."

Jack frowned. "Her driver? A hundred dollars?"

"Yep. Did I do good? A hundred is a hundred, right?"

"At that rate, I'll never be able to support my wife and child."

"Jack, we don't have a child yet," Katherine pointed out.

"But we will, and I have to provide for you."

"We have plenty of money," Katherine assured him.

"*You* have plenty of money. We are not touching that."

"Don't be so macho. What's mine is yours. You know that."

"We'll discuss that later—in the bedroom."

Kate shook her head.

"If worse comes to worst, I could always do live psychic readings or tarot readings," Juliette offered. "I *am* a certified psychic."

"It's not going to come to that," Jack promised. "But speaking of pets, Juliette, will you please go get that welcome-home surprise I arranged for Kate?"

"Of course." Juliette went into Jack's new office and brought back a squirming white ball of fur and handed him to Jack.

Katherine's hands flew to her face. "Jack? What is this?"

"Your surprise, sweetheart. Meet Romeo, the newest member of the Hale family. Romeo, meet your new mommy." Jack handed a mewling Romeo to Katherine.

"Why Romeo?"

"We already have a Juliette. We can't have a Juliette without a Romeo."

Katherine squealed. "I love her."

"Him," Jack corrected.

Katherine snuggled the Bichon Frise puppy against her face. Romeo proceeded to lick her nose and eyes.

"Lucky dog," Jack said.

"Romeo, Romeo, wherefore art thou, Romeo?" Katherine intoned dramatically. "I've always wanted a dog."

"Well, now you have one. Every boy needs a dog."

"But we don't have a boy."

"We will," Jack said, patting Katherine's tummy. "He, or she, could be in there right now."

"Isn't that a little premature?"

"I believe in the power of positive thinking," Jack said.

"You're impossible, Jack Hale, but I love him. And I love you. Thank you." She planted a kiss on Jack's cheek.

"I have all the things the little master needs—his doggie bed, chew toys, food and water bowl—and he's going to stay here with us during the day and then move to the main house at night," said Juliette, who now had her own wing in the main house.

Kate and Juliette had grown very close since they'd discovered each other. They even dressed alike. These days, Kate wore frothy, swishy, sparkly clothing and preferred purple—Juliette's favorite color. Miss Junior League had definitely left the building. She was growing more comfortable with herself. Jack loved Kate's gypsy look, her style, and everything about his new wife.

"Okay, Juliette, you can take him now," Jack said.

Katherine kissed Romeo quickly on the nose. "Parting is such sweet sorrow."

Juliette hooked a leash onto Romeo's collar.

"I'm going to take Master Romeo for a walk around the garden," she called as she walked out the door. "I'm trying to potty train him."

"I want to play with him," Katherine pouted.

"We don't have time for games, Kate," Jack stated. "I dropped by the precinct and finalized my paperwork. I'm officially off the force."

"What did they say when you told them you were leaving?"

"They were upset, of course, but they were thrilled they'd still have access to Crystal Ball Kate, so they plan to keep Crystal & Hale very busy. In fact, we just got our first real assignment based on their referral."

"Oh, Jack, that's wonderful. What is it?"

"Let's go into the conference room and I'll give you the details."

Jack slapped a thick manila folder onto the mahogany conference desk.

"The APD got a call from the Graysville, Florida, Police Department. While we were out of town, there have been more brutal murders in that college town.

The psychopath is murdering members of the college's new homecoming court."

"Oh, no."

"Yes, and after three months, they have no leads. The campus, in fact the entire city, is in the grip of an unknown serial killer."

"Jack, not another one."

"Sarge said girls are carrying pepper spray in their purses. Business is booming at all the Graysville sporting goods stores. Coeds are traveling in pairs or large groups, arming themselves with guns and knives and any weapon they can get their hands on. They're all scared of being grabbed next. The girls' parents are up in arms, five girls are dead, and one is missing. There's already a media feeding frenzy. Kate, we're going to be involved with the biggest murder case in Graysville, Florida, certainly in the South, maybe even in the entire country. The tabloids say the case is shaping up to be one of the biggest killing sprees in modern history."

"Why are we just now hearing about this?"

"We were a little tied up catching our own serial killer in Sydney, falling in love, and getting married."

"Sounds a little selfish of us, with all this going on in the next state."

"Well, law enforcement has been doing its best to keep a lid on it, but things are heating up," said Jack. "It's being broadcast nonstop to the whole wide world from the situation room and streaming out across cyberspace. Complete with pictures of the six beautiful dead or missing girls, of their bereaved parents mourning their losses, of the candlelight vigils, and of the remaining homecoming pageant contestants, under headlines that scream, "Who's Next?" The grief of the bereaved parents is bleeding into every living room in the world.

"They're calling this case 'The Homecoming Homicides.' Everything is spinning out of control, and the murder investigation has stalled. The campus and city police have hit a roadblock after months of fruitless investigation, and the death toll continues to rise. The FBI has been salivating to gain access, and now that they've established a joint task force, the university and the city police are forced to beef up their efforts or lose total control of their case. And to make matters worse, the city and campus police are fighting over jurisdiction. Yhey were in the middle of a turf war even before they called in the FBI."

"Why is jurisdiction such a muddy issue?" Katherine asked.

"The bodies of the five victims were found on landmark sites around the campus, so that's University turf. The Graysville Police Department claim the girls weren't necessarily murdered on campus, that they're responsible for forensic examination of the crime scenes, and that the University is overstepping. They can use all the assistance they can get. That's where we come in."

"What do they want us to do?"

"They want you to work with the girl who's the director of this year's homecoming pageant. She's a former pageant contestant."

Katherine felt sick. She was in over her head. And she was sinking deeper every minute.

"But Jack, we just got back from our honeymoon. We have a million things to do around the house and the office. I haven't written my thank-you notes. I can't just drop everything and leave town. I don't want to leave you."

"That's the best part. You won't have to. I'm coming with you. I would never let you go down there alone. I'm going to protect the mother of my child."

"Aren't you jumping the gun?"

"I don't think so. I have this feeling."

"Are you a psychic now?"

"No, just an optimist."

Katherine bit her lip. She tried hard not to show it, but deep down, she was scared to death, and Jack could probably see right through her act of false bravado.

"Just so you know, I can't pull the killer's name out of my head. It's not that simple."

"I know how it works. I've seen you in action, and I know you can produce results." Jack stared at her face and saw right through her. "But, sweetheart. We don't have to do this if you don't want to. You don't have to do this. You are more important to me than any case or any business."

Just then, Juliette walked through the door with Romeo.

"Romeo is exhausted. I'm going to put him down for a nap."

"Hurry back. I want to go over some crime scene photos with you and Katherine to see if you get any vibes."

"Vibes?" asked Katherine.

"You know, any psychic-type feelings."

Katherine shook her head and Juliette sighed.

When Juliette returned, Jack brought Juliette up to speed on the case and the three of them sat at Juliette's desk with the file between them.

"The city is crawling with media. And unfortunately they want all the gory details. The Graysville police department has faxed over the crime scene photos, the police reports, and the ME reports and photos. A lot of blood and guts."

Jack opened the file and arranged some graphic photos on the table that made Katherine want to puke.

"Let's start with twenty-one-year-old Meredith Henning. Tortured, throat slit, what was left of her dumped into Alice Springs. What the alligators didn't get was recovered there. Burned on the left side of her face, *while* she was still alive."

"Then there's pretty little twenty-year-old blond Montana Rountree. Tortured—butchered, really—left naked in a pool of her own blood in the fountain in front of Richert Hall. Same pre-mortem burn marks on the left side of her face."

The queasy feeling in the pit of Katherine's stomach persisted as Jack slipped more photos out of the file.

"And twenty-two-year-old Natasha Hemmingway? Tall, tan and shapely, Tash was stripped naked, almost decapitated, and let's not forget tortured, before she was hurled off the top of Centennial Tower. She was pretty smashed up, but even broken bones can't hide burn marks."

Jack held the third handful of grisly photos right up to Katherine's face, and if she didn't get out of there this minute, she was going to vomit all over them.

"Oh, my god," Katherine whispered, rising out of her swivel chair, swaying as she gripped the edge of the desk.

"What are you trying to do to the girl?" Juliette

protested. "She's not one of your cops, she's your wife!"

"Don't you think I know that? I'm trying to prep her for what she's going to be up against in Florida, so she vomits in this office and not all over the Graysville police chief."

"Will you excuse me for a moment?" Katherine managed.

"Take all the time you want, sweetheart."

Katherine avoided looking at the black-and-whites and barely made it to the bathroom before she tossed the remainder of her airplane lunch. Dammit, Jack knew he'd get this reaction. It was just what she didn't want to happen. She would not lose her cool again, she promised herself, rinsing out her mouth with water. She splashed more water on her face until the room stopped spinning and she could catch her breath.

When she returned to the conference room, Jack had strategically spread out the rest of the photos in glorious, gory detail across the table.

"Gee, Kate, you don't look so good. Maybe you should go and lie down."

Juliette flashed him the evil eye and Jack relented.

"I'm not going to let anything happen to you, Kate," he said, his tone softening. "I won't let you end up like Meredith, Montana, and Natasha, or the rest of the girls. But if we can solve these murders, more cases will come our way."

"And if we can't?"

"I have faith in you, honey, and you have to have faith in me. We solved the Sydney Strangler case together, and we can solve this one. It's very high profile."

Katherine closed her eyes and fought to regain what was left of her dignity.

The eyes of the country were on Graysville. Which meant the eyes of the country would now be on her, again.

Why was she, an inexperienced thirty-year-old, tapped by the Homecoming Homicides task force to work such a high profile case? Simply put, she was in the right place at the right time, or the wrong place at the right time, depending on how you looked at it. Jack had tried scaring her away with those gory crime scene shots, but she was sticking. She'd committed to their detective agency—Jack's dream—and she wasn't going to let him down.

"When do we have to leave?"

"I've booked us on the first flight out in the morning."

"Jack, that's too soon. What about Romeo? We just got him and now we're leaving him alone?"

"Juliette will watch Romeo. Now go to the house and unpack, and then pack again. We're due at Mama's for a welcome-back dinner. You too, Juliette."

"Jack, this is such short notice. It's a little too much. I was counting on some more alone time, just the two of us."

Jack gathered her into his arms and squeezed her tightly before he kissed her forehead and whispered against her hair, "I know, honey, and I want that, too. You are my top priority. But we can't just think of ourselves. Lives are at stake." Then he released her and smiled. "Besides, Mama won't take no for an answer, *and* she's making her special-recipe fried chicken."

If you have enjoyed *Sixth Sense*, you will want to read the sequel:

Homecoming Homicides

by

Marilyn Baron

A Psychic Crystal Mystery
Book Two

Prologue

Rodney Willis inhaled the aroma of fresh blood. In his opinion, nothing else even came close to the scent of suffering. The blood was slick and sticky and velvety, and he was practically swimming in it. He'd nearly slipped on the floor this morning while he was in full clean-up mode, getting ready for the new contestant.

The candidate on the table had been a real trooper. He had to give her credit. She'd performed superbly, even exceeded his expectations, although she was rather noisy. He'd had to muffle her screams. The bitch had bitten him, had probably given him rabies, if that was possible. He'd have to research that on the Internet. He was finally forced to drug the little vixen, and after that it wasn't nearly as much fun.

When she'd come around again, she complained of the cold. He had to keep the temperature of his workshop near freezing, so he'd obligingly covered her with a blanket and softly soothed her with meaningless prattle while he continued his work. She was pathetically grateful, probably holding out hope that he wouldn't kill her if he was considerate enough to cover her. It suited him to kill her with kindness for the time being. It made it easier for him in the end. He nearly swooned as he remembered the touch of his hand on her naked breast, the feel of her pulsating heartbeat as it tripped like a frightened rabbit and then slowed in resignation, finally sliding into defeat as it stopped altogether when all the blood had drained from her body.

And speaking of hearts, he was going to have to have a long overdue heart-to-heart with his big brother, Donny. Last night had been too close for comfort. The screams and moans and tiresome begging sounds coming out of his workshop had drawn the idiot to the door, and he'd had to do some fancy footwork to get him to go away. Donny knew the workshop was off limits and yet he couldn't help poking around. He had been looking for Traci; he wouldn't have wanted to see what was left of her.

Donny was dangerously fixated on that girl. Rodney had allowed him to stay for the contest and watch Traci model Queenie's dresses, but he didn't get to view the aftermath. Someone of Donny's delicate nature would never understand what had to be done. He always wondered where the girls had gone, and he'd always been satisfied when Rodney had said, "They had a previous engagement." But not this time. Not with Traci Farris.

Donny had to be kept in the dark. Rodney needed Donny's help in carrying the bodies, which Rodney would lovingly clean and delicately wrap. Donny was stronger than an ox. Donny's father had been big and strong, too, at least from what Rodney remembered. His own father had left them a long time ago, left Queenie to raise her two boys alone. Donny was special, but Queenie always said both her boys were special to her.

Rodney had inherited his mother's slimness and dark good looks. Everyone said he favored Queenie.

And that, Rodney took as a supreme compliment. After all, Queenie was a winner.

He looked over at his mother's picture and smiled. "There's no one like you, Queenie. Never was before, never will be again. Only one even comes close."

He'd promised his brother another scavenger hunt tonight. This one was a reverse scavenger hunt. They weren't hunting for anyone. Instead, they were delivering something. Donny wasn't to ask what was in the package. That would ruin the fun. He'd picked out the new dump site, and he couldn't wait until it got dark.

He knew the rules of jurisdiction. As long as he continued to dump the bodies on campus, the FBI couldn't get involved unless they were invited in. And the campus police and city cops—more like the Keystone Kops—were clueless. They had no intention of asking the Feds to their party. In the end, they'd bowed to public pressure. With the notoriety of the case, the outraged parents had demanded it. But as far as he was concerned, even with the FBI intervention, it wasn't an even match. He was already on Number Six, and they had no idea who he was or when he would strike next or why he was doing what he was doing. At this rate, he'd rack up his goal of thirty girls in no time.

He was rather enjoying this little contest of wits. Of course, now that the FBI was involved, he'd have to be more careful. FBI or no FBI, the campus police and city police were engaged in a pissing contest, and they were so busy getting in each other's way they'd left the field wide open for him. Unfortunately, they had thrown a wrench into his plans when they called in Crystal Ball Kate, that psychic he'd seen all over the news. But she was no match for someone of his skills and abilities. And, just for fun, he might teach her a lesson, too.

Tomorrow, after work, he would go trolling for Number Seven, and he would save the best—Katherine Crystal—now Katherine Crystal Hale—for last, unless an opportunity to snatch his prize came along earlier. Then he wouldn't be able to resist her. He'd jump right on it.

It would be more difficult, considering she was now a consultant for the Graysville Police Department. And that big brute of a husband of hers, Beauregard somebody or other—the one with all the names, who called himself Jack—would be guarding her around the clock.

But he was smarter than they were. And eventually the Atlanta cop would let his guard down, and then he would make his move at exactly the right time and the right place.

Chapter One

One week earlier

Traci Farris had been running for what seemed like miles. Running away from Jack Armstrong's apartment. Running away from what easily would have been an ugly confrontation with Jack's fiancée, Philippa Tannenbaum. Running away because she'd rather die than face Flippy and relive that look of shock and betrayal on her best friend's face.

"Wait," a man's voice called out. Traci turned toward the sound in midstride and nearly collided with a concrete bus bench.

Gasping for breath, she stopped short and grabbed the bench post for support while her heart raced to play catch-up with her feet. She just wanted to disappear, to be swallowed up by the earth as twilight settled like a shroud over the ghostly quiet town of Graysville.

The man at the bus stop—he was more of a big hulk of a boy—flashed her a dazzling smile that transformed his flabby face and lit up the night. It was a friendly face, and right now Traci desperately needed a friend. She'd seen him around campus from time to time. Hard to miss. He was very slow, but sweet, helpless, and harmless. He'd waved to her a number of times on her way to and from classes, and she'd waved back. She recalled helping him count out change once at the University bookstore.

The boy fixed her with an endearing look.

"Don't you remember? I saw you in the show. You signed your picture for me."

Puzzled at first, Traci suddenly remembered where she'd last seen the boy-man. He'd approached her after last year's homecoming pageant with his program in hand, asking for her autograph, just another star-struck fan, a backstage hanger-on. He'd been shy and appreciative when she signed his program. She'd been flattered. The boy had been lost in the crowd of people that night, agitated and confused when the cameras started flashing and the well-wishers surrounded her, almost crushing the two of them.

"I'm waiting for my brother to pick me up," the boy announced in a monotone. "He's late."

"I'm sorry," Traci managed, leaning against the post of the bus bench, still winded. "I really have to be going, but if you need to call your brother I have my cell phone right—" She realized then that she'd run out of Jack's apartment without her purse or her cell phone. She wasn't going back there anytime soon. "Well, I'm sure he'll be along soon," Traci said, happy to focus on someone else's problems for a moment. "But I've got to be going."

"Where are you going?"

Traci couldn't answer because she didn't know.

"I'm going to the end of the world," the boy announced, smiling.

Perhaps she hadn't heard him correctly. "The end of the world?"

"That's where I live," said the boy. "Here." He placed his right hand over his heart and then pointed a fat forefinger to a yellowing piece of paper pinned to his pitifully outdated flowered shirt. Didn't the boy own a coat? It was freezing outside. At least she'd had the presence of mind to grab hers before leaving the "scene of the crime." A Miami girl, born and bred in the sun, she hated the cold with a passion.

Traci followed the boy's black button eyes as they moved down insistently to the note. Did he want her to read it?

"My name is Donny Willis," she obliged. "I live at 5555 Skyline Road. Please take me home."

"You're real pretty," said Donny. "Just like my mama. My mama was real pretty, too."

"Thank you," Traci said, her heart beating back to a near-normal pace. "But I really need to go now."

"If my brother doesn't come, I'm supposed to take the bus."

Looking around, Traci suddenly felt exposed standing at the isolated bus stop as darkness got a choke hold on the sky. She'd passed a few stragglers, girls walking in pairs, scurrying home before curfew, probably packing heat. Normally the campus would have been alive with people. But nothing was normal anymore in Graysville. Every girl on campus was scared and wondering who the killer would grab next.

If she had her cell phone she could call one of her sorority sisters for a ride home. Or one of those walking or driving student safe escorts services. Or 9-1-1. She looked around. There wasn't a pay phone or a policeman in sight. Where were the cops when you needed them?

But if she went back to the sorority house, Flippy would find her and demand an explanation. Her friend, her *former* friend, deserved an explanation. But Traci had no excuse for her actions.

A fresh set of hot tears streamed from Traci's eyes. Flippy had every right to hate her. Traci knew from the beginning she'd been wrong to poach what belonged to someone else. But she'd done it anyway.

Jack had been depressed about his football injury. He'd needed sympathy and a shoulder to cry on, and Traci had been more than available.

Tired of Jack's self-pity routine, Flippy was too busy now with her own life to babysit him. Once, she'd even let it slip to Traci that she wasn't sure she was doing the right thing by marrying Jack. That she'd waited so long for love to come along and it never had. That her mother had been thrilled when Jack finally proposed. Barbara Tannenbaum was a force of nature. Flippy had spent her entire life trying to please her mother, so she and Jack had set a date. But that could have been just girl talk, pre-wedding jitters. Jitters or not, Flippy's uncertainty didn't give Traci a license to steal. Or stab her best friend in the back.

It didn't matter that Traci had secretly nursed a crush on Jack from the moment Flippy had introduced them and that Jack had fanned the flames by flirting with her every chance he got, especially when Flippy's back was turned. One thing had led to another, and they'd become involved on the sly. And then Traci was in too deep, up to her neck in love with him. And now she'd lost them both.

Earlier that evening, Flippy had walked in on them in bed, and the whole house of cards had come crashing down. The last words she heard were Jack's, feebly begging Flippy to come back to him. He hadn't even been concerned about Traci's fragile feelings.

"Are you taking the bus?" Donny interrupted her thoughts.

"No," Traci said softly, her eyes looking away from Donny's beady ones, her mouth closed clam tight, her breath coming now in rapid, shallow bursts.

"Will you wait with me?"

Traci shrugged and began to shiver. Her body had started to shut down after the adrenalin rush. She needed time to think about what to do next. Maybe riding the bus to the end of the world wasn't such a bad idea. No, it was a really stupid idea.

She contemplated bolting from the bench when the blue city bus screeched to a stop in front of them and the driver cranked open the heavy steel doors.

"Donny? Your brother late again? Hop on. I'll take you on home."

"He says he lives at the end of the world," Traci told the bus driver. "But there's an address pinned to his shirt."

The bus driver chuckled. "He's been wearing that raggedy old note for years. It's a wonder anyone can still read it. Says his mother wrote it. He lives at the last stop, the end of the bus line. He calls it the end of the world. Probably never been anyplace else."

"I want to wait for my brother," Donny said. "She can wait with me." The boy turned to face Traci and nudged her, creeping uncomfortably closer into her personal space.

"I—uh, need to go," said Traci, noticing that the full moon was on the rise.

"She can wait with me," Donny repeated.

Then Donny started to rock. Back and forth. And

rant. And refused to get on the bus.

"Wait with me," Donny wailed, touching his face over and over as tears puddled on his puffy cheeks. His nostrils flared and dripped and his pupils dilated. And he continued to rock, while remaining bolted to the ground.

"You a friend of Donny's or Rodney's?" asked the driver.

"I don't know any Rodney. He looked lost and I just wanted to help."

"Look, miss, sometimes he gets like this. And he won't stop. I hate to leave him here alone like this. No telling when that smart-ass brother of his will come back for him. But I have to keep to my schedule. Don't want to lose my job, do I? And you can't wait here. It's not safe for a pretty girl like you, what with everything that's going on around campus. You can ride along with us and I'll drop you where you need to go after I finish my route."

Traci shook her head hesitantly. Her every instinct told her it was definitely not a good idea.

"Please," Donny sniffled, sensing victory.

Mentally challenged or not, he was nothing but a big manipulative mama's boy, Traci realized as she started to ease away from the bus. But if Donny left, she'd be alone. That's what it came down to. She didn't want to get on the bus. Neither did she want to be alone.

"I might be able to stay for a few more minutes, just until his brother comes," Traci relented, although everything in her argued against it.

"Thanks, miss. Now be careful out here. Why don't you call the campus police to come pick you up, walk you home?"

Flippy worked for the campus police. Traci wouldn't be calling anybody in that place.

Donny wiped his eyes on his shirt sleeve and looked back at her with that hundred-watt smile, like everything was all right again in his world.

"You're pretty," Donny repeated. "Just like my mama."

The double doors closed with a loud whoosh, and the bus pulled away just as a green Thunderbird came roaring out of nowhere and pulled up in front of the bus stop.

"You're late," the boy accused, pointing his finger at the car, his fat face red and splotchy from crying.

"Sorry, bro. Hey, who's your pretty little girlfriend?"

Donny blushed and stammered. "Sh-she's not my girlfriend."

"Did the bus driver happen to get a look at your new girlfriend?" Donny's brother asked.

"I told you, she's not my girlfriend."

"Too bad."

Traci leaned into the car, trying to get a look at the man inside, but it was dark and the man turned his face away as he switched off his headlights. "I was afraid to leave your brother alone. He was really upset."

"She's beautiful *and* she's a Good Samaritan," said the driver. "We hit the jackpot this time, big bro. Get in the car, Donny. Say thank you to your pretty little girlfriend."

"She's not my girlfriend," Donny insisted as he opened the car door and lumbered into the front seat.

"Donny doesn't exactly have a way with words, does he?" mocked the faceless voice that floated from the car. "But I appreciate you waiting with my brother. I'd like to show my gratitude. Can I give you a lift anywhere?"

"N-no," Traci stammered. "Th-thank you. Goodbye, Donny." Traci edged away from the bus stop, gave a half-hearted wave, and started walking in the opposite direction of the car. The Thunderbird swerved, spun around in a cloud of dust and pulled up alongside her. A frisson of fear climbed up her spine and lodged in her brain. The car windows opened and the vehicle tracked Traci as she began to run.

The car kept rolling. Traci kept running. But she could still hear the man's voice.

"I offered you a ride home. Are you always this rude? Don't you know it's not safe to be out alone at night?"

Traci kept up her pace.

"Grab her, Donny. Your girlfriend needs a lesson in manners."

"But why?" the boy asked.

"Don't ask questions. Don't I always know what's best for you? We're just taking her home for a short visit. Wouldn't you like a little company? It gets pretty lonely with just us guys around the house way out at the end of the world."

"Don't hurt her."

"Now where would you get an idea like that? You watch too many movies, bro. Go ahead and get her, and be quick about it before someone else sees you."

Traci risked a peek back as Donny stepped out of the car. He was as big as a giant, but he moved quickly and he was gaining on her.

"No, please." Traci tried to shout, but the words

12

came out as a strangled whisper. A sick knot of fear twisted in her throat, festered in the pit of her stomach, choking her as it rose into her mouth. A slick band of sweat glistened on her chest, pooled under her arms and froze there. Her knees buckled. Each breath tore out of her with the force of a jagged knife. But still she ran. She ran like her life depended on it.

A word about the author...

Marilyn Baron is a public relations consultant in Atlanta. She's a PRO member of Romance Writers of America (RWA) and Georgia Romance Writers (GRW) and winner of the GRW 2009 Chapter Service Award.

She writes humorous women's fiction, romantic suspense, historical romance and paranormal. She graduated from The University of Florida in Gainesville, Florida, with a Bachelor of Science degree in Journalism and a minor in Creative Writing.

Born in Miami, Florida, Marilyn lives in Roswell, Georgia, with her husband, and they have two daughters. She loves to travel. Her favorite place to visit is Italy, where she studied for six months in her junior year of college.

Read Marilyn's other two books published by The Wild Rose Press, Inc.: Her historical (romantic thriller) *Under the Moon Gate*, and its prequel, a historical, *Destiny: A Bermuda Love Story*.

Author e-mail:
marilyn@marilynbaron.com
Petit Fours and Hot Tamales blog:
www.petitfoursandhottamales.com
To find out more about Marilyn and her books, visit her Web site at:
www.marilynbaron.com